I0662936

DISORDER

Peter Jensen

Martin Sisters Publishing

Published by

Martin Sisters Publishing, LLC

www. martinsisterspublishing. com

Copyright © 2013 Peter Jensen

All rights reserved. Published in the United States by
Martin Sisters Publishing, LLC, Kentucky.
ISBN: 978-1-62553-029-5
Mystery/Suspense
Printed in the United States of America
Martin Sisters Publishing, LLC

To my son, Keith, who is my compass.

Chapter 1

Zach sat in the visitor's waiting room, leaning forward with elbows on knees and hands clasped together. He stared down at the Lucchese alligator boots that his uncle had sent him, along with the faded jeans, and the maroon T-shirt with "Louisiana" embroidered across the chest. Leaning back on the plastic bench, he ran his fingers through his hair, and felt a nervous anticipation grip him.

Foxmire sauntered in from the courtyard, stomping dirt from his boots onto the welcome mat. Zach watched as the huge guard walked toward him. The man withdrew his nightstick from its holster, pointed it at Zach's head, and then swept the weapon toward the glass doors. "You're outta here, young man," he boomed. "We got the press blocked off."

Zach stood and walked toward the tall African-American man, held up his right arm, and smacked Foxmire's right hand with his own. He said, "Thanks for that. See ya, Foxy," and continued walking toward the welcoming sunlight.

"Not if I see ya first, Flicka," Foxmire hollered, his laughter echoing in the large, concrete and tiled space.

It was noon on the last Monday of December. The temperature in Baton Rouge, Louisiana, was sixty-five, and the sky was devoid of clouds.

Zach turned to take one last look at the Jetson Center for Youth. "*Sayo* fuckin' *Nara*," he said aloud, turned back, and walked toward the limo. A corner of the parking lot contained a CNN van with a satellite dish on the roof, and a "Fox Eight News" van, both trapped behind a temporary wooden barricade. A pack of reporters and cameramen were milling about behind it.

Zach watched as Remy opened the rear passenger's door and stepped out.

Remy leaned against the car, tall and wiry, in his usual garb—cowboy attire with a Stetson hat sitting precariously to the right of dead center. He stretched out his arms. "Come to Remy, birthday boy," he said, his mouth transforming into a grin.

Zach walked into his uncle's arms and hugged him. "I missed you, Remy," he said, trying hard not to reveal his emotions.

Remy slid into the backseat of the limo and patted the seat facing him. "Sit," he ordered.

Zach pointed at a reporter and cameraman who had stormed the blockade. "Fox Eight News." He slipped into the seat, closed the door, and the limo driver swung the car around toward the street.

A reporter began screaming words at Zach as she ran alongside the car, her voice muffled by the air-tight window Zach was looking through. He stared at a vein popping from the woman's sweaty forehead, the perspiration glistening on her upper lip, and turned to look at his uncle's weathered face.

6

Remy had thick eyebrows over deep-set green eyes, a straight nose, and square jaw. His long black hair was pulled tight in a braided ponytail, and the close-cropped moustache and goatee showed no signs of graying.

"Thanks for the threads," Zach said.

"Wanna drink?"

"Whatcha got?"

"Southern Comfort."

"No beer?" Zach asked.

Remy maneuvered forward to sit and pour. He returned with a bottle of Abita Amber and a drinking glass full of ice and liquor.

"Here's to my twenty-one-year-old nephew on his birthday. Happy birthday, Zachary, and welcome home."

"Thanks, Remy." He touched the neck of his bottle to Remy's glass.

"So, you remember Claude?" Remy asked, nodding toward the front of the limo.

"Claude," Zach said, turning his head to look at the driver, "is dat cho up dere?"

"Yes, Massa."

"You got any dem nappy-headed kids witcho?"

"No, Massa, dem kids dey in prep school now."

"No shit, Claude?" Zach asked, sipping his beer. "They're all at New Orleans College Prep?"

"All three of 'em."

"Congratulations." Zach looked out the window and stared at Tiger Stadium off in the distance.

"Claude will join us tonight," Remy said. "It'll be boy's night out." He took a pull of Southern Comfort.

"And where will us boys be staying tonight?"

"I booked the twenty-sixth floor of Harrah's two years ago. There'll be chefs, butlers, and twenty-four-hour dining inside and out. We'll have a great view of the fireworks display."

"It's good to be out, Remy."

"They screw with your head in there?"

"I felt like a POW."

"Just chill for a while," Remy said, drinking Southern Comfort and placing the glass in a holder. He slipped a Cohiba between his lips and lit it. Puffing on the thin cigar and enjoying the aroma, he said, "Wanna smoke?"

"No, thanks."

"Good. Keep it that way."

"Anyone I know gonna be there tonight?"

Remy reached into his jacket, withdrew a cell phone, and handed it to him. "Your number is on the back. The phone is yours. Invite anyone you want."

"I guess I'm just wondering what the climate will be like."

Remy shook his head. "People think what they want. You don't have to prove anything to anyone."

"Miss Julie?"

Remy pulled an iPhone from his pocket and scrolled through a directory. He handed the phone over. "You invite her."

Zach put the phone to his ear and waited. "Miss Julie?"

"It's Zachary." He smiled.

"Thanks. Come to our New Year's Eve party tonight."

"The top floor of Harrah's. Bring anyone you want."

"Bye." He handed the phone back.

Remy handed him a credit card. "Use it for anything. The PIN is seven, seven, nine, nine. We'll go over the books in the next few days."

Zach looked at the face of the card. The name on it read "Mr. Bujold."

"What's the limit on this card?"

"No limit. Buy what you want."

"I'd like to get a good haircut and some clothes for tonight."

"No problem. You've got all afternoon."

Zach leaned back in the leather seat, stretching his legs, and looking out the window. He watched as a pretty blonde in a convertible entered Route 10 South, her hair swirling above the windshield.

"Any unattached women?" Zach asked.

"There'll be girls and boys eighteen and older. I wasn't sure if you'd switched teams durin' your stay."

"I've seen enough swingin' dicks for a lifetime, thanks."

"Glad to hear it, Zach."

Depressing a button to lower the window, Zach breathed in a combination of fresh air and sweet cigar smoke. He smiled at the blonde as she drove by on the inside lane.

"Have you sold Father's mansion?"

"It's still sittin' there, Zach. It's all yours. The corporation owns it, and I can quit claim it to you anytime you want. There'll be no probate."

"You've kept it maintained?" he asked, taking a swig of beer.

"I had a guy livin' there, keepin' it up. He left last week."

"So, it's furnished as it was seven years ago?"

"Sure," Remy said, puffing on the cigar, "minus a few things."

"You can say it, Remy."

"What?"

"Bodies, Remy. Minus a few bodies."

*

9

Lionel sat back in the oversized leather chair, his shoed feet resting on his desk, and unfolded the *Times-Picayune* newspaper. He sipped Starbucks coffee and looked out his office window to the Homicide Division bullpen. It was early, and only Mulroney had arrived. He put the coffee down and lit a Perique cigarette. He yelled, "Mulroney."

Mulroney picked up his coffee and walked to the office doorway.

"What, boss?"

Lionel held up his cigarette and said, "Last chance."

Mulroney walked in and sat down in a leather armchair facing Lionel. He lit a Marlboro and blew out the match. Lionel moved the ashtray to the center of the desk and said, "Bujold gets out today."

"I saw it on Nancy Grace last night," Mulroney said, taking a deep drag and holding the smoke in like it was a joint. "You gonna talk to him?"

"About what?" Lionel asked. "How were your accommodations, Zachary?"

"I dunno, maybe, 'keep your nose clean.'"

"That was the stupidest damned trial I ever saw."

"Why? He didn't exactly get off."

"Yes, he did. He just got off—today."

"Seven years in Jetson isn't a cakewalk, Sergeant."

"I don't care if it was a chain gang of pedophiles. He's now twenty-one and a multi-millionaire." Lionel spit a grain of tobacco onto the floor.

"Nancy Grace said he should have been acquitted—said there was insufficient evidence to convict."

Lionel stared at Mulroney. "Insufficient evidence, my black ass." He dragged hard on the cigarette.

"He was a minor. There was no jury, and Nancy Grace said the judge had biases."

"Don't you have work to do?" Lionel asked, turning back to read his newspaper.

Mulroney took one last hit on the Marlboro and snuffed it out. He grabbed his coffee and said, "I'll be in the Lower Ninth, Sergeant."

Lionel shook his head and thought back to the days of the trial. He could picture himself on the witness stand, seven years younger with no gray hair. New Orleans had a reputation for doing that—prematurely graying law enforcement hair.

*

She stood under the showerhead and rinsed her hair. *He's still calling me Miss Julie.* She began stepping down the Bujold family tree and forced herself to stop. It was too agonizing— like nails on a chalkboard—only the scraping never stopped.

She stepped from the shower and grabbed a towel. Blotting her skin dry, she critically appraised her naked body in the full-length mirror attached to the back of the bathroom door. *We're still okay.* She was five-foot-nine and one-hundred-ten pounds, with a flat stomach and perky breasts. Her pubic hair was bikini waxed, and she was attractive at twenty-eight. She had perfectly straight blond hair that reached the small of her back, and a vagina to die for, or so she'd been told.

She walked out to the master bedroom and surveyed the room—ten of her seventeen cats were in attendance, crouched or skulking about, waiting for their lesson in dog avoidance to commence. She threw herself on the king-sized bed, laid on her back with eyes closed, spread her arms and legs, and waited. The cats began sneaking up, smelling her soap-scented skin, purring, and sliding whiskers against her bare body. She could hear Newbie, the kitten, grabbing at the bedspread and pulling her way up, her razor-sharp nails getting stuck in the thick comforter. She felt the arrival of cats as they jumped from the dressing table and dresser onto the mattress.

She began her throaty growl—low at first, more like a gurgle. She then increased the volume a decibel or two. The sudden mattress slump told her that Hamilton was at her side. She could smell his bird breath and feel his wide paws, then his weight, as he cautiously took his position between her breasts. Hamilton was hunting now, and he had gained considerable weight. She squinted and watched him as he looked down at her. She increased the volume of the growl. Abruptly, it became a bark. "Arf, arf, arf," she shouted out as she began flailing her arms and legs. Newbie bailed first, followed by the faint of heart felines. She was left with Hamilton, whom she grabbed and kissed on the nose.

"Okay, everybody off Miss Julie," she commanded. "Class is over for today."

She scrutinized her eveningwear in the walk-in closet while wondering if she should invite a guest tonight. If this was a normal party, she would attend with someone, but this party would be far from normal. It was New Year's Eve in New Orleans, Zach's coming-out birthday party, and, to top it off, the Bujold clan would be hosting. She'd go stag, not willing to commit to someone who would be puking on her shoes before midnight. Julie knew how to pace herself through an evening of debauched drinking and drug-taking, and didn't want an amateur hanging on to her for support.

She chose a flowered, purple silk dress which stopped at her knees, and grabbed a pair of red shoes with three-inch heels. She searched for a suitable hat on the shelf above the hanging garments. Laying her selections on the bed, she slipped on a cotton bathrobe. Sitting at the dressing table, she took the time to blow-dry her hair and run hair cream through it. Men could never keep their hands off her hair. It was the first thing they reached for if she was clothed.

Walking downstairs and into the kitchen, she pulled a plate of peeled shrimp from the fridge. Grabbing a can of Bud, she walked to the back porch and sat at the table. She ate shrimp and drank beer, looking out at her garden, and thinking back to the time when Zachary was her student.

He was the most handsome boy in the sophomore class. It wasn't surprising—with the darker French-Cajun good looks of his father and the Hollywood starlet corn-fed looks of his mother. He had black, wavy hair and long, thick eyebrows over big, brown eyes, a straight nose, chiseled chin, and a beautiful mouth. His smile stopped her dead in her tracks. His skin color was mocha. She had to admit—her first day in class—she wanted to kiss that boy.

Zach had been a straight "A" student and a natural athlete, and, even while being a year younger than the other boys, excelled in baseball and football. Of course, the cutest girls were after him tooth and nail. What Julie had found so unusual was the way he held himself—he'd seem to be interested in a girl, but always appeared as though he needed more information. It drove them wild.

He had given her the "Miss Julie" handle. It was her first year of teaching, and she had called on him to comment on a racially motivated statement made by a senator from the south. Zach had stood up, scratched his head of wavy hair, shaken his head, and said, "Why, Miss Julie, I just don't know 'bout things like that goin' on anymore. Us Cajuns are still two rungs down the ladder from the blacks." Most of the class was African-American, and Zach brought the house down. Within a few days, other teachers were referring to her as "Miss Julie." The handle had stuck to this day.

As Julie looked out over the garden, watching Hamilton assume his position on the brick wall that divided backyards, she thought back to that New Year's Day, seven years ago, when she got the news that Zachary had murdered his parents.

Chapter 2

Zach got caught up in a game of Texas Hold'em and couldn't leave the table until he won or lost.

His interest in the game had faded midway through, but he forced himself to pay attention and play his cards the best way he knew. Out of a table of nine, it was now down to him and a young woman. He finally won, going all-in after a heart was dealt on the river. His adversary had no choice but to go all-in, holding two pair. Zach turned over his two hearts for the flush. He walked with eight hundred dollars. Countless hours of card games at Jetson had finally paid off.

He stopped for a beer before going to the party. The casino was crowded with gamblers, all of whom seemed certain that New Year's Eve was going to bring them untold riches. He sipped beer and thought about the current economy faced by the middle class. Obama was about to begin his lame duck term, and Zach wondered what was in store for the poor of New Orleans. The fiscal cliff was fast approaching.

He watched as a news reporter approached him with a cameraman in tow. He threw a ten on the bar and began walking fast. Slipping through a crowd of people, he stood at a craps table with his back to the aisle and watched as the reporter walked past him. He double-backed to the elevators and stepped in as the door was closing.

Getting off on the twenty-sixth floor, he passed through security by showing his credit card. He didn't have a driver's license or photo ID yet. It was eight-thirty in the evening, and the festivities were in full swing. Walking from room to room, he smiled or nodded at familiar faces. Some people were wearing facemasks, a few in costumes, and Zach was grateful for their anonymity. He stepped out onto the rooftop balcony and watched as Remy finished kissing a young woman—Remy holding a cherry stem between his perfect teeth, the stem rolled neatly in a knot, to the applause of onlookers.

Watching Remy in action, flirtatiously laughing with women, brought back memories of the family get-togethers—Cajun women dancing seductively and Cajun men with their slow burns. There was always an arbitrary, self-proclaimed line that better not be crossed. It seemed to him that every adult male had it when he walked in through the front doorway. Zach would watch someone's line being crossed and the slow burn that followed—then the stare you just didn't want aimed at you—dark eyes.

He grabbed two plastic glasses of champagne from the tray of a passing waitress and walked to Remy, handing him one. He held his drink up in the air and said, "To the best man I know, my Uncle Remy," and downed the champagne. Remy's circle of guests applauded, beginning a "For He's a Jolly Good Fellow" refrain.

Remy walked over to Zach and put a hand on his shoulder. "Nice suit, Zach, and beautiful stitching. Clean shaven, fresh haircut, and manicured nails. You look great, kiddo."

"Remy, how do you tell the hired girls from the guests?"

"Feel that urge, do ya?"

"Call it the seven year itch. I gotta scratch soon."

"The escort girls all have red heels on," Remy said as he walked to a young woman standing in red heels.

Zach walked away and Remy began laughing. "What's so funny, Remy?" the woman asked.

"Victoria, if Zach hits on you, it's 'cause he thinks you're a hooker."

"Why would he think that, Remy?"

"I dunno. Kids nowadays—who the hell knows what they're thinkin'?"

*

Zach lay on his back and took a hit off the joint, passing it back to Nadine. She seemed to have been pleased with his debut performance. She had her head tucked under his chin, stroking the hair on his chest, and flicking his left nipple with her tongue.

"So, how does the escort service treat you?" he asked.

"What? What escort service? You think I'm a hooker?"

"Aw, shit, Nadine. I should have seen that coming."

"What are you talking about?" She began to raise her head from his chest and he gently forced her head back down.

"It's Uncle Remy. Do you know him?" he asked as he slid a hand over her breast and gently pinched her nipple.

"I know of him more than having had actual contact," she replied. "Why?"

"He told me all girls wearing red heels were escorts."

She raised her head from his chest and looked into his eyes. "Well, then, lucky me. I just thought you were the determined type—a bit presumptuous, but charming." She took a hit and moved her mouth over his, sharing the harsh tasting smoke.

"I've been away for seven years," he said, expelling smoke.

"Ooh. Very lucky me. You're not done yet, are you?"

"If girls were hors d'oevres, Nadine," he said, "you'd be caviar." He scooted down some and slid his head between her legs.

*

He was sitting outside on the rooftop balcony, watching sporadic fireworks off in the distance. The moon was full and bright in the sky, and the smell of gunpowder wafted in the breeze. He thought back to his birthdays as a youth, each one accompanied by a flurry of fireworks. This birthday marked a new chapter in his life—freedom—and all that it offered.

He was drinking beer when Julie walked out. He placed the bottle on an end table and stood. She smiled and walked to him. "Happy birthday, Zach," she said, kissing him demurely on the lips.

"Are you still pissed at me for calling you 'Miss Julie'?"

"How did you know I was pissed?"

"You glared at me every time a student called you that."

She laughed. She had a throaty laugh. He'd never heard her laugh that way before. He put his hands to the sides of her face, scooped her hair up, and flipped it back over her shoulders. Looking in her eyes, he kissed her full on the lips. He held the kiss, and she didn't push him away.

She slid her hands between his shirt and suit jacket and brought them up his back. Her nails raked his muscles. He slipped his tongue into her mouth, and she moved her body into his. She brought her nails back down until her hands were cupping the cheeks of his ass. She felt his erection and moved her pelvis against it. With her three-inch heels, their privates were perfectly aligned.

"Let's get a drink and find a room, Miss Julie."

"You're gonna pay for that, Mister Bujold."

*

Zach lay on his side and ran his hand down from her neck to her pubic hair. He grabbed some hair from her shoulder and spread it over a breast. "You're more beautiful naked than I ever imagined, and I imagined you often."

"If I had done half the things I wanted to do to you when you were fourteen, I'd still be serving time," she said.

He grabbed the glass of Stoli's from the nightstand and offered it to her. She took a sip, and he placed it back on the stand. "Well, did I meet your expectations?"

"Christ," she replied. "I came before you were fully in me."

"You know, when I was in juvy, you were the only person I explained things to." He looked her in the eyes and whispered, "I knew you weren't actually there."

"That's a relief."

He drank beer and said, "I just didn't have a sole to discuss things with, other than the shrinks and lawyers. In a certain way, you saved me from going insane."

"Which the doctors thought you were."

"Absolutely. The psycho-babble was nonstop. Did you know they gave me acid?"

"Wasn't your appeal about that?"

"It was one of a number of bulleted events. They were all hell-bent on keeping me in there. I began thinking it was personal, you know, my family's history being thrown in my face. I told Remy I felt like a POW, you know, guilt by association."

"Did you get in a lot of fights?"

"At first, I did. Jetson was about eighty percent black, and many of them were big boys. Slower than me, but if they connected with a punch, I'd be in the next room."

"African-American," she said.

"What?"

"The proper term is 'African-American,' not 'black.'"

"You're right," he said, "and I'm half French-Cajun-American and half African-American. Why do they call me 'Cajun'?"

"Sorry. It's just the teacher in me."

"Put your middle finger just under your thumb."

Julie did so.

He said, "It works better without long nails. Now flick it hard."

She pushed her middle finger off the bottom of her thumb.

"Like you're flicking away a booger, right?"

"I'm guessing so. School teachers don't flick boogers. They do give good blowjobs, though, don't they?"

"The very best," he said as he kissed her. "Anyway, that's what I'd do to a big guy. Quick, before he saw it coming, I'd flick him hard in the eyeball. Then I'd hit him in his larynx."

"Jesus. And that would do it?"

"Anyone will go down if you have the opportunity to do that to them. Of course, once he was down, I had to beat the shit out of him before he got up. The guards gave me the nickname 'Flicka.'"

Julie put her hand to the side of his face and brought his mouth to hers. She kissed him sensually and said, "I'm sorry."

"Let's take a shower and join the others. I've spent one third of my life dealing with this shit. I don't want to waste another minute."

"This wasn't a waste, was it?"

"Oh, God, no," he said, touching her cheek. "This was the best birthday present I've ever been given—by my school teacher, no less."

*

They separated and mingled with others, watched the fireworks intensify as New Year's Eve came to a close, and began kissing and hugging other guests. The faceless took off their masks and ditched their costumes. Zach found her and spun her around, put his hands on the sides of her face and kissed her hard. "You're not leaving me tonight, are you?" he asked.

Julie shook her head and looked in his eyes. "No, I'm not leaving you."

He felt her shiver and led her inside. He put his jacket over her shoulders and steered her to a living room. Pulling two armchairs close together in front of a fireplace, he stoked the flames. It was a gas burner, and he found the remote and turned it up.

"Have you eaten enough? Did you try the Beluga?"

She shook her head, shivering. "No, I haven't."

"And some brandy?"

"That sounds scrumptious."

He left her, and returned with a silver tray containing two snifters of brandy, a bowl of caviar, some crackers, and silverware. He placed it on a small coffee table and moved the table between the chairs and the fire.

"Are you warm now?"

"Blissfully," she replied, sliding his jacket from her shoulders and draping it over the arm of a couch.

He turned the flame down and sat in the chair facing her. He held the snifter in the air and she touched hers to his. "I can't think of a better way to start the New Year," he said, reaching over to kiss her. She met him halfway.

"Do you have many suitors?" he asked.

"No, but if they suit me, I fuck 'em. Listen to me. I'm getting schnockered."

"Are you Jewish?" he asked.

"I'm a Jewess."

"A sexy Jewess."

"You're a beautiful young man, Zach. That's not the liquor talking."

"I've fantasized about you since sophomore class," he said.

She scooped some caviar onto a cracker. "You actually give off a heat."

He dipped a cracker in caviar and said, "I'm glad you feel that way. I don't want this to be it with you."

"It won't be, Zach. And I do want to hear your story very much."

"Soon. I have to shake Jetson off. I've gotta begin working out, running, maybe some swimming. It'll clear my head."

"Have you given any thought to what you'd like to do with the rest of your life?"

"Not so much. I'm a felon, now. I've thought about getting a captain's license."

"Commercial fishing?"

Zach shook his head. "Definitely for personal or private tours. I read a lot of Michener in Jetson, and, eventually, I'd like to travel. New Orleans would always be my home base."

"Have you picked out a bedroom for us?"

"Remy took care of that."

"I want to massage you."

"Would you spread your legs just a little bit for me before we leave?"

Julie stood and angled the armchair more in his direction. She sat and adjusted her dress, spreading her legs to give him six inches from knee to knee. "Enough?"

"Little more," he instructed.

She complied. "How do you think Remy will react when he sees us together tomorrow morning?"

"You're wearing red heels. What else would he expect?"

"I don't get it," she said, giving him just a little more.

Chapter 3

Remy and Claude were sitting on the rooftop balcony the morning of January 1, drinking bloody Marys at a table under a canvas awning. The sky was overcast, and a light rain fell. Zach and Julie walked out and joined them. A waiter took their orders, and Zach turned to look through the glass sliding doors of the rec room. Stragglers inside walked through the room, looking for articles misplaced in the melee. A young woman walked around stark naked, picking through clothes scattered on the floor. A semi-naked couple lay sleeping on top of a quilt on the rec room floor.

The early morning breeze was cool and brought with it smells from the Mississippi River. Zach walked over to the railing and looked down to where Poydras joined Canal. The day after, and the streets looked like a hurricane had hit. He joined them at the table and sat, holding the cup of steaming coffee to his lips and blowing.

"Well, Miss Julie," Remy said, "did my nephew receive a passing grade for the night?" He flashed his teeth and gave her an officious look.

"Remy," Julie said, "I'm afraid Zach is gonna hafta stay after school. He's been away from his studies far too long. I'm gonna hafta bone him up." She returned Remy's look with an innocuous stare.

Claude said, "Remy, we went to school twenty years too soon. There's a new breed of school marm out today, and I'm likin' her."

"Thank you, Claude," Julie said. "How are your children doing?"

"Straight 'A' students, Julie, thanks to you."

"I'm glad to hear it."

"You live in a predominantly black neighborhood, don't you, Julie?"

"I do, Claude."

"Nobody on the streets messed with you since Katrina?"

"That's right."

"Know why?" Claude asked.

She sipped coffee and replied, "I know it's not 'cause they think I'm the Virgin Mary."

"It's 'cause you're their kid's lottery ticket outta here."

"Ooh, wait. I hear Seger singing, 'Feel Like a Number.'"

"Don't sell yourself short, Missy," Claude said, raising an eyebrow.

"Thanks, Claude," she replied, grabbing Zach by the collar. "One more lesson and I gotta check on the cats."

*

Claude dropped them off at Remy's house in the Garden District. Remy owned a Greek revival double-galleried mansion on St. Charles Avenue. On either side of the property a smaller Queen Anne Victorian house had been built, both of which

Remy owned. His staff lived in one house, and the other remained unoccupied until guests arrived.

Zach followed Remy through the wrought-iron gate and up the steps to the front porch. Four wide columns adorned the front of the mansion, supporting the roof and the second-floor balcony. They walked into the vestibule and through to the kitchen.

"Fareeba, meet my nephew, Zachary."

Fareeba turned from the sink and gazed at Zach. He felt his knees weaken and his heart pick up a pace. She wiped her hands over her breasts, on an apron which ended inches below where her long legs met. She was a beautiful Creole woman. She smiled and walked up to Zach, ran her open hands over his pectorals, and kissed him on the mouth. "What's cookin', sugar?"

Zach looked at Remy, and said, "I gotta hand it to ya, Remy—you can certainly pick 'em."

Remy smiled and raised his eyebrows. "Reba, baby, would you bring Zach and me some coffee and Kahlua?"

"Sure, honey."

Remy led Zach to his study. He turned on a light over a small conference table, walked to a desk, and returned with a crystal ashtray. He walked to a shelf of books and returned with two hardbound ledgers. Finally, he retrieved a humidor from the desk and placed it on the table.

"Let's sit side by side," he said, bringing a chair to Zach's right side, and sitting. He opened the humidor and rolled out two cigars. "Cubans," he said. "Put up with me, Zach. This is a ritual your father and I went through once a month for many years."

Remy adjusted himself in the chair and said, "Henri and I always split everything down the middle. Now, that's what I'm doing with you."

Fareeba walked in and Remy stopped talking. She placed a glass mug of coffee to Remy's right and then one to Zach's left. He smelled a lilac scent coming off her. His head was at the level of her belly, and he breathed through his nose and felt light-headed. She bent and kissed Remy on the ear and let an index finger trail over Zach's shoulder as she walked out of the room.

Remy handed Zach a cigar and stuck one between his teeth. He produced a lighter and lit them. Leaning back in the chair, he blew out a smoke ring and took a minute to himself.

Reaching for the ledgers, he placed the ledger labeled "Henri Bujold" in front of Zach. He slid the ledger labeled "Remy Bujold" in front of him and opened it. Zach followed suit. The pages were held together by small, round metal rings.

"Every page represents a year of income and expenses. You're looking at last year. Go back nine years in time." Remy counted pages and laid the ledger open. He watched as Zach did the same.

"This was two years before Katrina and your being sent away. See the balance forward amount?"

Zach looked at the opening balance at the top of the page and counted the zeroes. "Two million dollars," he said.

"Every dollar amount is rounded off by one hundred. It makes things easier."

"Two-hundred million dollars?" Zach's voice increased an octave.

"Look at my balance forward."

"Two-hundred million dollars," Zach repeated.

"That's what we had nine years ago—four-hundred million dollars. Two years later, Katrina hit and you went to Jetson. Go forward in time two years."

They both turned pages.

Zack studied the page. "The opening balance was around one-hundred-fifty million dollars. You lost one-hundred million dollars in two years."

"That was the cost of us going legit. Isn't that fuckin' insane?"

Zach puffed on the cigar and looked at his uncle. "Remy, these numbers are insane to begin with. You guys racked up four-hundred million dollars?"

"More. Turn to the front page again. Last year. What's the current balance forward?"

"Three-hundred million," Zach said.

"Each."

"Fuck!"

Remy nodded and drank some coffee. "You know, there's a lot of Bujolds out there. It's a very big family which has been here since the colonies. We had slave traders, plantation owners, cotton and tobacco, stills, and more. Most of the big money was made during Prohibition. We had prostitution, drugs, gambling, cock fighting, boxing, and hooch. When mobsters tried to muscle in, we slit their throats and dumped their bodies in a bayou. We owned banks strictly for laundering money. Every generation passed the wealth forward."

He drank more coffee and puffed on the cigar. "Anyway, Henri and I knew it was only a matter of time before the IRS caught up with us. We went to the families we were involved with and negotiated our getting out. It was worth it. We could sleep at night.

29

"Our money and possessions are held in a corporate account. Investments are very conservative—gold, silver, and oil. You basically get around ten percent on your invested money every year, and you have to pay taxes on it. We never went crazy with tax-sheltered money, and we donated big to local charities. Guess what money you earned while you were in Jetson."

Zach shook his head and said, "I don't have a clue."

"Around twenty million a year, give or take. Of course, every year you paid the IRS a good share, but it's all positive growth. So, you made fifteen million net the first year. The next year, the principal was higher. Look at it this way for now—if you only spend five million a year, you'll never run out of money in your lifetime."

"Jesus!" Zach exclaimed.

"And it's good to be rich. You think I'd have a girl like Fareeba in my bed every night without a ton of money?"

"Does she have a sister?"

Remy laughed. "She's irresistible, isn't she?"

"I haven't met that many Creole women. Is she Spanish Creole?"

"A mix of French and Spanish. It's like mixing Italian and Puerto Rican. That's why they're kept barefoot and pregnant."

*

They sat in the cab, and Zach paid the driver. He and Julie stared at the mansion. It was three stories high, with a wrap-around deck on the first floor, and balconies on the second and third floors. Two gables jutted out from the roof. The entire mansion was painted white. A tall, wrought-iron fence ran along the sidewalk. "This was my parent's house," he said. A crack of thunder finished his sentence, and they looked at each other in surprise, and then laughed. Rain was coming down in torrents.

"Ready?" he asked.

He opened the door of the cab and held his hand for Julie to grab. They ran to the gate and he pushed it inward. Julie ran along the flagstone walkway to the porch, turned, and waited for him. "I thought the rain was gonna stop," he said, wiping his face clear of rainwater and walking to the front doors. He opened one large door and let Julie walk into the vestibule. The interior smelled of fresh paint and ginger blossoms. He noticed that windows were opened several inches to keep the house from getting stale.

A long staircase led to a second-floor balcony. They walked past it, on polished, hardwood floors through toward the back of the house. Entering a large kitchen, he brought her to a bay window overlooking a garden. Tall hedges lined the property, and the corners held thirty-foot high palm trees. A few bushes were flowered, but the garden wasn't thriving as it would be in three or four months.

He opened a pantry door and pulled out two towels. He handed her one, and they both wiped their hair dry. "I'll get some rain slickers from upstairs before we leave," he said.

Wide doors were open to a living room off to the left and a formal dining room off to the right. He steered her to the living room. A couch faced two armchairs and the backyard.

"That's where my parents were found, shot dead," he said, pointing to the couch.

He led her back into the kitchen and to the hallway leading down to the vestibule. He pointed to the floor. "That's where they found me, drunk, and unconscious."

They walked to the rear-wall of the kitchen, and he opened the door to the back porch. They stood on the porch, and he pointed into the garden. "Past that hedge, there's a sitting area with concrete benches and a birdbath."

They walked back in and he closed the door. Standing at a pantry door, he asked, "What's your pleasure?"

"Why don't we have scotch?"

He grabbed a bottle of Johnny Walker Black. The fridge looked new and had an ice dispenser on the door. He grabbed two drinking glasses from a cabinet and filled them with ice. Pouring scotch and adding some water, he handed her a glass and said, "Let's go upstairs and find something warm to wear."

They walked up the staircase. "My bedroom is down that way," he said, pointing to the left. "I'm not ready to look in there right now. I'll show you my parent's bedroom." He began walking down the hallway to the right.

"Zack," she said.

He turned to look at her. "What?"

"Why don't you take your time and I'll be in the kitchen. Okay?"

"Feeling creepy?" he asked.

"Not at all," she replied. "Just take some time for yourself. You've been away a long time." She began walking down the stairs.

Zach walked to his parent's bedroom and opened the door. The room looked exactly as he remembered it, with the canopied, king-sized bed, dark Victorian furniture, draped windows, and French doors to a balcony. He inhaled deeply, exhaled slowly and sat at the foot of the bed. He leaned back until his head was resting on the bedspread, and let the warm memories of his childhood flood back to him. He could vividly remember walking into this room in the middle of the night, at a young age, climbing up and into his mother's arms, the smell of her as she drew him to her body, and the feeling of being in a safe place.

Julie was sitting at the kitchen table, sipping her drink when he walked downstairs.

"How do you feel about wearing dead people's clothing?" he asked, laying some garments on the back of a wooden chair and grabbing the bottle of scotch.

"I shop at Good Will, Zach. They sell clothes that date back to the Great Plague."

"It's not really cold outside, and I thought rain slickers would be enough. I brought down some light sweaters if you think you might need one."

He refreshed their drinks and they donned the rain gear. He led her out to the front porch. They sat on high-backed cushioned chairs, and watched as the rain subsided and finally stopped. The sun broke through the cloud formations, and thunder could be heard off in the distance.

They sat next to each other and drank scotch. There was little activity on the street—an occasional mother walking with an infant in a stroller, people biking, and the sounds of laughter at a neighboring outdoor party.

"Did you ever meet my father, Henri?" he asked.

"Yes, at a PTA meeting in October of your sophomore year."

"And my mother, Annette?"

Julie nodded. "Strikingly beautiful woman."

"Did you know that Henri and Remy were identical twins?"

"No. I don't remember your father as looking like Remy."

"They decided early on that Remy would have the facial hair—moustache and goatee. My father liked to be clean-shaven."

"Your father was a classy man," Julie said.

"He had a quick temper, like all the Bujold men. Remember when Katrina hit New Orleans in late August?"

"I'll never forget it. Nobody will."

"Remember all the chaos surrounding that time? Then Rita hit. Neighborhoods were destroyed. Dead bodies were being counted. Families and lives were being shuffled around. My family and I had it easy—the Garden District didn't flood."

"I had to relocate," she said.

"That December, around the fifteenth, someone paid me a visit."

"Who was that?"

He shook his head and said, "I can't do this here. Let's walk and grab something to eat."

"Who came to visit you, Zach?"

"My twin brother, Louis." Zach stood and took Julie by the hand. They walked to the sidewalk and down St. Charles Avenue.

Chapter 4

They ended up taking a cab to the French Quarter. Zach wanted to eat at Broussard's. The cab pulled up on Rue Conti and he paid the driver. They had several hours of daylight available, and asked to be seated in the courtyard. The hostess led them to a wrought-iron table, outside, on a flagstone patio. A flower garden surrounded a water fountain, and the patio was lined with trees and shrubs.

"Are you cold?" he asked her.

"Not at all, Zach. Are you hungry?"

"I'm starved. How 'bout you?"

"I can eat."

Julie ordered vodka and Zach ordered beer and some appetizers. He looked around. "Some places haven't changed at all since Katrina."

"Well, it's been over seven years. Some areas are still a mess," she said. "I'll show you around sometime soon. We call it Obamafiction."

"Being back here is a mixed bag for me. It's conjuring up so many good and bad memories."

"We don't have to talk about it now, Zach, or ever."

"Oh, I have to talk to you about it, now. I've waited a long time to tell you about what happened, hoping you might make some sense of it all."

Their drinks arrived, and he said, "I was sitting in the garden when Louis approached me. He walked up to me and said, 'Hi, brother.' I said, 'Hi, my name is Zach.' I wasn't looking at him at that moment. I'd been watching a cardinal which had lit down on the birdbath, and had started washing itself."

He drank beer. "He said, 'My name is Louis. Don't you think we look alike?' I stopped looking at the bird and looked at him. Julie, it was like looking in a mirror.

"He said that his parents had told him about us being twins. According to him, our mother and his adoptive mother had shared photos of the two of us as we developed. He said he had just started prep school. Anyway, I was very skeptical at this point. I figured he wanted something from me, or that it was some sort of a con."

He took a drink of beer. "Louis said that he was on winter break, and had decided to come down and see if I existed, and if I had survived the hurricane. I asked him where he went to school, and he wouldn't tell me. I asked him where he lived, and he wouldn't tell me that, either. He walked away after saying he'd see me again. Pretty strange, eh?"

Julie had been listening intently, and she took a long drink of vodka. She watched as the waiter deposited shrimp Remoulade and crabmeat Broussard's on their table. He asked if they would be ordering an entrée. They both decided on the Louisiana bouillabaisse.

Zach stabbed a shrimp and ate it. "He showed up a week later. I was in the garden, studying for exams. He told me the story that his parents had told him—that I was born on New Year's Eve at ten-thirty in the evening, and he was born four minutes later. His parents had given him his birth certificate, and he showed it to me. He was born Louis Bujold, four minutes after my birth. Louis's adoptive mother could not conceive a child. I guess she was infertile. At least, that's what he told me."

He sipped beer and asked, "Any questions?"

"Did you ask him his parent's names?"

"I did. He wouldn't tell me. What he said was that his father was a movie producer, and his mother was a well-known actress. They were wealthy people, and he wasn't looking for anything but answers. He left at that point."

He picked at the shrimp and said, "This is where I lost the shrinks. They couldn't believe that I didn't approach my parents at this point, demanding answers. I told them that I respected my parent's privacy. They all thought I would have confronted my parents if I were telling the truth."

"I understand how you felt. You loved your parents, didn't you?"

"I did, very much. So, anyway, he returned on New Year's Eve. It was still early, around nine in the evening. My parents were home. They had plans to go out later, and I had a date. He said he thought we should approach them together and ask them what happened fourteen years ago.

"We entered the house and walked into the living room. I went to the stairway and called for them. I said I had to talk to them in the living room, together. My mother came down first and stood in front of the couch, staring at us sitting in the two armchairs, our backs to the garden. Then my father came down and joined her. He was staring at the two of us, and then they both sat on the couch."

Zach stopped talking as the bouillabaisse was delivered in two large bowls. He smelled the aroma of seafood, tomato sauce, and Cajun spices. "Let's eat," he said. The seafood tasted fresh and spicy.

He resumed ten minutes later, after dipping some French bread into the bowl, letting it absorb the tasty sauce, and eating it.

"I said to my parents that they were looking at Louis, and that he wanted to understand what made them decide to give him away. My father was usually the talker in the family, but he waited for Annette to explain.

"She said that she didn't want to raise twins. She used my father and Remy as an example. She said that there's a bond between twins that interferes with all other relationships, and that Henri's relationship with Remy almost broke up their marriage. She said she wasn't thinking of herself, but rather the relationships we would ruin with women if we were allowed to grow up together."

He finished his beer and asked if she wanted something else. She suggested cognac, and Zach hailed the waiter.

"My mother said that after a week with both of us, she decided to call an actress friend of hers, a woman who couldn't conceive children but wanted one. She wouldn't say the name of the woman, as she had taken an oath to never divulge that information. Louis nodded and walked to the kitchen. I followed him and he suggested that we have a drink. I poured scotch into two glasses, and he asked my parents to wait, 'cause he wanted to say goodbye before he left. We walked outside and sat in the garden."

He held his snifter of cognac in the air, and she touched her glass to his. He sipped the strong liquor.

"What I haven't conveyed is the tension that gripped us throughout all of this—both my parents and me, but especially Louis. My mother was actually trembling, and Henri looked very upset. As we walked out to the backyard, I saw my father head for the liquor cabinet. I was in shock, realizing that Louis had been telling me the truth. I was extremely nervous, and I had a feeling that things were about to escalate. I wasn't even sure that my father had known what my mother did. I expected Henri to explode at any minute.

"Outside, Louis became angry. He said, 'Doesn't that make you mad?' I asked why and he said, 'Because they kept us apart. It's not fair to keep twins apart, especially identical twins.' He said he felt betrayed.

"I was drinking to steady my nerves. He took my empty glass and walked into the house, said something to my parents, and returned with a fresh drink for me. At this point I was anxious and feeling nauseous. He was acting so animated, walking around the birdbath, throwing his arms in the air, saying that it just wasn't fair. I remember thinking that he was getting out of control."

Zach looked up from the table and stared at Julie. "That's it," he said.

She scowled at him. "What's it?"

"The next thing I knew, a police officer was putting handcuffs on my wrists. My parents were dead, and Louis was gone."

*

Zach paid for a room at the Windsor Court Hotel on Gravier Street, and they walked slowly through the French

39

Quarter. The full moon was waning, but shone brightly. He began talking about the psychologists and their take on his story. He said they all concurred that there was no twin, and that he had a psychotic break from reality. Some called him schizophrenic, while others felt he suffered from a psychiatric disorder known as multiple personality syndrome. "Psychosis" was a word bandied about a lot.

"The one thing in common I heard from all the shrinks was 'borderline.' In time, I realized what that was—it was their safety net. They hid behind the word. If one psychologist questioned another on his diagnosis, he could just say, 'Well, I said he was borderline.'

"I made a mistake with a psychiatrist early on, and I got stuck with it. His name was Doctor Fadon. I had been having nightmares in my cell, always involving a figure I labeled the Grim Reaper. He appeared before me in a long, black cape with a frightening death mask on his face. He would always end up crouching over me, and sometimes opening my mouth. It was a very scary dream for me, and I discussed it with the doctor. He used that dream against me, declaring that I had unknowingly invented a character that triggered my psychotic break from reality. Then my delusion that Louis existed in my life was born. The Grim Reaper was the catalyst for my psychotic split. I kept telling him the nightmare started after the murders, not before, but when a psychiatrist gets to thinking a certain way, there's just no convincing him otherwise. He was starving for an explanation."

Julie walked ahead of him and turned, stopping him in his tracks. She put her arms around his waist and then up his back. She said, "They put you through the ringer, didn't they?" She kissed him softly.

He put an arm around her back and continued walking. "Remy got me this lawyer who was supposed to be good, but I wasn't impressed. I told him to go get the certificates of birth for me and Louis. He did that. Louis's certificate showed him being born four minutes after me, just like Louis showed me. There were no further medical records on Louis, and the speculation was that he died early in his infancy and my parents had kept it a secret. No one, neither family nor friends, had ever heard of my having a twin. Not even Remy.

"There was some searching done regarding the possible adoption of Louis Bujold, both in Louisiana and California, which turned up nothing. Foster care agencies were questioned, but nothing was found to indicate that Louis was adopted.

"I told my lawyer I was innocent. He said, based on my age, I could be out by my eighteenth birthday if I confessed to the murders. None of the shrinks were talking 'premeditated' and most, if not all of them, were considering me to be a victim. Acquittal, however, was not a word anyone was mentioning. I was a minor, in a juvenile court, so there was no jury. I pled innocent before the judge. I wasn't convicted—I was an 'adjudicated delinquent.' It amounts to the same thing."

They ended up standing in front of the Windsor. "You'll stay with me tonight, won't you, Julie?"

"No, Zach. School resumes tomorrow. I have to get home tonight."

They kissed goodnight and he walked into the hotel and took the elevator to his room. He looked in the hospitality fridge and found a beer. Taking the can out, he walked to a recliner and sat down. Popping the top, he sipped the beer and tried to free his mind from the emotions stirred up by recounting the events as he remembered them. *That was the problem, though, wasn't it?* All this was the way he remembered it—perceived it—not necessarily the way it really happened.

Early on in his incarceration and ensuing psychological evaluations, one psychologist after another described the psychotic break from reality and the hallucinations that could follow. They described how he could be sitting in the garden and holding a conversation with himself, and how he would absolutely, positively swear that he was talking with another person.

He had asked the psychologists that if they were right, then why hadn't his parents freaked out if he was sitting alone, talking with them in the living room, and pointing to an empty chair that he saw Louis sitting in? They all agreed that such a conversation never really happened, just in his delusional mind. They all concurred that he called his parents down from upstairs, and, after they sat on the couch, he shot them both in the chest.

How could he prove that they were wrong? He never had a psychotic break in the seven years at Jetson, but that proved nothing. The insurmountable problem was that no one alive had seen him and Louis together. He was sure that Louis had structured it that way—always approaching him when he was alone in the garden. How could he prove that? His lawyer certainly couldn't.

The shrinks had discussed the statistical infrequency of a twin birth, but Zach had researched that in Jetson. Considering his race to be non-Hispanic black, due to his African-American grandmother, his chance of having a twin was the highest. Many genetics experts felt that twins often spawned twins, and his father was a twin. In all, Zach had felt certain that statistics were on his side.

Chapter 5

The following morning, Zach called Remy and asked if they could get together. Remy said he'd have Claude drive them to a place on the river he liked to frequent. They had great Creole food, and he'd have Fareeba join them. She knew the owners.

Zach put on his jeans and the maroon T-shirt, with a gray windbreaker he had found in his father's closet. Slipping on a new pair of sneakers, he realized he needed to spend a day shopping for clothes and shoes. He brought a laundry bag with his suit, shirt, and shoes down to the front desk and asked that they be dry-cleaned and held for him, and he checked out.

He waited at the entrance to the hotel, and hopped in the back seat when the limo pulled up. Remy was wearing his usual western attire, and Fareeba was wearing a peasant dress, with long legs crossed and a heeled shoe dangling from her foot. She had a sweater over her shoulders.

"Morning, sugar," she said to Zach.

"Morning, Fareeba. You look lovely today."

"Why, thank you, sir."

"Hungry, Zach?" Remy asked.

"I'm always hungry now. I can't get enough of the food around here. Try eating institutional food for seven years."

"We'll fatten you up, boy."

Claude drove them to a restaurant on the river. The place was ramshackle, but it was crowded with locals, which was always a good sign. The rain had slowed to a drizzle. Fareeba sauntered in through the front door, shimmied through the crowd of people waiting to be seated, and disappeared from sight. A few minutes later she reappeared at the side of the restaurant, waving for them to join her. Zach followed Remy and Claude, catching angry glances from hungry people wondering what made them so special.

They were greeted by a skinny woman of striking looks—a completely angular face with large, oval eyes and a haunting mouth. Her facial features all seemed to be exaggerated. Her teeth were straight but badly decayed. *A little inbreeding going on there?* Zach thought. She led them to a circular table at the corner of a large, crooked deck over water. An umbrella kept the table and chairs dry. The woman fussed over Fareeba, whispering something in her ear. Fareeba laughed and put an index finger to her lips, signaling a secret to be kept.

The menu was small. Fareeba said, "May I, Remy?"

"Of course, baby," he replied.

Fareeba walked to a backdoor and entered the restaurant's kitchen. Remy said, "Let's let Reba order for us. Any objections?"

Zach looked at Claude. Both men smiled and shook their heads.

"So, Zach. Wanna buy a car?"

Zach looked at his uncle, and replied, "Remy, what I need is a place to live. It's not gonna be the mansion. Based on where I live, I'll decide if I need a car. Sound okay?"

"Sure," Remy said, lighting a Cohiba and placing the pack on the table.

Fareeba walked back and sat between Remy and Claude. "Strawberry daiquiris and Creole omelets," she announced.

Remy said, "Reba, Zach wants a place to live. What are your thoughts?"

She reached for a Cohiba and Remy lit it. Looking at Zach, she studied him for a moment, and said, "I see Zach on a yacht."

Zach laughed and said, "I was thinking houseboat, but a yacht sounds a whole lot better."

"You know," Remy said, "you could live in a penthouse and have a staff of people take care of you. How do you plan on spending your time?"

"I might try getting a captain's license."

The daiquiris were delivered, and they all sucked their drinks through straws. *Ambrosia*, Zach thought. He said, "What do you think, Claude?"

Claude laughed. "I'm the wrong person to ask, Zach. I've never lived in a house that wasn't more than ten feet from another man's house. At forty-five, I wouldn't want to live any other way. My wife and I would be lost anywhere else. But if I were you, a single man in New Orleans, I'd be right in the thick of it. Get me a nice room with a balcony in the French Quarter, and leave me be."

"Claude," Zach said, holding his glass in the air, "you were just the right person to ask."

Claude smiled and touched his glass to Zach's, then sucked hard through his straw.

The omelets were brought out and they began eating. All conversation ceased, and each of them savored the taste of eggs with seafood and Creole spices.

*

Fareeba was having a conversation with some Creole women at another table, and Claude was on his cell phone talking with his wife. Zach asked Remy if they could walk off the omelets. They rose and headed for a pier that jutted out over the water.

"What made you stick with me, Remy?"

"You mean, after it all went down?"

"Yeah."

"You're my blood, Zach. You know, over the years, I spent at least as much time with you as your father did, maybe more. Henri was always busy with something, especially with Annette trying to find success in Hollywood. You were at my house all the time, remember?"

"Of course I remember, but everyone was sayin' how I did it, and there was no proof that I didn't. You loved Henri so much, I mean, how can you even stand looking at me?"

Remy slung his arm over Zach's shoulder. He said, "Like I told you—you're my blood. If you did it, it's not because you're evil. Something happened, and you split in half. Personally, I believed your story."

"How was it that you never knew my mother gave birth to twins?"

"That still confuses me, Zach. Your father and I told each other everything. With a twin, it's not like you're talking to someone else—it's like you're thinking to yourself, out loud.

46

There's no judgment. That's the way it was with us. I guess that's what almost drove them apart, as a couple—that closeness Henri and I had. Annette must have laid down the law—there would be no discussion with Remy about twins or this thing that we're gonna do."

"You mean, giving Louis up?"

"Yeah."

"So, you never came by the hospital to see your new sweet little nephew when we were born?"

"Nothing could have stopped me except for the fact that I was in jail."

"I never heard about that," Zach said.

"I punched a police officer. I'd been driving the back roads in my Lincoln. A deer jumped out of the marsh and I hit it. The deer ended up on the hood of my car. It wasn't dead, and I kept driving, knowing there was a gas station a mile away. This trooper stopped me. He gave me shit for not stopping, and he called me a dumb Cajun. I clocked him and he went down hard. I ended up calling it in from the phone in his cruiser. I said, 'Code red. Officer down. Veterinarian needed immediately.'"

Zach began laughing. "You're a piece of work, Remy."

"Aw, it's good to see ya laugh, kiddo. Lighten up. Keep them hangin' loose."

*

Zach spent the afternoon walking Bourbon Street. He enjoyed watching the interactions between local merchants and the tourist trade. The marks were easy to spot, and the locals were just trying to get their fair share. Hookers would slowly pass a lone, male tourist and whisper, "Wanna date?" or "Blowjob?" He encountered a black boy, no more than ten years old, tap dancing on the sidewalk. Zach stopped, watched, and waited until the boy took a break, and then handed him a twenty.

It was a cold afternoon, and he stopped to buy a black leather coat. It had a nice cut to it, with a warm lining that could be removed. He wore it out of the shop, stopped in a bar for a quick Abita Amber beer and continued to walk.

He entered the Inn on Bourbon and asked to see their best accommodations. He was led upstairs to what they called a petite suite. It had a king-sized bed and ornate bedroom furniture, with a sitting area and a desk next to a small balcony. It was impressive, and certainly had all the amenities—a flat-screen with HBO, free WiFi, and Internet access. He thanked the woman for her time and continued down Bourbon Street.

He walked into the Desire Oyster Bar of the Royal Sonesta Hotel. It was a casual, street-front bistro. He was seated at a table facing Bourbon Street, and he checked out the menu. Louisiana seafood was their specialty. He ordered a dozen oysters and a Stoli's martini, chilled.

The waitress brought his drink, and he sipped the vodka. A pamphlet provided an overview of the Sonesta, and he read it while looking up occasionally to watch people walking by. The hotel had a jazz band which played seven days a week, and a coffee café. There was a courtyard, a heated swimming pool, and almost five hundred guest rooms and thirty-five unique suites. That sounded interesting, and after talking with Remy, Zach knew it was affordable.

The oysters were delicious. He sat for an hour, sipping the drink and beginning to feel excited about his prospects. He could take lessons in piloting and begin researching boats. He had nothing but time and nothing to lose.

He paid the tab and walked to the hotel reception desk. A young woman greeted him, and he said he was looking for something special in a suite, perhaps one of the thirty-five suites they advertised. She made a phone call, and within minutes Zach was talking with a concierge named Philippe. He was taken on a tour of the various specialty suites that the hotel offered on the sixth and seventh floors.

Julie called him as he was ending the tour. It was approaching six o'clock in the evening, and he asked if she would join him. He needed help deciding on a living space at the Sonesta. They could dine at the Restaurant R'evolution and take in Irvin Mayfield's jazz music.

He was standing on Bourbon Street as Julie approached. She was wearing blue jeans with knee-high black leather boots and a black woolen sweater. Her blond hair fell down over her breasts and almost to her navel. Her hair bounced as she walked quickly. She smiled and gave him a secretive, down-low wave of her hand. Walking up to him, almost at eye level, she gave him a sensuous kiss.

"I need a drink," she said, feeling the leather of his coat. "Nice coat. Soft leather."

"Let's go to the restaurant and look over the menu. I might be eating their food a lot."

They began walking. She said, "You're thinking of staying at the Sonesta?"

"More than thinking, Julie. I want to live here."

"No more mansion?"

"I can't do it. There's just too much that went on in that house which is no longer part of my life. Maybe I can donate it to some charity—perhaps an abused women's shelter. I'll have to talk to Remy about it."

They waited for a table in the restaurant. Julie ordered a double scotch on the rocks and Zach ordered a draught beer. He began describing the luxury suites available at the Sonesta. He placed a hand over hers and asked how her day was.

"My days are almost always good, Zach. I love living here, and I love teaching. I'm studying to be a criminologist, and there's no better city in America for something like that. I'm not one to get depressed, although I can get lonely sometimes. I have no family to speak of. You're so fortunate to have your uncle."

Zach nodded and said, "I am. He's stood by me through everything, and he's being very generous to me now."

They were seated and given menus. Asking for another scotch for Julie, he ordered crawfish etoufee and she ordered stuffed lobster tail.

"Do you mind talking about the incident?" she asked.

"Is that how we'll refer to my parents being murdered? The incident? Why not Callanwolde?"

"Don't take that tone of voice with me, young man." She laughed and said, "It's good to know you read the book, though."

"Are you kidding? With a family tree like mine? I read that book when I was twelve. I thought I was Tom Wingo. After the incident," he said, staring at her, "I felt more like Savannah."

"May I ask you a question about Callanwolde?"

"Shoot," he responded.

"Funny you should say that. I want to know about the murder weapon. Did they find it?"

"Nope."

"Did they test your hands for powder burns?"

"Yep."

"And?" she asked.

"There were no powder burns. However, I could have worn gloves, and I could have disposed of all the evidence, or hidden it somewhere in the house."

"While you were drunk?"

"Or drugged. That's what I think happened. Louis dropped something into my glass of scotch that knocked me out. Then he carried me inside the house and laid me in the hallway."

"How did the police happen to find you on New Year's Day?"

"An anonymous phone call tipped them off. Wasn't that thoughtful of Louis?"

"They couldn't trace the call?" she asked.

"Not from a prepaid cell phone. I asked the shrinks if they thought I made the call, seeing as how Louis only existed in my imagination. They never offered an explanation for the call."

They took their time eating dinner. The food was delicious. Zach knew he had found his next home.

Chapter 6

Zach awoke the following morning to the beat of the street—cars honking, trucks grinding gears, and people yelling to one another while starting their day. Sun filtered in through the French doors of a balcony. Thin drapes flapped in the breeze that drifted into the bedroom. He lay on his back in the middle of the king-sized bed, smelling jasmine. There were potted plants on the balcony, and he figured one might be the fragrance's source. He reluctantly swung his legs out of bed.

He walked between the drapes to the railing of the balcony. Standing there in boxer briefs, he looked up at a crystal clear sky. The temperature was around fifty degrees. It was January 3, and the second day back to work for most people in the country. Looking down, it just looked like another day in the French Quarter.

Walking down the spiral staircase to the living area, he started the coffee-maker. He sat on the couch and switched on the flat-screen. Scrolling down the menu of channels, he selected local news. Police were escorting handcuffed men into a cruiser.

Julie had suggested he try the two-level suite for a while, to see if the spiral staircase would become a nuisance. She thought it was nice to have the bedroom separated from the living area, with both levels having balconies. Zach didn't care one way or another—the Sonesta had two bedroom suites on one level, some with larger balconies. He could make the second bedroom an office. Philippe said he'd work with them to come up with a suitable floor plan as suites became available. He was aware that money was not an object, and that Zach had long term plans to live there.

Julie had been wonderful to be with last night. She loved the jazz, and was intrigued by the Sonesta Hotel. She'd been there before—to parties held on the concierge floor—but had never seen the private suites. He'd only been with her for a few days now, which was usually his threshold for girls when he was younger, but with Julie he found himself wanting more.

He slipped on bathing trunks and walked down to the pool area. Diving into the deep end, he began doing laps. The water was heated but cool, and he swam at a fair clip. He stood at the shallow end and waited until the cold air made him shiver. He began swimming more laps, and finally dried himself with a hotel towel and returned to his suite.

He dressed and took the elevator to the lobby. Tourists were coming and going, and he entered PJ's. He poured a cup of coffee into a to-go container, and walked over to the business center. A computer was available, and he sat down and accessed the Internet. He spent an hour on Dell's website, selecting a state of the art laptop computer, cordless mouse, laser printer, and memory stick. Filling in the billing and shipping information, he entered his credit card number and specified overnight delivery.

Walking along Bourbon, he headed to St. Philip Street. Julie now taught at the KIPP McDonogh School on St. Philip, seven blocks from the Sonesta Hotel. The school was relatively new, and he thought he'd take a look at it. He walked toward Jackson Square, stopping to buy a silver watch and wristband in one store and a copper bracelet in a small jewelry store. Several musicians were setting up in the square, next to palm trees and rhododendrons, with a backdrop of the St. Louis Cathedral.

He sat on the grass and watched the musicians work. His senses seemed more alive today, as if they were relearning their craft after a seven year hiatus. In Jetson, he had dumbed-down his senses, allowing himself to read without distraction. Remy kept his subscriptions current, and he enjoyed most articles in *Newsweek*, *USA Today*, and *National Geographic*. He had become a minimalist, disregarding money Remy had transferred to his commissary account. It was a self-induced game that he could play at and win in a world where he was a loser.

He watched as a group of local youths tossed a football as they crisscrossed the expanse of lawn. A tall, good-looking guy broke from the others and threw a football at Zach. "Heads up!" he hollered.

Zach jumped up and scrambled for the ball. He caught it with one hand in the air, his sneakered feet off the ground. He landed and threw the football back to the black guy.

"You still got it, Zach," the young man said, sauntering over in the typical "I'm a brotha" fashion.

"Robbie!" Zach exclaimed, walking fast and opening his arms. They did a full-frontal chest-bumping and slammed each other's backs with open hands.

Robbie waved at his friends, indicating he'd catch up. Sitting on the grass, he said, "How the hell have ya been, Zach?"

"I just got out, Robbie. How are you doin'?"

"Workin' hard or hardly. I just got back. After you went to juvy, my father got a job in Houston. I had to leave New Orleans, Zach. Houston really sucked."

"Where are you staying?"

"A small place on Decatur. It's temporary, 'til my father starts work and I get a job."

"Seen any of the old gang?"

"I hooked up with Sanchez and Pounder a few days ago. I thought I saw you yesterday walking on Bourbon. I yelled your name, but the guy kept walking. I ran and looked at his face. He looked like you with blond hair. He just kept walking."

"That's odd," Zach said.

"Seen Miss Julie?"

"I have. Have you?"

Robbie shook his head. "I thought I'd try to catch her after school."

"Let's trade numbers. Maybe we'll meet her together, if I'm not bein' a third wheel."

Robbie laughed. "If you become a third wheel, brother, I'll keep Miranda and roll you into the river."

*

Zach was standing on the sidewalk, eating a chilidog when he got a call from Remy. It was one o'clock in the afternoon, and the weather was crisp. "What's up, Uncle?"

"You took refuge at the Sonesta?" Remy asked.

"Yeah. I'm gonna stay there for now. Is there a problem?"

"Not at all. I just got a call from the concierge there, checkin' on you, makin' sure you are who you say you are."

"That makes sense," Zach said, wiping his hands with a napkin and tossing it into a trash receptacle, "the suite is probably three hundred a day."

"You know you don't have to worry about that. You're talkin' two hundred grand a year to live and eat well. It was a good choice, if you like living in all that commotion."

"You like it, Remy, just not every day."

"I've got twenty years on you, Zach. I'm comfortable in my little oasis here."

"What are you doing today?"

"Reba feels lucky and she loves the slots. Wanna meet us at Harrah's?"

"Sure. Where are you gonna be?"

"She wants Sushi. We'll see you at Bambu."

Zach walked down Iberville Street toward the casino. Clouds had taken over the skies, and the temperature was conducive to walking. He made a vow to walk at least two hours a day. He stopped at a bookstore and purchased *No Easy Day*.

Bambu was all set up for lunch, and he took a seat at the bar. A pretty Japanese bartender walked over, and Zach ordered a Sapporo beer. He realized it was a five-star Asian restaurant. *Remy knew his eateries.*

He watched them enter the restaurant, looking like a Hollywood couple. Remy was wearing a light blue suit Zach figured had to go for a grand, with great stitching and breast pockets with flaps. His slacks fell down over brown leather boots. He had on a white shirt and western string tie. Fareeba was wearing a sleek one piece silver dress with a slit up the side, and showing modest cleavage. Her beautiful face and long, thin arms and legs had a healthy-looking complexion. Her long, black hair was pulled tight against the sides of her face, emphasizing her high cheekbones, and the hair cascaded down her bare back.

Remy walked over to Zach and put a hand on his shoulder while Fareeba made arrangements with the maître d'. Zach placed a ten on the bar and followed Remy as they were led to a remote corner booth. It had a horseshoe shaped bench, and Fareeba slid in first. Remy and Zach sat on either side of her.

"I'm dying for Sushi," Fareeba said. "What are you interested in, Zach?" she asked, turning to stare at him with her big, green eyes.

Zach laughed. "I just had a chilidog when Remy called, but I'll find room for something." He reviewed the menu. "The Wasabi shrimp looks delicious. What do you like here, Remy?"

"The Cantonese barbeque duck."

A waitress approached the table, asking for their drink orders.

"Is Taruzake okay with y'all?" Fareeba asked.

"Is it sake?" Zach asked.

She nodded. "Aged in wood. It's nice."

"Sounds okay to me," Zach replied. "I bought a laptop and printer today, Remy."

"Good. Ever play Texas Hold'em?"

Zach nodded. "I played on New Year's Eve, before the party. It was a limit game."

"You learned to play in Jetson?"

"Every card game imaginable."

"Wanna play no limit today?"

"How high do the pots get?"

Remy looked at Zach. "What do you care? You play the cards and the players, right? If you want, set a mental limit as to how much you're willing to lose."

"We won't be playing against each other, will we?"

"Not if we establish signals," Remy said, smirking at Zach.

"Just straight, flush, boat, and four of a kind?"

"And get the hell out now, motherfucker." Remy laughed as they were poured sake.

*

The high-stakes table had nine players. Zach thought that four of the players looked serious, and three looked like they just stepped off the bus. Remy sat across the table from Zach. They had each invested twenty grand in chips, and each had ten grand cash on them.

Zach planned to play tight and aggressive. He liked to bet when the blind was just to his left, so he could watch the players view their down cards and make their bets before he had to commit—trying to determine a tell. Aggressive meant when he stayed in, he'd normally raise the bet. His betting would change when he felt he had a lock, and then he'd just match the bet, hoping to sucker in the remaining players.

After the first nine hands, he had tossed his cards in eight times and stayed in for the turn once. Remy was also playing it tight. One of the tourists had gone all-in, and was now getting back on the bus. Zach was only concentrating on two players at the table now.

He watched as a flop came down, and he glanced at his uncle. Remy had his index finger rubbing his right eye, indicating, "Get the hell out, now." Zach tossed in his cards and watched Remy masterfully ponder the pot, hesitate, and finally decide to stay in the hand. Other players bet heavy, and one went all-in. There had to be fifty grand in the pot. Remy went all-in immediately. It was now Remy and one of the serious players. The player flipped over his down cards, resulting in an ace-high flush. Remy flipped over his down cards to reveal four of a kind. He must have won eighty grand on that hand alone.

Zach hit a streak where he was pairing up on the down cards and catching a third on the flop. By the river, he usually had a boat. He never went all-in, but was up forty grand after three wins in a row.

After an hour or so of gambling, Zach and Remy sat alone with the dealer. Remy tossed her a thousand-dollar chip and Zach followed suit.

"Thank you, darlin'," Remy said.

They stood and placed their chips in trays, then walked out into the casino. Remy found a smoking area and lit up. He laughed and said, "You just earned your room and board for a couple of months."

"What a country," Zach said, grinning.

"Let's cash in these chips and have a drink. What time is it, Zach?"

"Almost six. Shit, I forgot to call Robbie. We were going to see Julie together."

They cashed in their chips and sat on barstools at a casino bar. They both ordered vodka on ice.

"I'm leaving town for a few days, Zach. Care to stay at my place with Fareeba?"

Zach leaned back and looked at his uncle. He said, "I don't know how to say this, Remy, so I'll just say it. I wouldn't feel comfortable doing that."

Remy looked at Zach and said, "'Cause Reba's so hot, right?"

"Right."

"And you don't want to hurt me, right?"

"Exactly. And Remy, I'm not suggesting that she'd come on to me, but, if she did, well, I wouldn't want that to happen."

"Fareeba's like a bitch in heat, Zach. Once men get the scent, they start sniffing around like bloodhounds. I realize she's twenty-five and I'm forty. We have a good time together, and she knows I'm not gonna marry her, but I keep her happy. She doesn't have to beg for money, shit like that. I know I'm not gonna keep her forever, Zach, but she's just too good to let go. I'd like to keep her around for at least another year."

"I hope you do, Remy."

"And I'm not telling you to fuck her, but, I'd rather it be you than some stranger. You know why?"

"I've got no idea why."

"'Cause a stranger is gonna come back for more, and won't take 'No' for an answer. There's not a doubt in my mind about that. When he comes back, it's gonna get messy. I don't want to die by lethal injection for a piece of tail."

"So where does that leave me?"

"If something happens, get it out of your system, and be discrete. Don't let me know anything about it."

"I'd prefer not to be put in that position to begin with."

"Well, suck it up, nephew. We're family."

"I'd like to keep it that way, Remy."

"Then think ugly and don't brush your teeth." Remy laughed and pinched Zach's cheek. "I'll give you her cell number in case you chicken out."

*

Zach spent the rest of the evening drinking coffee and reading *No Easy Day*. He found the book to be fascinating, and couldn't put it down until the story ended. He had read some of the hype about the book, and had expected to find some revelation regarding President Obama stealing glory, but was confused when no statement argued that issue. Weren't the SEALs supposed to engage in operations for which they didn't receive credit? Couldn't all the information regarding their physical training be helpful to terrorists? Didn't Obama approve a backup helicopter that proved essential to the operation? He fell asleep on the couch, after watching CNN report that Congress approved a bill that kept Americans from falling off the fiscal cliff for a few more months.

Chapter 7

Zach entered his suite Friday morning after swimming forty laps in the pool. He was feeling fit for the first time since high school. Jetson had a weight-lifting area outside, but he had stayed clear of it. It was dominated by the blacks, and he saw no reason to cause any provocation when it wasn't necessary. Most of them considered him a rich kid, which didn't endear him to anyone there.

He made coffee and took it to the balcony. His cell rang and he picked up the call.

"Can you tell who this is?" a female voice asked.

"Whoever you are, you have a very sexy voice," he replied, almost certain as to who it was—Odette.

"I'll give you a hint—you stood me up on New Year's Eve seven years ago."

"Odette, I thought it was you. Do you forgive me after all this time?"

"Not yet. We had a date and you blew it."

"How can I make it up to you?"

"Buy me lunch at Café Amelie."

"That's a block from where I'm staying."

"Where're you staying?"

"The Royal Sonesta."

"Ooh, they've got much better lunch there."

"They're open now—the Desire Oyster Bar."

"I'll be there soon." She disconnected.

Zach pictured Odette in sophomore class—five-ten and slender, with budding breasts, a beautiful face with perfect teeth, all encompassed in a black, silky-smooth skin. She was a mutt—like many kids Zach knew then—her mix being black and Spanish Creole. Her facial features where sharp, with high cheekbones and brown eyes. She had been a knockout, and she knew it. All the girls had despised her.

He showered and deliberated as to what he should wear. Odette always wore expensive clothing in high school, and he doubted that she had changed that aspect of her life. He decided on the suit he'd worn on New Year's Eve. It had been dry-cleaned, and was hanging in his closet. He slipped on a blue, long-sleeved shirt.

Taking the elevator to the lobby, he walked into the bar. There was an empty table facing Bourbon Street, and the hostess followed him with two menus. He asked for a shaker of Stoli's martinis and watched the street, looking for Odette. It was a sunny, cool day, and pedestrians walked by at a healthy clip. He saw her round the corner wearing a blouse and short skirt, with long legs in four-inch heels. Her black hair was cropped short and hugged her face. *You got legs right up to your neck*, he thought, hearing Rod Stewart singing "Hot Legs" in his mind.

He stood as she entered, and he smiled when she saw him. She walked to him with a confident stride, navigating waiters and diners, her long legs and heels completely in command of her body. She stood before him. He grabbed her hands and kissed her on the mouth. The kiss lingered before she moved her face back to look in his eyes.

"You're lookin' good, Zach—all grown up and handsome as ever."

"You look amazing, Odette. Let's sit."

Zach sat to her right. The table was small, and their knees touched. Zach saw a lot of slender leg under the table. She grabbed his left hand with her right and squeezed.

"I'm so glad to see you're okay."

"Thanks, Odette. It's been quite a ride."

A waiter brought the martini shaker and two glasses. The young man poured vodka and placed a small bowl of green and black olives on the table. They ordered two dozen oysters.

"How've you been?"

"I'm good, Zach. On my own, which is the way I always wanted it. You just got out, right?"

He nodded. "New Year's Eve. Seven years."

"How does it feel?"

"Strange. I went in four months after Katrina, and I got out four months after Isaac. When is this city gonna catch a break?"

"You missed the Deepwater Horizon oil spill. That was simply a horrific time for us locals."

"So what have you been doing?" he asked.

"I left New Orleans for two years after high school—New York City runway stuff. At seventeen, I was competing with fifteen-year-olds. I began the whole binging and purging routine, drugs, sex, and parties. I went to Paris once. I had an abortion once. By nineteen, I was all used up. I came back home and went through detox. I'm clear of all that now."

Zach held his martini glass in the air and Odette touched it with hers. "To new beginnings."

They sipped their drinks. She said, "Robbie gave me your number. I hope that's okay with you."

"Of course it's okay. I've got Robbie's and Miss Julie's numbers. That's it."

The oysters arrived and they began eating.

"You better be careful, Zach. Seven years in prison and you're eating oysters."

"And I'm sitting next to a goddess. Do you have plans this afternoon?" he asked, giving Odette a smirk with eyebrows high.

"Why, Zach. Is that anyway to talk to a lady?" she replied.

"Where?" he asked, looking around.

Odette scooped an oyster from its shell and into her mouth, and said, "Same ol' Zach— disrespectful of his elders."

"Your body may be twenty-two, Odette, but your mind is still back in sophomore class."

"I'm taking that as a compliment," she said.

"I meant it that way. Do you remember how you had all the boys drooling over you back then?"

"Vaguely," she quipped.

"I'm still drooling, Odette. It's out of my control."

"Well, Zach, we'll just have to see about that drooling problem of yours after you pour me another drink."

*

Odette was a very energetic lover, and Zach did his best at holding on. Their first bout ended too quickly, due to Zach's over-eagerness, so they took a break and began again. Their orgasms came close together, and he lay on his back, winded, and satisfied. Odette's moaning had seemed a bit theatrical to him.

He filled the Jacuzzi with hot water and mixed them both a rum and Coke. They sat across from each other in the tub. "What are you doing now, Odette?"

"What everyone figured I'd be doing—working for an escort service. Shocked?"

"Not at all. You're just using what God handed you. I say 'Bravo!'"

"It's not that bad. I'm given a choice on all customers. I pass as much as I play."

"I bet you get a lot of repeat business," he said.

"I'm welcomed to recruit my own business as well, as long as the agency gets their cut. It can be a pretty easy way to make money, if you can deal with the bullshit."

"Have you had any bad experiences?"

"Yes, but I'm not afraid to voice my opinion. If the john isn't listening, I'll grab his balls and get his attention."

"Here's another way," he said, showing her his flick to the eyeball gesture, "in case you can't reach his nuts."

"I wanted to see you for the obvious reasons, Zach—our unfinished business—but there's something else I want to discuss with you." She took a swig of her drink.

"What?"

"It's about your uncle, Remy."

"What about him?"

"He's been using the escort service quite a bit lately. There's a woman running the service named Edna. She wants to get her hooks into Remy. She believes he's worth a fortune."

"Have you ever been with Remy?"

Odette looked Zach in the eyes. "I have, Zach. Does that make you feel weird?"

"No," he replied, "I just wondered how he treats his women."

"He's a perfect gentleman. I'd tell you if he wasn't."

"Do you think this Edna wants to seduce him or blackmail him?"

"I don't know, but she's capable of either, or both."

Zach put his drink down and moved Odette's legs apart. He slid in close to her body and kissed her deeply.

"My uncle and I thank you, but I'm in a better position to thank you personally. Give me a little time to revitalize." He put his hands on her breasts and said, "No critiquing, please. My uncle has had a lot more time to get it right."

*

He spent Friday evening walking Bourbon Street, and ended up on Frenchmen Street. Dining on street vendor food, he popped into a bar for an Abita Amber beer and then continued walking. The temperature was around sixty degrees, keeping the crowd of pedestrians moving. Music filled the street, coming from a dozen different clubs.

He ended up at Snug Harbor, sitting at the bar, and listening to Charmaine Neville on the jukebox. He had read that she had been in bad health for a while, and he knew that she used to perform weekly at this club. She always kept the crowd in awe—slip-sliding through songs while displaying her technical versatility. *What genes that family has*, he thought.

He wondered about his own family's genetic mix—murderers, thieves, liars, and cheaters. When he had turned twelve, he'd heard rumors of Henri's sexual escapades, and Remy was an unleashed hound dog. In the Bujold family,

68

divorces occurred as frequently as weddings, and both occasions demanded a party.

Now, he had learned that Remy was cheating on Fareeba, and that was confusing him. He was sure that Fareeba was game for anything in the bedroom, and here's Remy looking for something different. And it's not like Remy's got a rubber ball in his mouth and getting his ass whipped—he's having gentlemanly sex with Odette. *What the hell is wrong with him?*

Zach had first experienced sex when he was ten years old. He was in the sixth grade with the eleven-year-olds. A girl new to the school had every guy ogling her. She dressed differently and had an attitude about her that reeked of sex. Zach had caught up with her in the hallway at lunchtime and said, "Feel like ditchin' class this afternoon?" The girl accepted and they strolled off the school grounds and began walking. He pulled her into any alley and pushed her against the side of a building, putting a hand on her breast and kissing her. She had said, "Fuck me," and he did just that—standing up in the alleyway, alongside a dumpster, eye to eye, her panties twisted around one ankle and lying in mud.

As he entered his teens, sex was easy to find with girls his age. Blowjobs were taken for granted on the first date, and by the third date it was their anus or vagina being offered up. As his confidence grew, he felt capable of winning over older women. Older females seemed more intriguing—their bodies were more developed and they weren't looking for guys to "go steady" with. They wanted to experience sex and experiment as well, and he found them less inhibited. For Zach, it was all a game of self-confidence. His buddies from school would watch as he approached a girl—respectful but also cocky. He was batting around four hundred. Most of his friends were batting zero. Robbie was batting one thousand.

By thirteen, Zach was bedding seventeen-year-olds. He also purchased some nasty looking ladies of the night. He was fascinated by women who threw caution to the wind and spread their legs for money.

Now, sitting at the bar at Snug Harbor, he realized that he was no different than his father or uncle. He had dreamed and lusted for Julie over a seven year period of time, and, after he had her, he's captivated by Odette. How does one even consider a life as a husband and father with a mind that works that way?

Chapter 8

The following morning, Philippe called to invite Zach up to the concierge floor. A suite had become available, and management authorized Philippe to offer it to Zach on a long term basis. He wanted to see if Zach approved of the suite's layout.

Zach joined him in the lobby and was escorted to a private elevator which took them to the concierge floor. As they exited the elevator, a concierge's desk faced them. Zach followed Philippe as he walked down a corridor and opened a door.

Zach walked slowly through a living room containing a couch, two armchairs, and a coffee table in front of a fireplace. The room had thick Berber carpeting. A TV room followed, with inlaid tile, offering another couch, and armchairs that swiveled in front of a flat-screen TV. Bedrooms were off to either side, and ahead was a kitchenette, balcony, and dining area. The suite smelled freshly painted and the furniture was modern—brown, leather couches and armchairs, glass tables, and recessed lighting controlled by dimmer switches.

There was an open feeling about the place, with a cool breeze blowing in from the balcony. Zach walked into the guest bedroom to find a queen-sized bed and a desk with the Dell computer hardware that he had ordered. It was still in the shipping containers.

"I took the liberty of having the computer hardware placed here. If you don't like the suite, I'll have it brought downstairs."

"I love the suite, Philippe." Zach entered the master bedroom to find another balcony with armchairs positioned on either side. A king-sized bed faced a long dresser and mirror. The room had wall to wall Berber carpeting. An inner wall contained a walk-in closet and access to the master bathroom. The bathroom contained a glass stall shower and a hot tub. A long vanity lined a wall with mirrors, and a private room contained a toilet.

"I'll take it," Zach said.

"Great. You won't be disappointed. You have the exclusive R Club on this level, open twenty-four hours a day, and available to members only. It's right across the hallway from you. Also, if you close the doors to the balcony, you won't hear much noise from the street."

"I'll sign whatever you want, Philippe. Will you have my things brought here?"

"Of course. If you leave the hotel, come back up using the private elevator and the concierge on duty will have your keycards. The suite is number four."

"Is it possible to leave you a list of liquor I need delivered?"

"I can take care of that for you."

Zach reached into his pocket and retrieved a list he'd been compiling, and he handed it to Philippe. "I can't thank you enough. I'll pay you back somehow," he said, shaking Philippe's hand with a folded hundred-dollar bill in his palm.

"Nonsense," Philippe said, pocketing the bill, "the pleasure of your company is more than enough."

"Stop blowin' smoke, Philippe. It's a smoke-free hotel, remember?"

*

Zach walked the streets, shopping for casual clothes. He found a store with great belts and belt buckles, and a store full of new jeans, T-shirts, and packages of Hanes boxer briefs. By lunchtime, he was hungry and thirsty. He stopped in Lafitte's Blacksmith Shop Bar on St. Philip. He figured he'd have lunch and walk by Julie's school. The school was just down the street.

As he entered the bar, he wasn't sure it was open for business—it was so dark it was difficult to determine if people were inside. As his eyes adjusted to the darkness, he saw a couple at the far end of the bar. He took a seat at the bar, on a stool near the entrance, where the bar picked up sunlight from the doorway. As he placed his shopping bag on the barroom floor, a bartender walked over and asked what he'd like to drink. He ordered a pint of draught beer and studied the menu. He ordered a bleu cheeseburger.

Sipping cold beer, he began reading a pamphlet describing the history of the bar. Someone walked in and blocked the sunlight. Zach looked up and stared at Louis, standing in the doorway, looking at him. He was wearing jeans and sneakers, a T-shirt, and a black leather coat exactly like the one Zach had purchased. His hair was dyed blond.

"What the fuck are you doing here?" Zach asked.

"Checking on your crazy ass," Louis said as he sat on the barstool to Zach's left.

"What does that mean?" Zach asked.

"It means I want to know if you're done murdering people. It will affect my life down here."

The bartender asked Louis what he wanted to drink, and he ordered a rum and Coke.

"Life down here?" Zach echoed.

"I just graduated from Harvard Law, and I want to practice law here. I can't do that if you plan on murdering more people."

"Louis, you fuck, you murdered our parents. What are you trying to do? Make me think I did it?"

"Zach, you may not realize it, but you did do it. That night, you were getting drunk in the garden and our parents were getting drunk in the house. I went in to tell our mother I thought it was shitty to keep twins apart. She apologized to me and began crying. I walked out and waved goodbye to you, but you were too busy talking to yourself to see me. I got on a plane and went back to prep school."

Zach looked at his brother. He said, "Louis, I don't believe one word of what you just said. You drugged me and shot our mother and father, then left me to take the heat. They locked me up for seven years, you motherfucker." Zach clenched his right hand, preparing to take a swing at Louis.

"Apparently, the clinical psychologists did a rotten job of treating you. They had so much time with you, and you're still in denial."

"I don't deny that I want to smash your face in."

"Look at you, Zach. All that rage and anger you demonstrate. Yet, you accuse me of murdering them."

Zach took a moment to compose himself. This was, after all, a psychological battle.

"What's with the blond hair?" Zach asked.

"I don't want anyone to think I'm you."

"Then why are you wearing the same clothes as me?"

"We're identical twins. Is it so unusual for us to like the same clothes?" Louis threw a ten-dollar bill on the bar and stood. "Don't mess with me, Zach. I'm perfectly within my rights to defend myself if you begin fucking with me." He walked out of the bar.

Zach fought an urge to follow him, but remained sitting. The bartender brought his plate of food and silverware.

"Did that guy look like me?" Zach asked.

"I didn't notice, buddy. Need anything else?"

"I'm good."

Zach ate, playing back his conversation with Louis. *What's he trying to accomplish?*

What frightened Zach was that Louis was dressing like him. What if the blond hair was a wig? He could look exactly like Zach in a few seconds. He thought about involving the cops, but discarded that option quickly. He'd have to have a lot more evidence before he approached the police. First, he'd have to follow Louis and find out where he was staying. Then, maybe, he would involve the cops.

He only ate half the meal. It was good, but he'd lost his appetite. He threw money on the bar and left.

*

They were welcomed into the R Club lounge and escorted to a table. Julie ordered vodka on ice and Zach ordered a beer.

"This is nice, Zach. It's open twenty-four hours a day?"

"I guess so. I know certain things are offered during set times, like hors d'oevres. Pick out some things to start with, and we'll decide where to eat dinner."

"The suite is outrageous. You're gonna be happy there."

"Did you see Robbie yesterday?"

"Yes. We talked for a while. I told him who to see about getting a job."

"Robbie's a good guy," he said. "He was my best friend in high school. He referred to you as 'Miranda'. Have you been called that before?"

"Not that I'm aware of," she said.

"It's the ultimate compliment for a woman—an unselfish, uncompromising woman who helps other people."

Their drinks arrived. They both took sips.

"May I ask you something about Callanwolde?"

"Go ahead," Zach replied.

"I was wondering about DNA with identical twins. Is it the same?"

"Identical twins are called monozygotic, meaning that they develop from one zygote that splits and forms two embryos. They say that the DNA of identical twins is virtually the same at birth, and that very small changes may take place due to environmental differences and the aging process. I have no idea if Louis's and mine are alike by now. We could just be fraternal twins that look alike."

"Did they find any DNA that was nearly the same as yours, but different?"

"All they found was my DNA and my parents. It's not like anyone thought to bring in Barry Scheck, though I wish they had."

"Fingerprints?"

"Just mine and my parents. Identical twins usually have the same fingerprints, but they can vary in terms of hair and eye color. My father was left-handed, and Remy is right-handed."

She sipped the vodka and they ordered appetizers.

"Louis approached me today," Zach said, watching her eyes.

Julie had the glass of vodka to her mouth, and she put it down on the table. She stared at him. "Why are you looking at me that way?" she asked.

"Just checking your reaction. I'm shocked myself, and a little scared."

"He's in New Orleans?"

He nodded and raised his eyebrows. "He says he graduated from Harvard Law and wants to set up practice here."

"And he actually approached you with other people around?"

"Julie, he really exists. I expected you to react this way. I kind of did myself."

"I'm not sure what you mean."

He drank beer and said, "After so much time, and so many shrinks telling me I had a psychotic split, I was actually thankful to see him. I felt exonerated. That feeling only lasted a short time before he had me feeling angry."

"Did other people see you together?"

"Just the bartender, Julie. I know what you're thinking—that I had another psychotic break from reality. It's natural for you to be thinking that way. All I can say is, the bartender brought him a rum and Coke, and he paid for it. There's no other proof that he exists."

"And you talked with him?" she asked.

"Oh, yeah, we talked."

"What did he say?"

"Why don't we eat here and go back to my place?"

"That's what he said?" she asked, trying not to grin.

"Very funny."

"Yes, let's go back to your place," she said. "I want to lay with you."

*

They made love and lay close to each other. Zach couldn't get enough holding and touching. He knew Jetson had much to do with that. He moved Julie so she was lying on her stomach. Brushing her long hair to the far side of her naked body, he ran his hand down her back to her ass. Bringing his hand back up, he began lightly touching her shoulders and back. He slid the tips of his fingers down the small of her back, his nails making lines on her skin that disappeared quickly.

"That feels nice, Zach."

"You've got a great body."

"You're a wonderful lover."

"We're good together," he stated.

"I'm seven years older than you."

"It's too early in our relationship to worry about that."

"I guess you're right. Let's just enjoy it."

"What do you think about my experience today?"

"I don't know what to make of it," she said. "I do believe you—I just don't know what Louis's intentions are. Is he trying to scare you?"

"He wants me to think I'm crazy, and he's trying to piss me off. Unfortunately, I'm documented as being just that—crazy and pissed-off."

"What if you got him in a place where you could be photographed together? I could snap a picture of you two."

"I've thought of that. It's not enough—not with Photoshop available. I have to get the police to see us both, so they can question us. That's a scary proposition, though."

"Why?"

"He could claim to be me."

"Did they give you a polygraph before your court case?"

"Sure," he answered.

"And?"

"I passed it."

"So, what was the problem?" she asked.

"Passing a lie detector test means nothing when you have a delusional disorder. Everything you're saying you believe to be true. All your body's chemistry indicates that you're telling the truth. The ink on the chart doesn't spike. That's why they didn't catch Gary Ridgway, the 'Green River Killer' using a polygraph."

"What can you do?" she asked.

"I can kill him, Julie. I can make him disappear. He's hounding me again—it's like déjà vu. The problem is that I don't know enough about him to know if he'd be missed."

"God, Zach, you can't allow yourself to think that way. There's always a better solution than murder."

"He said he graduated from Harvard Law. That would have to be in June of last year. I can try to find something on the Internet. There must be a service that can check that out. At least it's a start."

"I'm afraid for you, Zach. You've got a psychopath following you around. What if he decides to kill you and take over your identity? You're a wealthy man. There's no way to distinguish the two of you. You should consider hiring a detective."

"A private investigator. That's a good idea," he said.

"You need to protect yourself from him."

"I don't know how much of this I want to share with Remy, if anything."

"I wouldn't let anyone know yet. Not until you find a detective and have him check Louis out. It shouldn't be that hard to do."

"You're right," Zach said, moving her body so he could cup her breast. "Can I intrigue you into staying over tonight?"

"I gotta feed the cats, Zach, or they'll all start hunting birds."

"Your cats are interfering with my pussy," he said as he rolled her over onto her back.

Chapter 9

Zach planned to jog the streets early morning or late at night. It was early Sunday morning, seven days since his release, and his stamina was increasing. Between the swimming and jogging, he was feeling more mentally alert. He completed a six-block square jog and returned to the Sonesta.

Placing the laptop and printer on the desk in the guest bedroom, he loaded the software. He put batteries in the cordless mouse and laid it on the pad. Double-clicking on the Internet icon, the Google search panel was displayed.

He made coffee and sat down at the desk. Searching for private investigators in NOLA, he found an abundance of companies and others who advertised just their names. He found a private investigator named Andre Picard, more than likely Cajun, and punched the number into his cell.

"Andre Picard, private investigator."

"Hi, Andre, my name is Zach. I need to track down a guy I believe is staying in New Orleans."

"How much information do you have on this guy?"

"Basically, all I have is what he looks like."

"Something like that can get expensive. The more information you have, the cheaper it will be."

"It's gonna be what it's gonna be. I can afford it."

"I bill honestly, Zach. I look to make five hundred a day. It may sound like a lot, but I've got overhead."

"Were you a cop?"

"For twenty years, right here in The Big Easy."

"Good. That could help us later. For now, I just want to find out where this guy is staying."

"Where would you like to meet?" Andre asked.

"How about the Old Absinthe House? I hear they make a great bloody Mary."

"I can be there in an hour. What do you look like?"

"Tall, dark hair, wearing a black leather coat."

"If I can't find you, look for somebody better."

"Bring a digital camera with you."

"No problem."

Zach took a long shower, shampooing his hair and soaping his body. He rinsed and dried himself and shaved, then put on jeans, a T-shirt, and the alligator boots. He slipped a new belt on with a circular buckle made of black onyx, with a white circle in the center containing the number '8.' He put on his watch and bracelet and slipped on the leather coat.

He walked into the Absinthe House ten minutes early. He sat at the end of the bar and looked around. If Louis followed him here, Andre's job would get a lot easier.

A bartender asked for his drink order, and Zach ordered a bloody Mary.

"Make it two," someone standing to his right said.

Zach turned and looked at a man's body and then continued to look up.

"Did you play basketball in the cop's league, Andre?"

The man laughed, taking a seat. He was ruggedly handsome, with a head of black hair and a Fu Manchu moustache. His skin was darker than Zach's, almost black. *He's gotta be six-five*, Zach thought.

He extended his open hand to Andre for a shake. "I'm Zachary Bujold. Call me Zach."

"Glad to meetcha, Zach." Andre lit a cigarette. "So, what do you have?"

"Were you on the force when Henri and Annette Bujold were murdered?"

"I was. I wasn't part of the investigation. I didn't work Homicide. I was on the Drug Task Force."

"I'm their son, Andre. I was convicted of murdering them. I just got out of Jetson."

"Your uncle is Remy Bujold?"

Zach nodded.

"I know of him. He's said to be a good man."

"He is. He stuck by me through all of it. He believed my story."

"That you had a twin?" Andre asked.

Zach nodded. "Who murdered my parents."

"So, what do you have for me?"

"Louis is my brother, and he's back in New Orleans. He's confronted me. I need to know where he's staying. He says he graduated from Harvard Law. That would have to have been this last June. He's twenty-one years old."

"So, his name is Louis Bujold?"

"That's what it says on his birth certificate. My mother gave him to an actress friend of hers when Louis was a week old. I don't know what his last name might be now."

"And he looks like you?"

"Yes, with blond hair."

Andre reached into his jacket pocket and pulled out a digital camera. He aimed it at Zach's face and said, "Say shit."

He gave Andre a smile.

"Big shit."

Zach smiled with his teeth showing.

"No shit."

He gave Andre a deadpan look.

"I'll Photoshop these and make you blond. Wavy hair like yours?"

"Yeah. I don't think it's a wig."

"Where did he confront you?" Andre asked.

"At Lafitte's Bar. Yesterday."

"Zach, I'll give you a call when I have something. Did you call me from your cell?"

"Yeah."

"Good. I saved it. You save mine?"

"I've got it, Andre. Would you like a retainer?"

"Not yet. I'll pass the picture around, discretely, of course. We'll see what we have in a few days."

They shook hands and Andre left. Zach ordered another bloody Mary.

*

He received a call from Remy, saying he'd be on a plane in the early evening. He wanted Zach to have dinner at the house with Fareeba and then escort her to the casino.

"Is she expecting me, Remy?"

"Yeah, kiddo, she's cookin' up a Creole specialty of hers."

"When should I be there?"

"Six-ish. Don't bring anything. We have plenty of wine and booze."

"Have a safe trip, Remy."

Zach walked the streets until four in the afternoon. He'd turn occasionally, trying to catch Louis behind him. He'd round a corner and stand with his back against a building, waiting to see if Louis made the turn. He kept his eye on the drivers. Louis wasn't tailing him.

He showered and put on clean boxers and new jeans. He pulled on a shirt he'd bought downstairs in a men's boutique. It was a long-sleeved white silk shirt with a collar he liked. He slid his feet into the alligator boots and ran his fingers through his hair.

Standing outside, he hailed a cab. Sliding into the backseat, he gave the driver Remy's address and looked out the back window. He didn't want Louis following him to Remy's house.

He paid the driver and walked up to the front door of the mansion. Pressing the doorbell and opening the screen door, he heard Fareeba yell, "Come in," and he pushed one door open. Stepping into the vestibule, he closed the door and made his way down to the kitchen. Fareeba was slicing garlic cloves. She wore a simple housedress.

"Good evening, Fareeba."

"Hey, Zach, I'm almost done. Will you pour the wine?" She indicated a bottle of red wine on the counter.

"Sure. Remy got off okay?"

"Well, I got him off. I don't know if the airlines did."

"You're a naughty girl, Fareeba," Zach said as he poured wine into two goblets. "Want these at the dining room table?" he asked.

"Yes, and sit yourself down. I'll bring it in."

He walked into the formal dining room and placed the goblets next to two place settings. He sat on the long side of the table and sipped the wine. It had a smoky flavor he liked.

Fareeba walked in with two plates containing a steamy casserole. "Be careful, it's hot," she said. She sat down at the head of the table and held up her goblet. "Luck, be a lady tonight."

Zach held up his glass and touched it to hers. They drank the red wine.

"You like to gamble, eh?" he asked.

"I love it. I escape into it."

He put a fork to the food on his plate, raised it to his mouth and blew, then slipped it in and began chewing. The Creole spices mixed with the crawfish morsels and the creamed sauce, causing his taste buds to come alive. It was the best thing he'd tasted since he'd been out.

He wiped his mouth with a cloth napkin and said, "Fareeba, this is outrageous. Is this your recipe?"

"My father's. He had his own restaurant on the Mississippi until Katrina. Now he's head chef in a bigger restaurant, more inland, away from the river."

"It's all so fresh. You're a great cook."

"What I do, I try to do well. Remy isn't complaining."

Zach took his time and spoke little. He was so overwhelmed by the food he didn't contribute much to what she was saying. He stopped eating when his plate was empty.

"I'm sorry, Fareeba. I've been a pig, but I couldn't stop eating."

"There's more. Would you like me to refill your plate?"

"No, thanks, I'm stuffed."

"Good. Let's leave the dishes here and go sit in the living room. I have a zydeco CD I want to play."

He followed her into the living room and sat down in an armchair. She placed a crystal ashtray on the coffee table, turned on a CD player, and sat across from him on a couch. Chubby Carrier and the Bayou Swamp Band began playing "Zydeco Junkie." She put her bare feet up on the table, and he found himself staring between her legs at a pair of loose fitting panties. He grabbed the goblet of wine and put it to his mouth.

"What I want you to do now, Zach, is to put it up my ass."

He was in the middle of a swallow when he choked. He bent forward and put his elbows on his knees. Half the wine had gone down his windpipe, and the other half had flown out his nose. He groaned and put his face in his hands. He struggled to stabilize his breathing, and looked for something to wipe his nose with. The wine was burning his nostrils. He stood and ran into the dining room, grabbed his napkin, and blew his nose. He cleared his throat and wiped his eyes.

He walked back into the living room and stood in front of her, arms akimbo. "You did that on purpose." He cleared his throat again and began laughing.

"What?" Fareeba asked, innocently.

"You waited 'til I was drinking before you said that."

"Well, I've said that to other men, and they didn't get all huffy about it."

"You are bad, Fareeba."

"That's the whole idea, Zach. It's taboo."

"Not in grade school or high school, it isn't. It's called birth control, or a Cajun sizzler."

"Oh, so my idea isn't tawdry enough for you?"

Zach grabbed one of Fareeba's cigarettes, almost in self-defense. He lit it, coughed, and said, "Fareeba, nothing could be further from the truth. Of course it's exciting to think about, but you're my uncle's live-in girlfriend."

"Doesn't that make it even more taboo?" She grabbed a cigarette and lit it.

"Jesus. Are you fucking around on Remy?"

"Very seldom, Zach. First of all, I love him. I wouldn't want to hurt him. Secondly, I have an effect on men. I'm not complaining about it, I mean, let's be real. Every woman wants men to stare at her, to desire her. But strange men can be dangerous. I know you find me sexy."

"I do, Fareeba. I can't deny it. I'd love to have sex with you."

"You're a very handsome, twenty-one-year-old man. You know you're gonna excite me more than any forty-year-old man."

"But, Remy."

"No, butt me."

He laughed. "Is there a way we can keep this a one-time deal? I'm asking myself that as much as I'm asking you."

"Spend the night here with me, Zach. Let's put guilt in a safety deposit box, to be opened at another time. I want to enjoy this, and it's gonna take a while."

He could feel beads of sweat forming on his forehead. No man who has spent seven years in the can could resist this. *No pun intended*, he mused.

"So, Fareeba, we make a pact—lovers for one night only, okay? One and done?"

"Scout's honor," she said, raising her right hand in the air.

*

She was insatiable. They spent the night drinking and fucking. Zach reached a point at which he simply took orders from her. "Touch me here, lick me there, put it in now. Faster. Slower. Stop for a minute. Ooh, sugar!"

They ate more of the casserole and sat in the hot tub in the middle of the garden. Steam rose high in the cold air. She placed her long arms on the sides of the tub, her head back with her breasts breaking the swirling water's surface. He looked out into the garden, wondering if Remy had picked out a plot for his casket. No forty-year-old heart could survive this.

As the sun began to lighten the eastern skies, Fareeba said she was content and needed sleep. Zach said they'd keep it their little secret as he stared into her green eyes.

"Secret forever?" he asked.

She held out her little finger and Zach hooked his to hers.

"And we went to the casino last night. We both won, didn't we?"

"You bet we did, Zach. Thanks."

He hugged her after opening the front door. He said, "Thank you very much, Auntie Fareeba," and walked to the wrought-iron gate. He turned back as Fareeba raised her middle finger.

Chapter 10

Zach woke up to the noise of traffic in the city. The French doors were open to the balcony, and cars were honking. He figured it must be noon. He rolled over and looked at the alarm clock. It was 4:30 p.m. He had slept all day.

He placed a K-cup in the coffee-maker and a coffee cup under the dispenser. Yawning, he rubbed his face with his hands, and scratched his head. Taking the coffee to the balcony, he sat and listened to the sounds of the street.

He heard his cell phone ringing. Picking it up from the couch, he walked back to the balcony, and saw "Fareeba" displayed on the screen.

"Good morning, Fareeba."

"What time zone are you in?"

"I just woke up."

"Listen, Zach. I can't lie to Remy."

"Aw, shit, Fareeba. We've been through this."

"I can't tell Remy I won at gambling if I didn't go to the casino."

"I need time to shower and shave."

"I'll have Claude pick me up at six. Be ready and outside at six-ten."

"Yes, your highness."

He showered and shaved, then dressed. Pouring out the coffee, he pulled a bottle of Stoli's from the freezer and poured some in a small glass, adding orange juice. Sitting out on the balcony, he sipped the drink. He replayed the events of last evening, and realized how addicting sex with Fareeba could become. He didn't envy Remy. She would be very hard to relinquish. Her exquisite body was just so damned welcoming.

Standing on the sidewalk, he watched as the limo approached. He opened the back passenger's door and slid in. He closed the door and Claude took off. Fareeba was wearing a white, tight-fitting dress with a plunging neckline. Her well-proportioned breasts required no support.

"Good evening, Fareeba. You look especially enchanting tonight."

"And you, sir, are a heartbreaker. I do think you'll need my help in finding you a proper men's boutique, though."

"Claude, my man," he said, "are you gonna join us for some gambling?"

"I'm on my way home, Zach. I gotta work my real job once in a while. You kids will have to cab it back."

Claude pulled up to Harrah's and Zach opened the door and stepped out. He held his hand out for Fareeba to grab, and helped her exit the backseat. He closed the door and Claude drove off.

Fareeba grabbed his arm as they walked into the casino. She leaned her head against his upper arm and said, "Thanks for doing this."

Julie was sitting at a bar talking with a woman when Zach walked by. Fareeba was hanging on his arm and whispering something in his ear. He stopped and stared at Julie.

"Hey," he said. *Smooth*, he thought.

"Hey," Julie said, turning back to talk with her friend.

"Julie, this is Fareeba," Zach said as he disengaged himself from Fareeba's grasp.

Julie ignored him, continuing to converse with her friend.

Damn it! he thought. He looked at Fareeba and said, "Let's go gamble."

*

Zach called Julie several hours later. She didn't pick up. He walked through the casino and found Fareeba playing video poker.

"I'm leaving, Fareeba. Do you want to stay or leave with me?"

"I'll stay, Zach. I'm winning, just like you said I would. I'll be okay. Go see your Julie."

"Okay. Good luck."

The night air was brisk and windy, and Zach decided to walk to Julie's house. He headed north on Canal Street and walked seven blocks to Burgundy. He headed east on Burgundy toward Jackson Square. He hadn't seen her house before, but knew it to be a two-story pink house with black shutters on Burgundy, near the KIPP middle school.

He spotted a large cat with tiger stripes on the second-floor balcony of a pink house with black shutters. The cat had been crouched, ready to pounce on something when Zach's boot heel hit a metal storm cover and the cat's quarry flew away. The cat looked down at Zach indignantly. The French doors to the balcony were open, and Zach called out, "Julie." He watched as she walked to the railing and looked down at him.

"May I come up?"

She nodded. He walked along the side of the house and up the staircase to the second-floor wrap-around balcony. He walked to the front of the house and she rushed into his arms.

"I'm sorry, Zach. I got jealous. I'm so embarrassed," she said, nestling her head under his chin.

"There was no need to be jealous, Julie. Fareeba is Remy's girlfriend. He's out of town, and he asked me to watch over her."

"I knew this would happen, just not this soon. I reacted inappropriately, and I'm sorry."

"Don't be sorry. It was just a misunderstanding."

"Do you accept my apology?"

"Of course. By the way, you've got a tiger on your balcony."

"That's Hamilton. He's hunting now."

"I see why you don't have a car. You're in walking distance of everything."

"So are you, now."

"I love this city, Julie."

"Come in and let's have a drink."

She walked downstairs to the kitchen and Zach walked into a sitting area past the second-floor bedroom. It was a comfortable home, with planters everywhere—flowered plants hanging above the railing of the balcony, and from metal anchors in the bedroom and sitting room ceilings. He sat back in a comfortable, upholstered armchair.

She walked in and handed him a glass of vodka on ice. He set the glass down and grabbed her, bringing her onto his lap. He kissed her hard, slipping his hand between her hair and her back. He held her body to his, rocking softly. He slipped his hand between her legs. She pushed off and was gone, returning with her own drink, and then sitting in the other armchair.

"How did you get interested in criminology?" he asked.

She laughed. "I've got you to thank for that."

"How so?"

"I was only teaching four months when you were arrested. I was new to New Orleans, and had no friends. I'd teach during the day and try to follow the investigation regarding your parent's deaths in the evening. Because you were a minor, the court allowed no cameras. Reporters were more interested in the effects of Katrina and Rita than your trial. It was hard for me to follow the details of the investigation.

"I began searching the Internet, and finally spent a lot of time in the genealogy department at the public library. I wanted to know more about your parents, and their parents, and then the whole fucked-up Bujold family tree. I made some interesting discoveries."

He took a pull of vodka and said, "Like what?"

"Almost every generation of Bujold had the oldest male family member killed suspiciously—usually shot by an intruder, but also run over, drowned, or just gone missing. I went back eight generations."

"That is interesting. It was never discussed in my family— neither by my father nor Remy—at least, not in my presence."

"I began thinking about the exchange of money from one generation to the next. No males seemed to be dying of natural causes and willing their money, as would normally occur in a patriarch. I began wondering if the intended heirs were just too impatient to wait for the money."

"I know that a lot of money was passed from one generation to the next," Zach said.

"Did you know your grandfather? Your father's father."

Zach shook his head. "He was called Papa Pierre. He was shot to death when I was three or four years old."

"By an unidentified intruder," she added.

"I knew my father's mother. We called her Mama Teresa, you know, after Mother Teresa. She was African-American. I loved that woman crazy."

"She died of cancer when you were thirteen."

Zach nodded.

"Anyway, the whole process of your trial and incarceration drew me to the field of criminology. I enjoy it."

"You're young enough to switch careers," he said.

"Naw," she responded. "I enjoy the mystery of it all, but I'd hate to work with homicide cops."

*

Julie declined making love, stating she just wanted to be held. He held her until she fell asleep, and then slipped out of bed. Hamilton jumped up to occupy his spot, and Zach whispered, "Don't eat Miss Julie."

She had to work in the morning, and he felt like walking the streets. He slipped into his clothes and walked out to the balcony and down to the street.

Walking along Burgundy, he marveled at the jambalaya of homes which formed the neighborhood. Most of the structures were old houses, some were warehouses, but now and then a new home would be nestled in where a dilapidated structure had been put out of its misery. Everything, old and new, contributed to the personality of the block of dwellings.

He walked to Jackson Square and entered Muriel's, walking to the Courtyard Bar. He stood at the bar and ordered a Johnny Walker Black on the rocks with a water back, asking the bartender if there was any seating available outside. A waitress led him to a small table for two on the second-floor balcony. He sat and looked down at the corner of Chartres and Saint Ann, watching as cars and pedestrians wound their way through the streets.

He thought about Julie being jealous, and felt bad about that. Though he had never experienced the feeling of jealousy over a woman, he knew he was very capable of being swept away by such an emotion. The thought of someone else vying for the affections he held sacred could drive him to depths he didn't want to imagine.

He finished the scotch and asked the waitress for another. It felt good to be alone with his thoughts. He felt that he had accomplished more than he had expected since his release. No more mansion haunting his thoughts, new living quarters he looked forward to enjoying, and a relationship forming with Julie that he had only dreamed about in jail. He was among the adults, playing his cards like everyone else.

He heard steps behind him and Louis sat in the chair across the table from him, wearing the black leather coat and sporting the blond hair. He was holding a glass of scotch, and took a swig.

"I see you're still prowling around, Louis."

"I'm trying to figure out who you're going to kill next," Louis said, lighting a cigarette and inhaling.

"The only person I've thought of killing lately is you."

"There goes your element of surprise, Zach. You're not really very good at this, are you?"

"I'm certainly not as accomplished at it as you."

"Let's stop fucking around, Zach," Louis said, and then stopped talking. He took another swig of scotch as the waitress delivered Zach's drink and left.

"I want you to leave this city."

"This is where I grew up, Louis. Go back to wherever the rock is you crawled out from." Zach took a long pull of scotch.

"I'm not leaving, Zach. I told you, I'm setting up my practice here. Remember one thing about your situation now."

"And what is that, pray tell?"

"You're an adult now. The next murder you're involved in, you'll be going to a maximum-security prison, where you'll idle away your time until the day of your lethal injection."

"Are you threatening me, Louis?"

"I'm just stating the facts. All of a sudden, I'm back in your life, and you're ready for another split from reality. Borderline, my ass. You're a full-fledged psychopath. Get ready for the shit-storm, fucker." Louis stood up and walked away.

Zach wrapped the drinking glass Louis left on the table with a cloth napkin, and carefully placed it in his coat pocket. He'd see if Andre could establish if Louis's fingerprints were identical to his own.

Chapter 11

Zach completed jogging an eight-block square on Tuesday morning and returned to his suite. He put on coffee and took a shower. Slipping on jeans and a sweatshirt, he sat on the couch, drank coffee, and watched the local news.

He walked to the R Club for breakfast. They were having a breakfast buffet, and Zach was hungry. He piled on scrambled eggs, sausage, and pancakes, then took a seat at an empty table. He went back and poured orange juice and brought it back to the table.

He had not slept well through the night—his talk with Louis had thrown him off his pace. Why wouldn't Louis just leave him alone? What could Louis gain from badgering him? If he was telling the truth about wanting to live in New Orleans, which Zach highly doubted, why wouldn't he just hang up a shingle and practice law? If he was devious enough to get away with two murders, his practice should flourish.

He was impatient to hear from Andre, but had recruited his services on Sunday. Unless Andre worked the weekend, Zach would have to wait before hearing from the man. He expected that learning more about Louis and his past could uncover some answers to questions that had gone unanswered for seven years. He wondered what kind of upbringing Louis had experienced.

He walked to his suite and brewed another cup of coffee. He added Kahlua, which made him think of Remy. He took the cup to the couch and powered on the flat-screen. Finding CNN, he pressed the mute button and called Remy.

"Zach, how are ya?"

"I'm good. Where are you, Uncle?"

"I got home last night. Fareeba told me to tell you she won."

"Great. I had to leave her there. Sorry."

"Something about Julie?"

"That's 'cause there's something about Fareeba. She causes other women to get jealous."

"That's one of her problems—she's a Michelle. Have you heard the term?"

"Sure," Zach said. "All the pretty girls are named Michelle."

"She can't hang around with men without stirring the pot, and women want to keep her away from their men. For some reason, Creole women trust her."

"Well, you've got a nice girl there, Remy. I enjoyed her company very much." *If you only knew how much.*

"That's good to hear. What are you doing today?"

"Not much. I want to see Julie this evening, and thought about buying some nice clothes today."

"Try RaB-DaB's and Gentlemen's Quarter, on Royal Street. You'll find most of what you're looking for there. You can't beat Brooks Brothers for sweaters and jackets. I got your boots at Wehmeiers."

"Thanks, Remy. It sounds like a fun afternoon. See ya soon."

*

Julie walked into the Rampart Street Police Department and down the hall to the Homicide Division. She saw that Lionel was on the phone, and waited outside his office. She looked around the large room full of cops sitting at desks, making notes or taking calls. A few officers waved at her, and she smiled back, nodding in recognition.

Lionel opened the door to his office and shouted, "Oh, God, no, Miss Julie. Has someone kidnapped Lemar?"

She looked at Lionel then back at the bullpen. Officers were in various states of amusement.

She walked into his office and he closed the door. Locking it, he waved goodbye to the onlookers as he closed the vertical blinds. He took his seat behind the desk and Julie sat in an armchair facing him. He reached into a desk drawer and plopped a plastic ashtray in the center of the desk, fishing for a Perique from his pack and lighting it.

"No one stole Lemar yet, Sergeant, although the 'Take me' sign you stapled to his back doesn't help matters."

"He's just of that age," Lionel said.

"Twelve can be rough," she admitted.

"I'm talkin' about one through eighteen, after which he gets booted out of my house. That kid has his head up his ass." Lionel took a long drag on the cigarette. "How'd you spring an afternoon off, Miss Julie?"

"A field trip which I didn't have to chaperone."

"Where'd they go?"

"Lionel, when I'm offered an afternoon off, I don't ask questions."

"But you're gonna ask me some, right?"

"I know you're familiar with the Bujold murder cases."

"Pierre, Henri, and Annette."

Julie nodded. "Do you know if anyone checked ballistics on the bullets to see if they all could have come from the same gun?"

"No murder weapons were ever found in the murder of Pierre Bujold or in the murders of Henri and Annette Bujold."

"I know, but were the bullets compared in terms of caliber and striations?"

Lionel pulled the laptop in front of him and typed on the keyboard, studying the results.

"You're suggesting that Pierre Bujold, shot to death in nineteen-ninety-four, and Henri and Annette Bujold, shot to death in two-thousand-five, were murdered with the same weapon?"

"Well," she said, "if they were, it would be highly unlikely that Pierre Bujold was shot by an intruder. Are we to believe that the intruder also murdered Henri and Annette Bujold eleven years later with the same weapon?"

"I guess that would also prove that Zachary Bujold is innocent of the crime for which he was convicted. How could Zach, at fourteen, be in possession of the murder weapon that killed his grandfather? Unless he shot his grandfather when he was three years old and hid the weapon."

"It's an interesting theory that could easily be proven or refuted if we have the bullets, right?" she asked.

"You were here in New Orleans pre-Katrina, right?"

"Yes, just barely," she said.

"I came down just after Rita. After I got here, I found out that someone upstairs decided that the evidence room wasn't high enough if Katrina were to hit New Orleans. So, all of the evidence was moved to a warehouse on higher ground. Want to know the name of this warehouse?"

"Sure," she responded.

"It's referred to as the Pre-Katrina Evidence Warehouse. Want to know what I found out after a while?"

"Sure," she repeated.

"All the evidence for post-Katrina crimes was also being stored in the Pre-Katrina Evidence Warehouse. I stopped that and kept the current evidence here."

"Okay."

"Not okay. The two staff members who handled all evidence in the Pre-Katrina Evidence Warehouse left after I arrived—they had lost their homes. The guy upstairs who decided on the location of the Pre-Katrina Evidence Warehouse died during Katrina."

Lionel stood up from his chair, crushed his cigarette in the ashtray, and walked to the door. He unlocked it and opened it wide. He yelled, "Who knows where the Pre-Katrina Evidence Warehouse is?"

A chorus of "Nobody!" echoed throughout the bullpen. He walked back to his desk.

"It's not all that bad. The department is still paying for all warehousing, and sooner or later we'll track down the warehouse. Right now, the only need for such evidence is cold cases, and we're not investigating cold cases. Crime in New Orleans is way above the national average, and we're all investigating current cases."

"You'd think that Zach Bujold's attorney would have thought of this," Julie stated.

"Vanderhayden was an incompetent asshole. If it hadn't been a slam dunk case, Zachary would have walked."

"Remy Bujold hired Vanderhayden."

"Vanderhayden cross-examined me on the witness stand. He didn't ask the right questions."

"I think the judge was predisposed because of the Bujold family history," she offered.

"I've heard tell that you've been seen here and there with Zachary Bujold."

"So?" Julie said, defensively.

"So, we all love ya, Miss Julie. We wouldn't want to see anything happen to you."

Julie stood and looked at Lionel, saying, "I think you should find the bullets."

*

Zach met Julie at Fat Tuesday's. It was three blocks from the Sonesta and three blocks from her house. It was crowded at 6:30 p.m., but within minutes they had two seats at the end of the bar. They both ordered Hurricanes.

"That's a beautiful jacket, Zach," she said, fingering it. "Suede?"

"Yeah, thanks. I bought it today, along with a bunch of clothes." His fingers played with hers and he asked, "How was your day?"

Julie described the conversation she had with Lionel. She said, "You really got screwed by that attorney. Imagine, I thought of something that could have thrown a wrench in the DA's case, and your lawyer didn't think of it. That's criminal."

"Remy said the guy was good. Frankly, I just think they had it in for me. I remember the atmosphere surrounding the trial and the few newspaper articles I was able to read. Katrina had happened to the poor and indigent and little Lord Fauntleroy murdered his folks. That's how the guards treated me for years."

They sipped their Hurricanes. "Hungry?" he asked.

"I am," she replied.

"Let's eat at Muriel's at Jackson Square. They have Cajun and Creole."

"Sounds great," she said and leaned over to kiss him.

"Louis stopped by to see me last night on the balcony of Muriel's."

Julie put her drink down. "What did he say?"

"He kinda threatened me. He said to watch out, 'cause I'm an adult now, and if someone turns up dead, I'll be executed this time."

"We have to find out where he lives. He's just popping up out of nowhere whenever he chooses."

"I've got someone on that, and I'm hoping to hear from him soon."

*

After dinner, Zach walked Julie home. They entered through the first-floor threshold, and Julie led him through a nicely decorated living room to a small but renovated kitchen. She pulled a bottle of Kettle One from the freezer and made them each drinks. She brought him out to the back porch, overlooking a small garden.

"This is where Hamilton does most of his stalking for prey," she said.

"Are any of your cats feral?"

"They're in between feral and being domesticated. Some come in to eat but live outdoors. Others never leave the house. They all started as strays."

"Do you get them fixed?" he asked.

"If they hang around long enough, I do. I have the females spayed, but I don't have the heart to have the males neutered."

"How many cats have you got?"

"Officially, seventeen. A few are borderline."

"Are you fuckin' with me?" he said, then leaned and kissed her. "Can we take this conversation to bed? I miss holding you."

Chapter 12

Zach had finished doing laps in the pool, and was eating breakfast in the R Club when he received a call from Andre. It was Wednesday morning, and Andre said they should meet. Zach suggested they meet at his suite, and told Andre to take the private elevator and the concierge would show him the way.

When Andre arrived, Zach shook his hand and walked into the kitchenette.

"Would you like coffee or a drink, Andre?"

"Coffee, please."

"Straight or with Kahlua?"

"I can't pass up coffee and Kahlua. I'll have one, thanks."

Andre walked to the balcony while Zach made the drinks. He squirted whipped cream on each and brought them to Andre. He sat a drink on the coffee table in front of Andre, leaned against the railing, and said, "You can smoke out here."

"You've got a nice place here, Zach."

"Uncle Remy is very generous to me."

"Good. Here's what I got. Your twin brother was adopted by Bruce and Mary Snow. If you're a movie buff, you've heard of Mary Snow. Bruce Snow has produced a number of hit movies, all years ago.

"Your brother was raised as Louis Snow. He was a popular kid, and even appeared in bit parts of movies his mother starred in. He went to prep school in Hollywood, and graduated Harvard Law last year."

Andre opened the suitcase on his lap and handed Zach a photograph. "That's Louis, at graduation from law school. No blond hair. He was an excellent student, graduating in the top two percent of his class."

Andre put down the drink and lit a cigarette. "He's never been arrested in the states of California or Massachusetts. His parents are now divorced, and both are running on empty. Mary hasn't had a role in four years, and Bruce is seemingly washed up as a producer. His last two movies were flops. Louis got through Harvard on loans, and presently owes over two-hundred-fifty thousand in student loans. He might have some sort of nest egg, but, by all appearances, he's broke.

"I hired a computer hacker to try and determine how much money your uncle is worth. He couldn't gain access to any financial statements relative to Remy. There's a holding company that makes his actual financial records unavailable. My reason for doing this was to find a motive for Louis tracking you down. I don't believe he knows what Remy is worth, and I don't know what he would do if he had such information. It doesn't seem likely to me that Remy would be giving him any money, especially if Remy thinks you were telling the truth at your trial.

"You've got to consider Louis a threat. If he's capable of murder, he's in a position where his psychotic behavior or alter ego could take over again. You know the jargon better than I do. I think at this point he's dangerous to be around. If he's not crazy, he's doing it for the money."

Zach nodded. He remained silent, absorbing the information and trying to determine if any of his questions were answered. "He approached me two days ago, Andre."

"At Muriel's, on the balcony, Monday night," Andre said. "I've got the audio and video of that encounter."

"Where were you?"

"In a car parked on the street. I'd been following him while he was following you. Do you want to see the clip?"

"Not really. So, you know he somewhat threatened me," Zach said.

"It was a veiled threat, Zach. The police or psychologists may see it differently, but it might not be anything that would legally hold up in court."

"So what do you make of these brief encounters?"

"He's crazy, and he wants you to think you're crazy."

"How can he think I could be persuaded into thinking I'm the crazy one when I clearly know he killed our parents?"

"Before you had proof of his existence, didn't you ever buy into what the psychologists were telling you?"

Zach nodded. "I did, after a while. If you hear the same thing over and over, you eventually begin to believe it. I couldn't account for my time immediately prior to my parent's murders. I could have blacked out and killed them."

"The thing is," Andre said, "something else has to happen. What's the difference if you think you're crazy or not? You've already served your time for the murder of your parents. You can't be tried again for that crime."

"If he gets me to believe I'm crazy, and that I did kill my parents, perhaps he could fall into the good graces of Remy. He could be the victim instead of the murderer."

"The problem is, Zach, if he's crazy, we're not going to understand his rationale—we don't think crazy."

Zach emitted a grunt, and said, "I'm not so sure anymore."

"I'd like to see you get him to confess."

"It's funny, but he's so convincing when he talks about that night. It's almost as though he really believes that I did it. He'd never admit to killing them, especially since I was convicted of the murders."

"Don't you feel vindicated, Zach? After all those psychologists formed their opinions and considered you delusional. Don't you want to rub it in their faces?"

"I don't feel vindicated as much as I feel extremely angry at Louis. He set me up and fucked me good. I miss my parents, and I couldn't even attend their funerals."

"I would still want to take this videotape to the shrinks," Andre said.

Zach nodded. "I'd scream, 'Borderline, my ass!'"

"I want to keep following him," Andre said.

"Of course. By the way, what do I owe you?"

"I worked two days and hired the hacker for two hundred. Make it twelve hundred."

Zach went to the safe and withdrew five thousand dollars. He handed it to Andre. "That should buy me another week of your services. If you need to hire help, just let me know. By the way, I have Louis's fingerprints on a drinking glass in my safe."

"Keep it there." He withdrew the memory chip from the digital camera and said, "This is the video and audio of your encounter with Louis at Muriel's. Keep it in your safe."

"You do good work, Andre. I think you're gonna help me get through this. By the way, do you know Miss Julie?"

"Of course. Everyone knows her."

"She's the only one who knows what you're doing. I want to keep this a secret between the three of us, okay?"

"That's the best way, Zach. Hit them with the facts when we're ready. We can't let Louis know that he's being followed."

*

He visited the Lower 9th Ward in the afternoon. When he was young, his father would drive him to areas within the ward, and would show him where earlier generations of Bujolds owned plantations, cotton fields, and farmland. Now, he paid the cabbie and walked in St. Bernard Parish, a community that at one time had about seventy thousand residents, down to seven thousand after Katrina and now up to thirty-five thousand or so.

The eye of Katrina had passed over the parish, and a surge of water had breached the levees. Witnesses had reported that the parish flooded in fifteen minutes, with surge water higher than the roofs of some houses. Structures were blown off their foundations and crashed into other structures. Many homeowners ended up on their roofs, and many were swept away.

He had read that drugs were rampant throughout the ward. While in Jetson, he had read that The Army Corps of Engineers were exonerated from any liability in the billions lost in the ward due to a legal loophole—don't try to sue the federal government when a discretionary decision had been made— whatever that meant. The Corps had poorly maintained a shipping channel called "Mister Go," which eroded wetlands that represented a natural buffer against hurricanes. *Oops, sorry folks.*

Zach remembered watching CNN broadcasting the Katrina destruction, sitting with his parents and cursing President Bush for his lack of a response. Annette had said that Bush was sitting back in the oval office, saying, "That whole area needed a good enema, anyway, heh, heh, heh."

Then there was Bush's visit, with his arm around Brownie's shoulder, saying, "Hell of a job, Brownie." Then the government assistance which was available after Hurricane Andrew and missing after Katrina—the difference being the real estate involved and the brand of people living in that real estate.

He had read the *Times-Picayune* newspaper in November, while he was in Jetson. The headline read, "Obama Triumphs." He remembered his feeling of elation, not so much because Obama won but rather because Romney lost. He just couldn't see how a Republican president was going to help the fragmented families throughout the city. He wondered if Bobby Jindal had been the right choice for New Orleans as the Governor of Louisiana.

It was a mystery to the rest of the nation as to why people kept repopulating the area after three major hurricanes and a disastrous oil spill occurred in less than a ten year period of time. It was no mystery to the people who grew up in it—there was no place in the world like New Orleans. It was just a different way of living and thinking amidst a potpourri of people and culture.

After two hours of walking, Zach was hungry and depressed. He hadn't seen a person he recognized, and had spent plenty of time as a pre-teen with friends that lived in the ward. Every once in a while he'd see a "Make it Right" home, standing apart from the older homes, care of Brad Pitt. It was heartening to see, but only a drop in the bucket. He called for a cab and waited. He went back to the Sonesta and drank two martinis before ordering appetizers.

*

He took a two-hour nap and woke up invigorated. It was early evening, and the sun was going down. He checked his cell phone for messages, but had none. Julie had said she wanted them to eat at Harrah's and meet a friend of hers. He called her cell, but got no answer.

He began walking over to her house. The streets were crowded with people, many of them checking out menus on windows of restaurants. Zach was excited to tell Julie about Andre and the video clip of him and Louis sitting on the balcony of Muriel's. Finally, he had proof that Louis actually existed.

Julie's house was dark. He rang the doorbell but got no response. The front door was locked. He walked to the side of her house and up the staircase to the second-floor balcony. Walking to the front of the house, he looked in through the French doors. The inside was dark, with just one light on somewhere near the bedroom. He tried the door and it was unlocked. He swung it open and Hamilton jumped out, hissing at him.

"Julie," he said. No response. "Julie," he said louder, still getting no response. He walked through the bedroom to the sitting room. *Nobody home*, he thought. He walked to the bathroom—the only room on the floor with a light on.

"Julie?" he asked. He walked to the bathtub and pulled the shower curtain open. Julie was sprawled naked in the tub, eyes

113

open, with a look of horror on her face. "Julie!" he screamed and fell to his knees alongside the tub. He put his thumb and index finger to her throat and felt no pulse. He began to panic. He touched her cheek and her skin was cold. Her face had a bluish tint. He felt blood rushing to his face, and heard a pounding in his ears.

He fumbled to get his cell out of his coat pocket and pressed nine-one-one. Sobbing, he told the operator he needed an ambulance on Burgundy Street, number six-forty-five—pink house with black shutters. He kept the line open and felt her wrist, hoping for any faint sign of a pulse. He sat on the bathroom floor and put his arm on the side of the tub, staring at a dead Miss Julie.

The paramedics made it there to find Zach sitting in the corner of the bathroom, knees up tight to his chest, his arms hugging his legs, his forehead on his knees, and rocking back and forth. He stood up slowly and left the room, walking to the sitting area and flopping down into an armchair. He watched as they spent a few minutes in the bathroom and then began setting up a stretcher to carry Julie's body out of the house.

He followed them down to the street and asked if he could ride with them. He sat in the back of the ambulance, dazed, staring at her with an oxygen mask over her face and a white sheet covering her body. Her blue feet protruded from under the sheet. They said they were taking her to LSU Emergency Services.

At the hospital, Zach talked to a woman in ER admitting, asking her if she would have a doctor inform him of the condition of Miss Julie. The woman asked what Julie's last name was and Zach said, "Sykes." He sat down in the waiting room and phoned Remy.

"What's up, kiddo?" Remy asked.

"Remy, I think Julie is dead."

"Dead?" Remy repeated. "What happened to her?"

"I found her in her house, in the bathtub. She had no pulse and was turning blue. She's dead, Remy."

"Where are you now?"

"LSU on Perdido."

"I'll be there," Remy said.

Zach sat back on a plastic chair, wondering what could have happened to her. That look of horror on her face was unforgettable. Does one look like that after a heart attack? She didn't look like she had fallen. The water must have drained from the tub. He bent forward and put his elbows on his knees and his face in his hands. He knew Julie was dead, and began sobbing.

Claude, Remy, and Fareeba walked into the waiting room and over to Zach. He stood and hugged his uncle, beginning to weep again. He forced himself to stop, and looked from one to another, shaking his head. "A doctor told me she was dead."

They walked from the hospital and climbed into the limo. Remy poured Southern Comfort into three glasses. He handed them back to Fareeba, who passed one to Zach and held two, waiting for Remy to take a seat. Claude said, "I'm sorry, Zach. Do you want me to take you home?"

"Yeah, Claude. Thanks."

"What do you think happened to her, Zach?" Fareeba asked.

"The doctor said he couldn't arrive at a cause of death, and asked if she had any family. I said I didn't know. I don't think she has any family, 'least not around here."

"Will they perform an autopsy?" she asked.

Zach gagged and put his drink in a cup holder. The thought of them slicing open her beautiful body turned his stomach. He fought the urge to vomit.

"I don't know," he managed to reply.

Remy put his hand on Zach's shoulders, rocking him back and forth. "I'm sorry, Zach," he said, turning to look out the window. He said, "Reba, maybe you should stay with Zach tonight."

"I will, if it's okay with Zach."

He put one hand over Fareeba's and the other over Remy's. "Thanks, guys. I don't want to be alone right now."

Chapter 13

Zach woke up Thursday morning slouched down on the couch. The French doors were open, and it looked and sounded like early morning. He remembered talking with Fareeba well past midnight. He had been drinking vodka non-stop, and must have just passed out. His nightmare of the Grim Reaper had returned with a vengeance sometime during his sleep.

He stood up and walked to the balcony, looking down at Bourbon Street, not yet consumed by cars and pedestrians. He walked into the bedroom and found Fareeba on the bed, snuggled under a comforter. He undressed and slipped under the comforter, watching as Fareeba stirred. He moved into the curves of her body as she lay on her side with her back to him.

She said, "Hey."

"Let me just hold you, Fareeba." He ran his hand over the smooth skin of her arm and fell back to sleep.

He woke several hours later, with an erection, and heard Fareeba in the shower. He swung his legs out of bed and began to dress. *Did we fuck?* He walked out to the kitchenette and slid a K-cup into the coffee-maker. Grabbing a coffee cup, he placed it under the dispenser.

He walked to the balcony and stood at the railing. Fareeba walked out in a bathrobe courtesy of the Sonesta. She pulled a pack of cigarettes from the robe, slid a cigarette out and lit it. Inhaling, she walked to the railing and put a hand on Zach's shoulder, then looked down at the traffic. She walked to a chair and sat down. "It's cold this morning," she said.

Zach turned to her and said, "Fareeba, we didn't—"

"If we had, sugar, you would remember."

"My head's still fucked-up. It's like one big blur."

"Aw, Zach, you're still in shock."

"I just can't believe she's gone."

"Do you want the coffee you poured?"

"I forgot all about it," he replied.

"I'll make us a coupla good ones," she said and left him on the balcony.

He decided to turn the fireplace on. He walked through the kitchenette and TV room and into the living room, turning on the gas flames. Sinking down into soft leather, he watched the fire burn. Fareeba walked in with two coffee cups. She handed one to him and sat next to him on the couch, scooping her legs under her and modestly closing the bathrobe to cover her exposed cleavage.

"This city will miss her, Fareeba."

"You know, I never met her before the casino incident. I'd heard about her, though."

"She was one of the many to lend assistance after Katrina. I was falling in love with her."

"I know you were, Zach. I could see it in your eyes when you left me at the casino—that determined look a man gets when he wants his woman back."

"How'd you get so smart?"

"By livin', sugar, and watchin' the dyin'."

"So what am I gonna do now, oh wise one?" he asked, sipping the coffee.

"You're gonna keep livin', sugar," she said, reaching over to put a hand on his leg. "Keep on livin' and watchin' the dyin'."

*

Zach called Remy and asked if he'd have breakfast with them at the R Club. Remy was only a few blocks from the Sonesta, and said he'd join them.

They were looking at menus when Remy arrived. The waitress asked for their drink order and Remy asked for bloody Marys all around. He looked frayed at the edges.

"Is something wrong, honey?" Fareeba asked him.

"Let's wait for the drinks, Reba," he said, leaning back in the chair.

After the waitress delivered their bloody Marys, Remy took a long swig and said, "News travels fast down here, Zach. Bad news travels faster. The police want to speak with you."

"Why?" Zach asked.

"Miss Julie—she was strangled to death."

Zach stared at Remy. "Julie was murdered?"

Remy nodded. "I got a call from Sergeant Lionel Dugas. They performed an autopsy early this morning. There was an obstruction in her throat. Her larynx had been crushed. Someone strangled her."

"Jesus Christ," Zach said, putting his hands to his face. He stood up. "I can't eat now," he said, reaching for the bloody Mary. "This is Louis's doing," he spat out.

Remy stared up at Zach. He said, "Your twin brother?"

Zach nodded. "He's back in the city." He took a long drink of bloody Mary and stared at the floor.

Remy glanced at Fareeba. She pursed her lips and shrugged.

"Zach," Remy said, "look at me."

Zach looked up from the floor and into his uncle's eyes. "What?"

"You've been seeing Louis again?"

"Yeah."

"And he's in New Orleans?"

"Yeah. He's approached me several times."

Remy slid back in his chair. He stared at Fareeba. She returned his stare, eyebrows raised.

"Let's go, Zach. We have to go see Lionel right now."

*

Zach sat in a chair facing Lionel Dugas. The sergeant had not yet spoken. He had closed his office door, locked it, and closed the vertical blinds. The room was lit only by sunlight coming in through a dirt-encrusted window.

"I'm Sergeant Lionel Dugas, and you are?"

"Zachary Bujold."

"Just so you know—I'm recording our conversation. Do you understand?"

"You don't have to talk to me like I'm an idiot, Sergeant. I'm fully aware of what's going on around me. Besides, I remember you from my trial."

"Good. Your Uncle Remy mentioned to me that you've seen your twin brother, Louis, recently. Is that correct?"

"Yes, that is correct."

"And you haven't seen your brother before?"

"You know I have, Sergeant. I saw him before my parents were murdered."

"And now, you've seen him before Miss Julie was murdered."

"That's right."

"Did you see him in the seven years you were in Jetson?"

"No," Zach replied.

"So, you admit that you see Louis shortly before someone you know is murdered?"

"That's correct, Sergeant."

"And your doctors at Jetson all agreed that you have a multiple personality disorder, right?"

"That's right, Sergeant."

"Do you think now that they may have been correct in their diagnosis?"

Zach reached into his coat pocket and withdrew his cell phone. He dialed Andre, praying the man would answer his cell.

"Zach?"

"Andre. Have you heard about Miss Julie?"

"I have, Zach. I'm sorry."

"You know Sergeant Lionel Dugas?"

"Sure."

"Speak with him, please," Zach said and handed the phone to Lionel.

Zach sat back in the leather armchair and watched as Lionel talked with Andre. Lionel reached into a drawer and placed an ashtray on his desk. He tapped on a pack of cigarettes and one fell on the desk. He lit it and leaned back in his chair, listening to Andre speak.

He handed the cell phone back to Zach, saying, "You were smart to have recruited Andre to monitor Louis. He says he left a memory card with you. You still have it?"

"Yes, sir."

"Let's go to your place. Andre will meet us there. He'll play it for us."

*

Zach asked Fareeba if she'd help him serve drinks. His guests were acting impatient, waiting for show time. Andre and Lionel were sitting on the balcony. Claude and Remy were sitting on the couch in the TV room, watching a local news channel. Everyone wanted coffee and Kahlua. Zach had asked room service for a lunch that would feed six hungry people, and added shrimp and crawfish to the order. He was extremely hungry yet wasn't sure if he could eat.

He walked to the kitchenette and poured diet Coke into a glass. Fareeba carried glass mugs of coffee and Kahlua with whipped cream to the men on the balcony.

She shook her head when she returned to make two more coffee drinks, saying, "Cops."

"Actually, Andre is a retired cop. He's a PI now."

"Same macho mentality," she said.

"What do you want to drink?" he asked.

"Vodka on ice, please," she said, as she poured Kahlua into a coffee mug.

Zach made her drink and placed it on the kitchenette counter. He sat in an armchair to Remy's right.

When everyone had a drink and food in front of them, Andre patched his digital camera into the flat-screen and turned on the TV. They all watched as Zach sat on Muriel's balcony. As Louis came into view, with his black coat and blond hair, Zach turned to Remy. Remy looked at him and winked, smirking.

The clip only lasted five minutes, and Andre replayed the video after turning up the volume. Street noise on the recorded audio interfered with a few sentences on the clip. They all watched and listened to the two brothers interact again. Andre turned the TV off and looked at Lionel.

"What did you mean when you asked Louis if he was threatening you?" Lionel asked Zach.

Zach finished chewing and drank some Coke. "He had killed my parents and got me seven years. He was threatening that he could do it again, with someone else. I should have warned Julie."

"He appears to be angry at you. How can he pull off being angry at you if you both know he killed your parents?"

"Sergeant, he's crazy, and he wants me to believe I'm crazy. He maintains that he didn't kill our parents. Andre, what do you think?"

Andre looked at Zach and then Lionel. "I told Zach I thought Louis was dangerous. You know, all the psychologists in juvy told Zach he had imagined Louis. I'd like to show this video to them."

"Oh, we will. Don't you fuckin' worry about that." He paused and said, "Sorry about the language, ma'am."

"You fuckin' well aughta be," Fareeba said, looking at Remy and laughing.

"Zach," Remy said, "I always believed your story, but you don't know how good it is to see proof of it."

Lionel said, "This ain't proof of anything yet, Remy. I'm gonna need a lot more information. Andre, can you come with me?"

"Sure."

Zach went to the safe and unlocked it. He withdrew five thousand dollars and handed it to Andre when Lionel was in the bathroom. "A bonus, Andre, for bein' there when I needed you."

"You realize that if you hadn't been videotaped, you could be in detention, waiting to be indicted on murder one?"

"You gotta catch this fucker, Andre."

Chapter 14

That afternoon, Zach went with Remy and Fareeba to his uncle's mansion. He sat on the back porch with Remy while Fareeba made them drinks.

"I have to do something with Julie's cats, Remy."

"Put them in your mansion and hire a cat person to stay there."

"That's a great idea. I'll call the SPCA."

"Call Lionel first and get his permission. That house is a crime scene now."

Zach didn't have a number for Lionel. He called Andre.

"What is it, Zach?"

"Are you still with Lionel?"

"Yeah."

"May I speak with him, please?"

Zach heard grumbling, then, "What?"

"I want to get Julie's cats over to my place in the Garden District. Can I have the SPCA enter her house?"

"We have the house cordoned off. We can't have people traipsing through it." Lionel had an edge on his voice.

"How about one SPCA worker under your officer's supervision?"

There was silence on the connection.

"I know Julie would have wanted this, Sergeant. Please, just one person."

"It's three o'clock. Have it set up for four. The guy will need gloves and a cage, taking one cat out at a time. This can't become a circus."

"Thanks, Sergeant." Zach nodded to Remy.

Zach called the SPCA and asked to talk with a supervisor. He waited and sipped the Mimosa Fareeba had brought him. Remy followed Fareeba into the house.

"Can I help you?" a woman asked.

"Yes. I need help with a house full of cats."

"What kind of help?"

"Have you heard of Miss Julie?" he asked.

"I know Julie Sykes."

"Did you hear that she died?"

"Oh, my God, no!" she said in alarm.

"I want to look after her cats until we figure out what's best for them. Is it possible to have the cats rounded up and brought to a mansion in the Garden District?"

"A mansion? Who am I speaking with?" the woman asked.

"Zachary Bujold. I own the mansion on St. Charles Avenue, number five-ninety."

"I was supposed to meet you and Julie at Harrah's yesterday evening."

"I went to her house to pick her up and found her."

"I don't think she has any family," the woman said.

"What's your name?" Zach asked.

"Virginia. Ginny."

"Do you know where her house is, Ginny?"

"Sure. I've been there."

"Can we get a truck over there with some cages, and a guy with gloves on?"

"We can be there in fifteen minutes."

"No. The police have taped off entry to the house. I'll meet you there at four. The police will accompany one of your people into the house. It's a crime scene."

"What happened to Julie?"

"She was strangled. I'll see you at four."

*

He walked the streets to Julie's house, still shocked over her murder. Could Louis really be so evil, so insane, that he could murder a woman he didn't even know? How can a person be that fucked-up?

The Grim Reaper was invading his sleep once again. He could visualize the dark presence, crouching over him and opening his mouth with long, slender fingers. He could feel an aura of evilness surrounding the illusion and couldn't forget the horrific look of the death mask. *Why was this dream occurring after each murder?*

He found Ginny and a worker sitting in a truck in front of Julie's house. They exited the vehicle and shook hands with Zach. An officer pulled up in a cruiser and joined them on the sidewalk. Zach and Ginny waited outside, as the worker entered the home with a cage, followed by the officer, both wearing plastic booties and gloves. Each cat that was retrieved was placed in the truck. Zach took a snapshot of each cat using his cell phone, and he hoped that Hamilton would be one of the evacuees. The cat was nowhere to be seen.

"Did you ever meet Hamilton, Ginny?"

She turned her back to the truckload of caged cats and whispered, "He was Julie's favorite."

"I'll come back for him," he said. "Let's get this truck to St. Charles Avenue."

The drive took less than ten minutes. He opened up the front doors to the mansion, and he, Ginny, and the worker carried in the caged cats. Zach poured water and milk into bowls and put down some of the cat food taken from Julie's house. He set up litter boxes in the kitchen and opened a back window to the porch.

Alone on the back porch, drinking a beer, Zach watched as cats came and went. He knew that cats didn't like to be relocated, but the smells of the garden seemed of great interest to them. He updated the snapshots on his cell, wanting to distinguish the indoor from the outdoor cats.

Finally, he walked to Julie's house with a leash given to him by Ginny. He would sit on the back porch of Julie's house until Hamilton came home.

*

Zach had a childhood alive with animals. Annette loved all creatures. Henri loved Annette enough to compromise—no critters in his study. The rest of the mansion was open range. Zach learned to love them all, though he preferred the haughty cats to the submissive dogs.

Hamilton taught Zach a few things he didn't know about cats—don't ever pick up a cat when its walking away, don't ever leash a cat, and don't ever put a cat in a cab. At one point, after prying Hamilton's nails from the driver's shoulders, Zach seriously thought about picking up the cat one last time and dropping him out the window. He paid the cabbie well and carried Hamilton to the mansion's front door and tossed him in.

He sat on the back porch, alternately dipping one hand in hydrogen peroxide while drinking a beer with the other. After drying his hands, he called Robbie.

"Zach. What's up?" Robbie asked.

"Do you like pussy?"

"As opposed to a sweaty ball sack? I'd have to say, 'Yes,' to that."

"How about the animal version. Can you abide by cats?"

"No way, MoFo. I like cats, and I loved Missy Julie, but there's no way I can take cats in our place on Decatur."

"You heard about Julie?"

"It made the late-edition papers today."

"I've gotta have someone take care of the cats, Robbie."

"I wish I could help, Zach."

"Did I mention the cats come with a mansion?"

"Say what?"

"My place on St. Charles Avenue. You can move the family in, rent free, and the position pays a healthy salary."

"Ca-ching."

"Can you really live with seventeen cats, Robbie?"

"The question will be whether they can put up with me and all the pussy I'll be bringin' home."

"Call me tomorrow and we'll set up a meet."

*

Against his better judgment, Zach had Andre invite Lionel to dine with them that evening. They agreed to meet at Broussard's for dinner.

Andre and Zach sat at a table in the restaurant, waiting for Lionel. They were both drinking vodka on ice.

"What's Lionel's take on this situation, Andre?"

"He's non-committal at this point, not wanting to say anything he can be quoted on later. He had a messenger deliver a copy of the videotape of you and Louis talking at Muriel's to Jetson, and he's waiting for the psychologists to comment. He may have been talking with them when I called him."

"I'm just afraid that the shrinks won't admit they were wrong. Regardless of their assessment of me, they'll have to admit that Louis does exist."

"Just remember, as far as Lionel goes, there now appears to be two brothers in the garden seven years ago. Either one of you could have murdered your parents, and either one of you could have murdered Miss Julie. The conversation on that tape is too vague for Lionel to draw any conclusions."

"So, all my testimony about my twin brother, disregarded by all, plus my years in prison, doesn't make Lionel believe me at all?"

"I suggest you don't harp on your seven years at Jetson to Lionel. He's Homicide, and his perceptions are aligned a certain way. We've been friendly over the years, but he's a hardened guy, especially concerning Miss Julie's murderer. If he was left alone with whoever murdered Miss Julie for two minutes, and if he could get away with it, I do believe he'd kill the guy."

Zach watched as Lionel entered the restaurant and surveyed the tables. He saw them and walked over. He was still wearing his police uniform. He took a seat across the table from Zach.

"Dinner's on you?" he asked Zach, still all attitude.

"Yes, Sergeant. Order anything you want."

"They serving up Miss Julie's murderer tonight?"

"Do you see Louis around, Sergeant?"

A waitress stopped to take Lionel's drink order. He ordered a Rum Runner.

"I have an initial report from the boys at Jetson, Zach," Lionel said.

"What was their analysis, Sergeant?"

"That you are one crazy motherfucker," Lionel said. He stared at Zach.

Zach looked at Lionel, then Andre. He looked back at Lionel, who burst into laughter.

Zach put his open palm to his heart and said, "Please don't do that."

"I'm sorry, Zach. Moments like this come so seldom in a career like mine."

"Please tell me what they said."

"Well, some of the conversation you brothers had could go either way. You said this, he said that. You did mention killing him, but the overwhelming statement made on that tape, according to the psychologists, is the threat that Louis made. It implied that if you didn't leave the city, another murder would occur, and you would appear to be responsible. They're assuming that Miss Julie's murder was the 'shit-storm' Louis mentioned."

Zach nodded. "Did they say anything about believing my story?"

Lionel shook his head. "The psychiatrist, Doctor Fadon, stands by his diagnosis of you."

They took a break and went outside to have a cigarette. Andre lit one for Zach.

"What did you do on Wednesday?" Lionel asked.

Zach dragged on his cigarette. "I met with Andre in the morning. I took a cab to the Lower Ninth Ward in the afternoon. I had appetizers at the Sonesta and took a nap for several hours before walking to Julie's. I guess that two-hour nap is the only time I can't account for."

"And that's the time frame we're looking at. Miss Julie ended her class at three o'clock and walked home. The coroner put the time of death at around five o'clock that evening. You called it in at six-thirty."

Zach looked at Andre. "You found Louis, right?"

Andre shook his head.

"Somehow, I assumed he was in custody. You know where he's staying, don't you?"

"Zach," Andre said, "I know where he stayed. He's not there anymore."

Zach took another drag on the cigarette and slipped it into a receptacle. "Louis is doing it to me again. He murders and takes off. He doesn't know you had surveillance equipment on him. He doesn't know anyone thinks he exists. He'll leave the city and let me hang again."

"We got an APB out on him," Lionel said. "Be prepared to be stopped by police. We posted two photos of Louis, one with blond hair and one with black hair. You better get some proper identification."

"And you'll keep looking for him, right, Andre?"

"If he's still in New Orleans, I'll find him, Zach."

They went back into Broussard's to eat dinner.

Chapter 15

On Friday morning, Zach wore some of the new clothing he had purchased. He slipped on socks, black slacks, and black leather shoes. He put on an olive-colored silk shirt and an off-white sports jacket, and slid on the eight-ball belt buckle and the silver and copper jewelry. He spent the morning getting a library card and driver's license. He was actually pleased at the "Convicted Felon" warning on the license. It was just another thing that distinguished him from Louis.

He called Robbie and they decided to meet on Frenchmen Street. Zach stood beside a street vendor's stand eating Cajun style crawfish boudin. A band was practicing jazz music somewhere nearby. Trumpets and saxophones attempted to strike an even cord. He watched as Robbie sauntered up and they locked hands.

"Let me catch up," Robbie said, ordering pork boudin with alligator meat on the side. He shook hot sauce over everything. They walked slowly, carrying their food on paper plates.

Zach pulled Robbie into Café Negril. They sat on barstools and placed their plates in front of them, continuing to eat.

"Remember Roz?" Zach asked.

"Ragin' Roz?" Robbie said and laughed. "Serving beer to minors 'cause they tipped so well?"

"We both missed seven years of this, Robbie."

"To endure our own private hells."

"You don't paint a pretty picture of Houston."

"Remember my father, Zach?"

"Leland? Of course. He was one of the funniest guys I ever met."

"He was happy as a lark before Katrina, doin' his carpentry thing. After the dust settled, he was countin' the money in his head, you know, the restoration. Then they imported workers, and we were homeless, and he couldn't get work. Houston ended up being a really bad experience for him. He was completely out of his element. He had a hard time making friends. My mom is making money and he's on the unemployment line. He lost his sense of humor, not to mention his pride."

A bartender walked in front of them. They both ordered Abita Amber beer.

"Is Roz still bartending?" Zach asked the bartender.

"Roz died in Katrina," the bartender said flatly and walked away.

They looked at each other. "Jesus," Zach said, shaking his head, "I may need some black tar heroin before this day is over."

"Cheer up, Zach. We're back."

He looked at Robbie. "So, how's Leland doing now?"

Robbie lit an American Spirit and said, "Day by day. It's just me and him now. My mom stayed in Houston. She has a good job there."

"Have you discussed the cat project with him?"

"Not yet. I wanted to talk with you first. I know he'd love to do it, and he likes cats, but if he perceives this as a handout, he'll never take it."

"Did he know Miss Julie?"

The bartender returned with two bottles of beer.

"Every parent after Katrina knew Miss Julie, Zach."

"Well, this project is in her memory. He'll be the keeper of 'Miss Julie's House of Wayward Pussy.' I know we can come up with something better than that."

"That would do wonders for his ego."

"Better than that—we could have him tear down the old porch in the back and build a deck surrounding a room for plants and cats, with plenty of glass, and access from the house and to the garden. There's a name for that," Zach said.

Robbie tilted his bottle of beer and clinked Zach's, saying, "Yeah—rooms for plants and cats, with plenty of glass."

"I was thinking of making this house kind of a halfway house for cats. Once we get Julie's cats adopted, we'll take in more. That would keep the job going on indefinitely."

"Aw, Zach, you don't know what this would mean for us."

"Is one-hundred grand a year salary okay?"

Robbie put his bottle of beer on the bar and stared at Zach.

"Okay, okay," Zach said. "One-hundred grand each, but that's my final offer."

Robbie grabbed Zach by the ears and kissed him full on the mouth.

"Hamilton stays put," Zach demanded, wiping his mouth on his sleeve. "I can't give up on him."

"Who's Hamilton?" Robbie asked.

"Oh, you'll find out." He reached in his pocket and pulled out a set of keys and handed them to Robbie. "Trust me. You'll find out who Hamilton is."

*

Zach walked into the Rampart Street Police Department at four o'clock in the afternoon. He asked the officer on watch if Sergeant Lionel Dugas was available. He identified himself. The officer picked up a phone and talked. Hanging up the phone, he said. "Down the hallway and to the left."

Zach saw Lionel sitting in his office and walked to the door. It was open, but he didn't walk in. He stood there looking at Lionel.

"Sit," Lionel said.

Zach walked over and sat in an armchair.

"What?" Lionel said.

"I'm just checking to see if you've had any luck finding Louis."

"You have Andre looking for him, right?"

"Yeah, but I guess I was hoping you'd have a team on it as well. I'm afraid he'll skip town."

"Look, Zach, I cared for Miss Julie as much as anyone, but we simply don't have the resource to put more than one man on this. Andre knows who that person is, and they should be working together. Beyond that, there's nothing more that can be done. We have no evidence against Louis at this point, but, trust me, if I had him now, I'd be sweating a confession out of him. I think he did it. Andre thinks he did it. The shrinks think he's capable of doing it. All we gotta do is locate the fucker."

Zach reached into his wallet and pulled out his library card and driver's license. He slid them across the desk to Lionel.

136

"I got those this morning. Notice the 'Felon' on the license? I'm hoping that will further identify me to your cops if they stop me."

Lionel passed the cards back to Zach. "Anything else? I'm busy."

Zach stood up and walked out of the sergeant's office.

*

He didn't want to go back to the Sonesta, and he decided to walk to the casino. He was thinking about Julie most of his time alone, and he wanted to stop that for a while. Missing her was not going to go away, but he still had urges to satisfy. He felt guilty at being horny so soon after her death, but he needed sex and he knew it was just a physical thing. He wouldn't be cheating on her, per se, more like cheating on her memory. *Who was he kidding?* He'd cheated on her while she was alive.

Walking into Harrah's, Zach wanted to see if he could strike up a conversation with an older woman. He was hoping for someone around thirty. Walking the aisles surrounding the blackjack tables, he began looking for a woman sitting by herself, grinding it out, trying to build a stash.

After fifteen minutes of walking and stopping to watch dealers sweep in chips, he found a very attractive Japanese woman. She was slim and well dressed, wearing a blue ensemble that tied at her neck and exposed the hint of small breasts. Her shiny hair was jet black and fell straight down her back. She wore a blue visor that kept her eyes shaded from the overhead lighting.

Zach sat to her left, not wanting to interfere in her play if he took a hit when it wasn't prudent. It was a fifty-dollar-minimum table, and he figured she had about five grand in chips in front of her. He placed a grand in hundreds on the table, and the dealer pushed him twenty chips.

"May I buy you a drink?" he asked her.

"Sure, but they're free if you're playing," she said, turning to him and smiling. "I'll have a Grasshopper, please."

They played side by side for a while. A waitress walked up to them and he ordered the Grasshopper and a beer.

"What's your name," she asked.

"Zach. What's yours?"

"Asami," she stated.

Asami was on a hot streak and Zach wasn't interfering in her game. He was losing, down about five hundred.

They were brought their drinks. Asami said, "Good luck," and smiled at him.

"What's Asami mean in Japanese?"

"Morning beauty," she said.

"Hit," Zach said to the dealer. He was dealt a seven and made twenty-one.

"I'd love to find out if that's true," he said, turning to look her in the eyes.

They played for an hour or more. He was down several grand and she had stacks of one-thousand-dollar chips in front of her.

"Want to grab some food at Bambu?" he asked.

"I've never been there," she said. "Is the food good?"

"It's five-star Asian. It doesn't get any better—at least, not in the States."

They both tipped the dealer and cashed in their chips. Asami was six inches shorter than Zach. He put a hand on the back of her arm and guided her through the casino to the restaurant.

There was no wait and they were led to a table. He pulled a chair out for her to be seated. He sat in the chair to her right.

"Do you live in New Orleans?" he asked.

"God, no," she said. "I'd gamble away the family fortune."

Asami was pleased with the menu. She said she wanted some Sushi and Sashimi. Zach suggested that she order for both of them. A waitress took their drink and food order.

"Are you married?" he asked her.

"No. Are you?"

"No."

"Are you a male prostitute?" she asked.

He looked at her. She had slices of green eyes squinting at him, her thin eyebrows raised.

"No, Asami. Unless you're looking for one, and then I am."

She laughed. "I'm pretty sure I can afford you, Zach."

"More importantly, I think you won't forget me."

"Young, handsome, well-dressed, and immodest. I hit the jackpot."

The talk and company was making him aroused. He put his hand under the table and onto her leg. He slid his hand upward, then back down to her knee.

Asami put her hand discretely under the table and onto Zach's leg. She moved it up and over the bulge in his slacks.

"Isn't the anticipation of sex almost as good as the sex itself?" she asked.

He looked at her and said, "No."

They ate leisurely, stopping often to converse. Asami was the daughter of a Japanese industrialist, and was vacationing in New Orleans for an indefinite period of time. Zach contributed little of his situation to her, not wanting to talk about any of it.

He paid the bill and followed her to her room. She was the first Asian woman he'd ever experienced, and she proved to be as sensual and eager as he had hoped. She brought him a drink and sat him in a chair while she slowly disrobed. She had him stand, and she removed the clothing from his body, kissing each exposed area until he was wearing only his erection. She spent considerable time kissing that. In bed, Asami was both an agile and aggressive lover. Zach brought her to orgasm and soon after she was sleeping. He slid out of bed, dressed, and walked home. He had her cell number, and was certain he'd call her.

Chapter 16

Zach received an early morning call on Saturday. He reached for the cell phone on the nightstand and answered, "Hello?"

"Rise and shine, kiddo. We've got a busy day ahead."

"What time is it, Remy?"

"Eight o'clock. We're hosting a jazz funeral for Miss Julie today."

Zach swung his legs out of bed and stood. He walked to the balcony and looked up to the sky. It was a clear and cool morning, showing no signs of rain.

"You're doing this?"

"It came to me yesterday. I called the funeral parlor and bought a casket. Julie was Jewish, so they'll be no Catholic Mass. I have the funeral home delivering her in a horse-driven hearse to her house on Burgundy. The jazz band will meet there at eleven. I figure the procession will begin before noon."

Zach put a K-cup in the coffee-maker and a cup underneath the dispenser. "Where will it head?"

"Down Burgundy, to Canal, then to Loyola. It'll pass by Tulane University—hell, half her students are in there. It'll proceed to the St. Louis Cemetery."

"Number one?"

"Yep," Remy replied proudly.

"How'd you swing that?"

Remy laughed. "Sometimes it's good to come from a criminal family. We've got three empty vaults in that graveyard—as far back as the nineteenth century. Some of your ancestors died under less than honorable circumstances, believe it or not. Two of them with vaults were never found. The third vault, to be occupied by your great grandfather, Jules, remains empty because they couldn't find his head."

"So you have an above ground vault for Julie?"

"Newly renovated, no less. Since there's been no wake, I was thinking of an open casket ceremony at the cemetery. What do you think about that?"

"She's been autopsied, Remy."

"The funeral director said her face is fine. They have her dressed in a green gown that covers her throat. She's been embalmed, and the director says she looks good. If you want, we can swing by and take a look at her before we go to Julie's house."

"I'm not sure I can look at her, Remy. Maybe I will. I'll trust your judgment."

"Lionel said her house is still off limits, so I'm having a caterer set up food on the sidewalks. I'll have beer, alcohol, and soft drinks delivered by ten-thirty. Burgundy Street will be shut down at ten o'clock, and Lionel will have police diverting traffic."

"I don't know what to say, Remy. Thank you for this."

"No problem," Remy said. "It's for the locals, too, as well as for her."

"You're a good man, Remy."

"Why don't we meet at the R Club soon and have breakfast, then we'll head to the funeral parlor."

"I don't have a tux or black suit."

"No need. Wear something casual. Most of the people Julie knew will be wearing jeans. It's not a sign of disrespect." He disconnected the call.

Zach took a few minutes to think about what his uncle was doing. What a tribute this was to Julie's life. The city that she loved and helped would be paying its respects to her. It would be a day that few in attendance would ever forget. It would also become an historical event.

He showered and dressed in a dark blue sports jacket with a white shirt and gray slacks. He knotted a Jerry Garcia tie and slipped on comfortable, black leather loafers. He poured out the coffee he never drank and popped open a beer. He waited for the crew to arrive.

The last jazz funeral he had witnessed took place just several months before Katrina—Chief Allison "Tootie" Montana, the Mardi Gras "chief of chiefs" had died at the age of eighty-two. An African-American, Tootie had begun making his own Indian costumes at the age of ten. The blacks had a connection to the Native American Indians as far back as the days of slavery, when Indians hid runaways from bounty hunters.

He had been in juvy when the one year anniversary jazz funeral was held to mourn the seventeen hundred victims of Katrina. He had seen pictures of the horse-drawn hearse and empty casket, with Mayor Nagin and Lieutenant General

Honoré leading the procession. There was a tolling of bells at 9:38 a.m. and a silent prayer where the first levee was breached.

Remy, Fareeba, and Claude walked in and Fareeba began making coffees with Kahlua. She was wearing a full-length black gown, with her long, black hair flowing down her neck and bare back. Remy wore western attire and Claude wore a black tux, white shirt, and bowtie. Zach walked in from the balcony and hugged Remy. "Hey, Claude," he said, over Remy's shoulder.

"Hi, Zach. You gonna be up for this?"

"Yeah. It's a good thing, remembering Julie this way. Thanks again, Remy."

"You know," Remy said, "she had no direct family. She would have been buried or cremated without any ceremony or fanfare. I feel good about this."

"You should. How are we doin' time-wise?"

"We're fine. Everything is set up. It'll happen with or without us. I got lucky with the brass band—the Hot Eight is in town. They agreed to play the procession."

"I won't even ask how much that cost you."

"They were very reasonable," Remy said.

They sat and drank their coffees and had breakfast at the R Club.

*

A police officer moved the wooden barricade to let Claude drive the limo down Burgundy Street. It was 10:45 a.m., and the closed casket containing Julie's body had been placed in the back bed of a horse-drawn, stagecoach-like hearse, allowing the casket to be viewed by spectators. It was a highly polished black coffin with gold handrails and white double-flowered lilacs covering the top. Mourners were placing signs and letters beside the coffin, wishing Julie a safe trip.

The neighborhood was alive with music playing from rooftops. Homeowners and tenants were out on their porches and balconies, and children were running down the traffic-free streets. The area was getting thick with pedestrians, and the buffet tables on the sidewalks were being monitored to keep the hungry in single lines. There was no sign of police officers, but Zach suspected that Lionel had some detectives working overtime to control the crowd.

They walked from the limo, through the crowd and toward the hearse. Lionel was standing at a table that served alcohol, a beer in his hand, wearing civilian attire, and talking with Mayor Landrieu. Lionel welcomed them, and introduced them all to the mayor. Apparently, Remy knew the man. They talked and laughed together.

The Hot Eight Brass Band arrived shortly after eleven, to cheers from the onlookers. "Rock with The Hot Eight!" was screamed out by someone behind Zach. It was the title of their first studio album. The band shook hands with the crowd and began setting up for the procession.

Zach walked out and away from the crowd. He sat on the front steps of a house, thinking about how much he missed Julie's laugh. A young African-American girl walked down the steps and sat beside him. He figured she couldn't be more than six years old. She wore a black dress with white socks and black shoes. Her nappy hair ended in pigtails. She was very cute, and smiled at him.

"Hi," he said, "I'm Zach."

"Hello, I'm Tameka."

"That's a pretty name for a pretty girl."

"Thank you. Are you going to Miss Julie's party?"

"Yes, I am," he said. "Are you?"

"Oh, yes. I know Miss Julie. She gave me a kitten."

"What's the kitten's name, Tameka?"

The girl looked at Zach incredulously, saying, "Miss Julie, of course. It's a girl kitten."

Zach smiled at the girl and stood. He walked away from her and began sobbing. He breathed in deeply and blew his breath out slowly, trying to contain his emotions. *Don't screw this up*, he thought. This was going to be Julie's last day, and he wanted to be part of it. He owed her that much. He could cry another day. He straightened his tie and wiped his eyes with index fingers.

As he walked back toward the girl, her parents joined her on the steps. Zach walked up and said, "Hi, I'm Zach. Tameka told me you knew Julie."

"We did," her mother said. "I'm Teresa, and this is my husband, John."

Zach shook their hands and said, "Have you eaten? There's a lot of food set up."

"We're new to the neighborhood, and don't really know anyone. Julie made a point of stopping by as soon as we moved in."

"Follow me," Zach said. He grabbed Tameka's hand and looked at her parents with his eyebrows raised. They nodded and walked down the steps. He walked through the crowd, finally swinging Tameka up onto his shoulders, and stopped at the first table of food.

"Why don't you two eat and I'll walk around with Tameka. Make her a plate when you're finished, and I'll be right there, where the band is setting up. Okay?"

Her parents happily agreed and Zach walked with Tameka clutching his hair while he held her by the knees. "What's your last name, Tameka?"

"Walker," she said.

"Thirsty, Miss Walker?"

"Very thirsty, Zach."

"Can you say 'Bujold'?"

"Bujold," she said.

"They call me Mister Bujold."

"I'm very thirsty, Mister Bujold."

Zach walked up behind Fareeba while she was drinking a bloody Mary, tapped her on the shoulder, and said, "Miss Fareeba, meet Miss Walker."

Fareeba turned to look at Zach and Tameka. She laughed. "We'll, aren't you two a couple." She looked at the young girl. "What would you like to drink, honey?"

"I'll have a Coke, please, and Mister Bujold will have what you're having."

Fareeba stared at the girl and burst out laughing. "Formal, and smart, aren't we? One Coke, coming up."

He walked over toward the two white horses. Two old African-American men in tuxedos and top hats were sitting up high and holding the reins. They smiled down at Tameka. She let go of his hair with one hand and waved at them from his shoulders.

"Watch you don't put a hand to their mouths, honey," one of the men said, making sure that Zach acknowledged the statement.

"They're hungry for chicken fingers," the other man said and laughed.

Zach walked back toward the crowd, put his hands up, and Tameka grabbed them. He swung her off his shoulders and to the ground. He looked around and saw the Walkers approaching. "Here comes your food, Miss Walker."

Fareeba walked over and handed Tameka a cold can of Coke. She handed Zach a can of Abita Amber, and kissed him on the cheek.

*

As the procession commenced, the band began with a traditional dirge. Zach didn't recognize the song, but it was slow and mournful. The band proceeded slowly down Burgundy, playing hymns and stepping slowly until they reached Canal Street. As they made a right turn up Canal, on their way to the university, the music became livelier. Tambourines and drums were added to the brass.

People threw streamers and confetti from balconies, and pedestrians stepped lively or began dancing on the sidewalk and the street. Normally, a procession wouldn't begin acting this way until after the cemetery, but Zach found it uplifting. They were all celebrating Julie's life, not just mourning her death.

By the time they reached Tulane University, the band was in full swing, sweeping their instruments from right to left and performing their well-known second line music. Zach scooped up Tameka as they marched behind the casket, letting her get a view of the mass of students lining the university campus. Tameka waved at the crowd.

When the procession reached the St. Louis Cemetery, Zach walked away from the crowd and set Tameka down on the sidewalk. Her parents walked up and Zach bent down in front of her. He said, "Miss Walker, you have to stop here. The rest is all grown up stuff you wouldn't like."

He kissed her on the cheek and rose. He looked at the Walkers and they both seemed relieved. The girl was too young to be dealing with death. They all hugged, and as Zach walked into the cemetery, Tameka yelled, "Thank you, Mister Bujold."

He waited on line to view Julie before the casket would be carried into the vault. He hadn't seen her at the funeral parlor, and still fretted looking at her this way, afraid that it would remain the last memory he would have of her. Determined that he would remember the times they had together, he stood and looked down at her beautiful face, resolute in the knowledge that Louis would atone for her murder. Whatever it took, Zach would find Louis and make him pay for this. He bent over and kissed Julie goodbye.

Chapter 17

Zach went jogging early Sunday morning. He alternated his route each day he jogged, but he kept the eight-block square a constant. The Mississippi River interfered with his south-easterly route, and he compensated by running around Jackson Square two times.

He returned to the Sonesta and took the elevator to his suite. Putting on coffee, he sat on the couch and watched "Fox Eight News." He relaxed and sipped coffee.

He showered and shaved, then dressed. The weather was cool, and he wore black slacks and a dark blue sweater he'd bought at Brooks Brothers. Slipping into leather loafers, he left the suite and entered the R Club for breakfast.

After eating an omelet, he left the table to pour more coffee. When he returned, a young woman was sitting at his table. He sat across from her and smiled.

"Do you mind?" she asked.

"Not at all," Zach replied. He studied the woman's face. "You look familiar to me."

"I'm Carol Charles, 'Fox Eight News.'"

Zach nodded. "So, you didn't sit down because you found me irresistible," he said, looking into the eyes of the pretty brunette.

Carol smiled. "You're a handsome young man, Zach, and I'm a working girl. I'm beginning to believe, however, that you've got an irresistible story to tell."

"What have you heard, Carol?"

"That an APB has been issued on one Louis Bujold, your twin brother."

"Listen, Carol, if Louis finds out the cops are looking for him, he'll run. I don't want that to happen."

"But the mere existence of Louis Bujold may prove that you were unjustly convicted of murdering your parents. That's news."

"It'll still be news when he's captured. Do other reporters know about the APB?"

"I can't say—it's just a habit of mine to check on APBs daily. There's no real great story without your input."

"Carol, I've never given an interview to a news reporter before—not during my trial, not during my incarceration, and not since I've been released. If you wait until Louis is caught, I'll give you an exclusive interview."

"Will you give me your phone number now?" she asked, handing him her card.

Zach recited his number to her and told her he was late for an engagement. He left her sitting at the table.

*

It was impossible to walk through Jackson Square, toward the St. Louis Cathedral, and not be inspired by the church—the white apparition in the morning mist, the three dark steeples, and the clock sitting up high. Its history dated back almost three hundred years, though the original structure looked nothing like what it was today. The church had been destroyed by fire in the eighteenth century, damaged by dynamite in the early twentieth century, and Katrina had blown a hole in the roof and the pipe organ had been water-damaged. The cathedral had gone through numerous expansions and had withstood the test of time. Pope John Paul VI had designated it to be a minor basilica.

Zach stood near the entrance and waited for Robbie. Mass began at 9:00 a.m. and Robbie said he wanted to join him. Robbie and his family were active churchgoers—Leland and his wife, Margaret, were always volunteering their time and labor to the Catholic Diocese.

He had been inside the cathedral only as a young boy, accompanied by his parents, on Easters and Christmas Eves. No one in his family was demonstratively religious, but Catholic guilt kept Annette in the game. Henri and Zach went along for the ride.

He watched as Robbie approached. He was wearing dress jeans and a sports jacket over a sweater, with loafers on his feet. Zach had never seen Robbie wearing anything but sneakers. He looked like a young college professor.

They walked inside and sat in a pew at the back, each of them anticipating an early departure—the mass being two hours long. The cathedral was dark inside, which made the golden altar even more awe inspiring. Zach took in the windows, the gold ornaments and statues, and the paintings on the ceiling. *All this wealth*, he thought, *with people near starvation only a few blocks away*. He reminded himself that he had not come to criticize, but rather to spend a quiet time remembering Julie. He was having a very hard time giving her up. He closed his eyes and thought of their times together, eventually pleased with the number of instances he could recall in which he had made her emit that throaty laugh.

From their vantage point in the back, it was difficult to view the sacristy, but Zach had seen it before—a priest wearing a surplice exorcises and blesses salt and water, then sprinkles the salt in the form of a cross over the water. The Tridentine Mass follows, beginning with the Mass of the Catechumens. Robbie hit Zach's leg before the Mass of the Faithful began, and they quietly slipped out of the cathedral.

"I can take so much," Robbie said, lighting a cigarette.

"I just went for Julie," Zach commented.

"In the mood for some boudin?"

"On Frenchmen Street?" Zach asked.

"It was good, wasn't it?"

"Let's go."

They walked briskly along the streets, stopping now and then to window shop.

"Have you discussed the cat project with Leland?"

"Well, he moved in yesterday. Our place on Decatur was a dump. He wants to see you to discuss paying rent."

"Tell him there is no rent. He's okay with the cats?"

"Sure. I haven't said anything to him about income. He's still working on a cabinet job, and I think it's something you have to offer him. He's very prideful."

"I'll get over there tomorrow."

The boudin vendor was still in business, and they took their food to Café Negril and ordered beer. Robbie had promised his father the afternoon, helping to put a new roof on a house in their neighborhood. They talked about common friends they had in high school, neither of them knowing how their lives were now. Robbie finished his beer and left. Zach stayed for another.

*

He paid the cabbie and walked into Harrah's. Sitting at a bar near the entrance, he ordered vodka and ice. He slipped a hundred-dollar bill in the video slot machine built into the bar, and selected video poker. As he played, he noticed that the computer would recommend cards to be kept and cards to be discarded. *Anything to quicken a player's loss of money.*

He played the game slowly, sometimes varying from what the computer recommended, and quickly became sucked into the game. He slid another hundred in and continued to play. The computer would wet his appetite with a straight, flush, or full house, but not the sacred ace high, straight flush. He lost two-hundred dollars in a short time.

Ordering a beer, he watched as Remy, Claude, and Uncle Etienne walked into the casino. He hadn't seen Etienne in over eight years, but knew him by the mole on his left cheekbone. It had grown larger and blacker with age. They didn't notice Zach off to their left, and they continued walking past the slot machines and in the direction of Besh Steakhouse.

He saw Fareeba as she walked in wearing a sleek, black dress and high heels. The dress stopped about three inches from her knees, and the front exposed considerable cleavage. Zach whistled and got her attention. She smiled and walked over to him.

"Thank God," she said. "Finally, someone to talk to." She sat to his left and waved at the bartender.

"Feeling ignored?"

"Men won't talk to me with Remy around. I met Etienne seven or eight months ago, and I just wanted to know what was up with him. He didn't even acknowledge my question."

"Etienne and his family work out of Lafayette County."

"Something is up with Etienne," she said.

"How are you doing otherwise?"

She reached for the glass of vodka as the bartender placed it on the bar and took a swig. "I wish I didn't need sex as much as I do," she said flatly, reaching into her handbag and pulling out a pack of cigarettes. She placed a cigarette between her lips and lit it.

"Remy doesn't satisfy you?"

"He can't always get it up. He's only forty years old. I started thinking he might be doing drugs."

"Do you think he could be using an escort service?" he asked.

"Maybe," she said and took a deep drag. "I try to dress sexy for him. What else can I do?"

"It's not you, Fareeba."

"I hate feeling so horny. It's an itch I just can't scratch myself."

"Are they going to eat at Besh's?"

"Yeah," she replied. "I told them I wasn't in the mood for steak. What I really need is a big sausage," she said, laughing.

"I don't know if I can measure up to that, but I'm willing to try," he said, knowing he was crossing the line.

"Put the pact on hold for an evening?" she replied, looking into his eyes.

"Let's get a cab and go to my place."

*

He could not understand how on earth Remy could tire of sex with Fareeba. Her face was so alluring and her body so welcoming. Lying between her legs, entering her, feeling her legs rise up and wrap around his upper thighs, he thrust hard and deep until she moaned. He kept thrusting until he knew she had reached an orgasm. He came quickly after her, and remained on top of her with his head beside hers until she kissed his ear. His penis made its slow withdrawal, and he rolled over onto his side. He ran his fingers over her still erect nipples.

"You sure know how to satisfy, mister," she said, slipping her body under the sheet.

"You better not get too comfortable. You've gotta go home."

"I know. Remy will be in late tonight. He and Claude are driving Etienne home."

"Do you know why they got together?" he asked.

"No, and Remy's not talking about it. It can't be anything good."

"Did Remy ever mention to you that he was out of the family business?"

"Yes, he did, but meetings like they're having now tell me he's not," Fareeba said.

"I'd just like to know if he's being forced to deal with his past, or he misses it."

"Why do you think he'd miss it?" she asked.

"The excitement of it all."

They napped for a while and then Fareeba dressed and kissed him goodbye. He made a cup of coffee and sat on the balcony. He looked out over the rooftops of the French Quarter, wondering where Louis might be staying if he hadn't already left the city. Andre had said he probably didn't have much money, but that didn't limit the search a great deal. There were cheap motels and boarding houses throughout the district. Many houses rented out rooms. Louis could be sleeping in his car if he had one.

He put on jeans, sneakers, and a sweatshirt and took the elevator to the street. He began a jog toward Frenchmen street. The night air was brisk and it felt good to be running. After the nap with Fareeba, and the coffee, he knew he'd be awake half the night. Slowing down to a fast walk on Frenchmen Street, he checked for a nightspot that wasn't too crowded. The club d.b.a. looked reasonable, and they were known for their eclectic choice of jazz and their single malt scotches. He paid the ten-dollar cover and walked in. Shamarr Allen was playing trumpet on stage. He had brass, trombone, keyboard, and drums accompanying him.

Zach sat at the bar and ordered an amber draft with a Jose Cuervo shot. He could see fresh oysters on the half-shell sitting on ice behind the bar, and ordered a dozen. Shamarr began his creation "Meet Me on Frenchmen Street."

This is what I've been missing, he thought. As young teens, Zach and Robbie would walk these streets and sit at a table until they were kicked out. On a good night, older guys would bring them into their group and buy them beers. For them, the grittier the club, the better the experience—watching bad girls dance seductively to good music. For Zach, it just felt like home. Speakeasies, and easy women. What could be better than that?

Chapter 18

Zach was walking on Canal Street Monday morning, window shopping. He stopped for a cup of coffee and then resumed walking. A red streetcar stopped and he jumped on, paid the driver, and sat upfront. The car was heading southeast in the direction of the Sonesta. He watched pedestrians weave their way along the Central Business District.

He caught a glimpse of someone wearing a black leather coat with blond hair. The figure turned left on the corner of Canal and Rampart, heading north. Zach jumped off at the next stop, ran to the corner, and looked up Rampart Street. Louis was standing three stores away, hands in coat pockets, looking into a store window. Zach slipped back onto Canal and bought a *Times-Picayune* newspaper from a street vendor. He peered around the corner and Louis was walking again.

Zach tailed him past Toulouse Street and up to Dumaine, pretending to read the newspaper when Louis stopped to light a cigarette at Congo Square, looked out over it, and then continued north to Ursulines Avenue. He made a left, and

Zach ran to the corner to watch him walk into the Empress Hotel. It was a sleazy hotel two blocks from Treme.

He waited five minutes and Louis didn't exit. He walked into the lobby and leaned against the counter. A young woman turned and noticed him.

"May I help you?"

"Yes. I'm supposed to meet Louis Bujold here. He's a guest."

The woman hit a few keys on the computer and shook her head. "Sorry, we don't have a guest by that name."

"You know, he also goes by the name of Louis Snow."

"Ah, room one-hundred-ten," she said, pointing to a hallway.

"Thanks," Zach said and walked on a mildewed and frayed carpet that smelled of vomit, checking room numbers. The fifth room on the left was one-hundred-ten. He stood with his ear to the door and listened. He put his hand on the doorknob and twisted his wrist slowly. The door was unlocked. He opened the door and slipped inside.

*

Lionel put down the newspaper and slid his feet off the desk. He took a sip of coffee and reached for the phone. "What?"

"Where?" he asked.

"I'll be there," he said and hung up the phone.

He dialed Andre from his cell phone.

"What's up, Lionel?"

"Zach has Louis detained at the Empress Hotel on Ursulines Avenue. Know where it is?"

"Sure. I can be there in ten minutes."

"I'll be there before you. Room one-hundred-ten."

160

Lionel walked out of the station house to his cruiser. He drove two minutes on North Rampart and turned on Ursulines. He drove two blocks and pulled into the parking lot in front of the hotel lobby. Walking through the entrance in uniform, he glanced at the woman behind the counter with a determined look that said, "Don't ask." He walked down the hallway to room one-hundred-ten and pushed the door open.

He saw Zach standing next to a couch that Louis was slumped on. Lionel walked in front of Louis and looked down. A syringe was sticking out of his left arm. His head was lowered with his chin against his chest. His blond hair was damp and disheveled. Lionel reached and pushed Louis's forehead back and saw foam oozing from the side of his mouth.

"You found him this way, Zach?" Lionel asked.

"Yeah. I've seen kits like that before," he said, pointing to a small leather bag on the coffee table, "as I'm sure you have. He's mainlining heroin."

Lionel bent to touch the side of his throat. "He's got a pulse." He pulled his phone from its holster and pressed a button. Andre walked in through the open door and looked down at Louis. He smiled at Zach and held a thumb up in the air.

"Ambulance to the Empress Hotel on Ursulines Avenue. Pronto. We got an overdose. Room one-hundred-ten."

Andre lit a cigarette and said, "Good job, Zach."

"I hope he lives. I want to hear him confess to murdering my parents."

"Andre," Lionel said, "would you take his belongings and place them in the trunk of my car?" He handed Andre his car keys.

161

Lionel looked down at Louis. *All dressed up and no place nice to go*, he thought. He looked at Zach and said, "Appropriate belt buckle he's wearing, eh?"

"Why?"

"The eight-ball. He's behind the eight-ball now, the motherfucker."

*

Zach woke from a dream that was so erotic he forced himself back into that deep slumber. He had Fareeba on a table outside, in the sun. She was naked and lying on her back, legs parted with knees up. Rain fell on their bodies, but it wasn't cold—rather, very warm and titillating. She was moving her hands over her breasts. He entered her and the dream ended again.

He was lying on his back, and, without opening his eyes, he turned to his left. The knuckle of his right hand scraped against something hard. He opened his eyelids and stared at yellow cinderblock. He opened his eyes wider and raised his head from the pillow. Looking around, he realized he was in a small, dark jail cell. He took a moment to assure himself that he wasn't still dreaming.

His head hurt, both inside and out. He swung his legs off the narrow bed and set his feet on the floor. As he raised his head, he felt dizzy and nauseous. He saw a small metal commode built into the wall to his right, and he fell to his knees and vomited. He missed the toilet completely.

He wiped his mouth with the sleeve of his shirt. He stared at the sleeve—it was a washed-out orange color. Raising himself up to a standing position, he looked down at a one-piece orange jumpsuit covering his body. His feet were bare. He rubbed the back of his head and felt a bump the size of a half-walnut.

He walked to the iron bars that confined him. Cinderblock walls obstructed his view to the right or left, and the view in front of him was a narrow walkway followed by more cinderblock. There were no windows to be seen, and he couldn't determine where the dim light was coming from. Walking back and sitting on the bed, he tried to remember his last conscious moments. Everything seemed clouded and vague. His mouth was extremely dry. *Had he dreamed that he was in an ambulance?*

Footsteps echoed through the hallway. Zach sat forward on the bed, elbows on knees, staring down at his bare feet. A uniformed guard walked up to the cell and said, "Walk up to the bars and show me your back."

Zach stood, walked to the bars, and turned.

"Arms behind your back."

Zach swung his arms behind him, wrist to wrist. He felt cold steel against his skin and the tight grip of handcuffs.

"Legs close to the bars."

Zach backed up against the bars. Leg irons were clasped around his ankles.

"Step forward."

Zach shuffled his feet forward. He heard the cell's door being unlocked and the creaking of metal as the door was opened. A firm grip pulled him around and led him out of the cell. He had to shuffle fast to keep up with the guard. He was led to an open door and then shoved into a room. The guard led him to a wooden chair at the end of a small conference table and forced him to sit down. The guard stepped back behind him.

There were windows to his left and he turned to them. It appeared to be near dusk—late afternoon sunlight shining into the room. The cell was so dark he had assumed it was nighttime.

Lionel walked in through a doorway at the far end of the room. He was in uniform, and sat at the other end of the table.

"Guard, state your name, the date and time," Lionel ordered.

The guard said, "Randall, Kenneth C., Monday, January fourteenth, two-thousand-thirteen, five-ten p.m."

Lionel said, "I am Sergeant Lionel Dugas, NOPD. I'm interrogating Louis Bujold."

Zach felt sick to his stomach. Blood pounded in his ears and he felt his heart fibrillate. Feeling nauseous, he turned his head left in case he vomited. He looked at the windows. A cloud had blocked the sun, and he could see his reflection in the window. He stared at the blond hair on top of his head and vomited on the tiled floor.

"Randall," Lionel said, "get that fucker back to his cell. We'll try this again on Wednesday morning."

*

Louis walked to the Royal Sonesta Hotel. He knew Zach was staying there, but didn't have any idea of the room number. He had Zach's wallet in his back pocket, and a keycard for the room, but there was no room number on it. He walked up to the reception counter and stood there, smiling politely at a young man behind the counter.

"Hi, Zach," the man said.

"Hey," Louis said. He placed the keycard on the counter. "This is a little embarrassing, but I was in an accident earlier today and had a concussion. The doctor told me I might have

164

periodic episodes of memory loss, and I don't remember my room number."

"I'm sorry to hear that, Zach. You're on the concierge floor, suite four. Take the private elevator over there," he said, pointing to his left. "I hope you feel better. If you think you need to see a doctor, call us."

Louis walked into the elevator and the doors closed. When the doors opened, he was looking at a man in a uniform, sitting at a desk facing him, with the nametag 'Philippe' over his chest pocket.

Louis smiled, and said, "Hi, Philippe." He saw a sign behind the man indicating that suites one through eight were to the left. He began to turn left.

"Hi, Zach. They're serving hors d'oevres in the R Club."

"Thanks, but I'm feeling like a nap." Louis walked down the hallway and saw the door to suite four. He inserted the keycard and entered the room. He stood, leaning his back against the closed door, looking at the furnishings of a well-maintained suite. Air freshener had been sprayed. He noticed the potted flowering plants and realized the smell of lilac and lavender was fresh.

He lit a cigarette and walked to the kitchenette, opening the door to the fridge. *No food, Zach? Just beer and orange juice?* He opened the freezer door and found several bottles of Stoli's. He pulled one out and looked for a drinking glass. Setting a crystal glass under the ice dispenser, he filled the glass with crushed ice and then poured vodka to the brim. He took his drink to the balcony and looked down. *Now this is living.*

He sat in a high-backed chair on the balcony and inhaled cigarette smoke deeply. He thought about the things he knew and the things he'd have to unravel. He didn't know the status

165

of the mansion, but knew where it was. He had never actually seen Uncle Remy, but knew where he lived and what he looked like. That was all information he had attained from the Internet and stored on his laptop, which now sat in a locker at the bus station. He didn't want the laptop to be found with his paltry possessions at the Empress Hotel. He'd have to get to the bus station soon.

He was concerned about his accent. Having studied the Cajun French language, and after listening to Zach during the few conversations they had seven years ago, Louis knew that Zach had inflections and used vocabulary that was strongly influenced by the Cajun dialect. Zach had the accent when he was incarcerated at fourteen, but he'd spent seven years with predominately black inmates. His whole approach to the spoken word could have changed significantly over that period of time. Their brief encounters recently didn't last long enough for Louis to close in on the inflections. He would have to keep his sentences short and simple. He'd have to put his Harvard public speaking education on a shelf.

He was confident their voices sounded the same. He'd be dealing with Remy soon, he was sure, and he decided he'd claim a sore throat that would develop into laryngitis. He could ease himself into conversations after he had digested more information.

The credit card in Zach's wallet intrigued him. As he refilled his glass with vodka, he decided he would dial the phone number on the back of the card and learn what sort of credit limit he was dealing with. The card simply read "Mr. Bujold."

For all accounts and purposes, Uncle Remy was probably a multi-millionaire. He was childless, and Zach was his only nephew. Louis knew in his heart that he had just stepped into a goldmine.

Chapter 19

Louis awoke to the sound of Zach's cell phone ringing. He had left it on the nightstand. He stretched his arm to reach it.

"Hello," he said.

"Hey, kiddo, how're you doin'?"

Remy? he thought. *Here goes.* "Remy."

"Have you had breakfast yet?"

"No, I just woke up. I have a sore throat," Louis rasped.

"Nothing some alcohol won't cure. How 'bout Claude and I pick you up in an hour? We'll celebrate your catching Louis."

"I don't know, Remy. I think I'm just going to eat at the R Club and stay close to home. I think I might have a fever." *Talking too much*, he warned himself.

"Okay. We'll join you there. Take a hot shower and sweat the fever out."

"I'll see you soon," Louis said and ended the call.

He took a shower and washed his hair. Drying himself in front of the mirror, he inspected the dye job. It was holding up well. His black hair had no signs of blond and no discolorations or streaking. He found Zach's shaving cream and razor in a bathroom pantry and began shaving. He took time to clip his eyebrows.

Walking to the bedroom closet, he entered and examined the hanging garments. Zach hadn't bought that much since he was released, but what he bought was quality goods. Louis grabbed a pair of beige slacks, a white silk shirt, and a sports jacket that rivaled anything he'd ever worn at Harvard. It was a light-weight dark blue blazer with nice stitching. He grabbed a pair of brown leather loafers and placed everything on the bed. He found Zach's sock and underwear drawer in the dresser. He got dressed leisurely. The clothing fit his body perfectly. *It's good to have an identical twin.*

Remy would be arriving with Claude. He had no clue as to who Claude was, but if all went well, he'd be the only man with Remy. Louis placed a K-cup in the Keurig and slid a cup under the dispenser. He opened a pantry door and reached for a bottle of Kahlua. He poured it liberally in the coffee and walked to the suite entrance door, leaving it ajar. Zach's cell phone rang.

"Hello?" he answered.

"Is this Zachary?" a female voice inquired.

"Yes, it is."

"This is Carol Charles, 'Fox Eight News.'"

"Hi, Carol," he said.

"Are you ready to give me an interview?"

"I'm not sure what you're talking about."

"Hey," she said, "you said you'd give me an interview after Louis was captured. I know he's in custody. You're not gonna welsh on me, are you?"

"No, Carol. I'm just tied up now. Can you call me back later?"

"You've still got my card, right?"

"I do. Listen, someone's at my door. Please call me later." He disconnected. *Interview, my ass*, he thought.

He sat on the couch in front of the flat-screen and pressed the power button on the remote, then selected "Fox Eight News." *Carol Charles*, he thought. Was she only a reporter or a newscaster as well? She had sounded like an attractive, young woman. Perhaps he would call her later. They could have dinner and he could fry "Louis's" ass real good.

He sat back, sipping the coffee, anxious to meet Remy, his new benefactor. He lit a cigarette and walked to the kitchenette for a bowl to use as an ashtray. As he resumed his position on the couch, he couldn't help but envision himself walking into a brothel, wearing Zach's fine clothes, with Zach's credit card in his wallet. He'd finally get to experience some of the exotic women he couldn't nearly afford up until now. He fanaticized what he would do with the hooker.

Remy walked in with a large African-American man in tow. Louis stood up and smiled at them.

"My boy!" Remy yelled and walked to Louis, pulling him into a long hug.

"Remy," Louis said. He looked over Remy's shoulder at the black man and said, "Hey, Claude, how have you been?"

"Congratulations, Zach," Claude said, "you not only proved them all wrong, you handed them Louis on a silver platter."

Remy eased up on the hug and kissed Louis on the cheek.

"You're smoking?" Remy asked.

Louis was caught off guard. He inhaled on the cigarette, giving himself time to think. "Well, my throat is sore anyway. Why not?"

Remy shook his head and laughed. "Fareeba's getting us a table at the R Club. Go join her, and we'll catch up in a few minutes. We've gotta make a call."

"Okay, Remy," Louis said, stubbing out his cigarette and walking to the entrance of the suite. He stepped into the hall and looked over at the R Club. It was crowded, and he had no idea how he was going to find Fareeba. He walked to the hostess and said, "Hi. Do you know where they sat Fareeba?"

"I don't know Fareeba, Zach, but we gave you a booth in the far left-hand corner."

"Thanks, honey," Louis said as he twisted his way through the crowd of people drinking and waiting to be seated.

As Louis approached the corner booth, a vision stood up and smiled at him. *Good Lord*, he thought. "Fareeba, you look stunning."

He walked to her and she put her palms on his pectorals, tilted her head and pursed her lips, waiting to be kissed. Tempting as it was, Louis said, "I've got a sore throat, Fareeba. I don't want to give you anything."

"Nice clothes, Zach," she said and kissed him on the lips. "I love the feel of silk on a man."

She grabbed his hand and led him into the horseshoe booth, pulling him in to sit at her right side. She looked and smelled incredible. He had a full erection running down his pant leg, and he turned to take her in. His eyes travelled down from her face to her cleavage. He sat back on the cushioned bench and tried not to get caught staring at her long, slender legs.

She waved at a waitress and the young woman came to the table. "Let us have four double bloody Marys to start with, honey." The girl walked off.

"I'm so proud of you, Zach, catching your brother when the police thought he left the city. You must feel so relieved."

"I spotted him on Canal and followed him to a cheap hotel near Treme. I gave him some time and then walked in on him."

"I heard he overdosed?"

"Yeah. I guess he uses heroin. He must have shot up as soon as he walked into his room. I don't even know if he's alive."

"Andre said he is. I like that man, Zach. I didn't initially think I would, but he seems to be very loyal to you. He is one tall drink of water."

Thanks for the heads up, Fareeba. Keep talking.

"I'm really happy you're safe, Zach," she said, leaning to kiss him on the cheek.

"Thanks, Fareeba."

"I've been with Remy a year now, and I haven't seen him this excited about anything before."

"Here he comes," Louis announced.

Fareeba put her hand on Louis's leg and ran it up toward his crotch. She encountered his erection and squeezed it. "I'm happy to see you, too, sugar," she said.

Remy slid into the booth and sat to Fareeba's left. Claude sat to Louis's right.

"I talked with Lionel," Remy said to Louis. "They found a sneaker print on Miss Julie's porch that exactly matches a sneaker taken from Louis's closet at the Empress Hotel. They got enough for the DA to charge him with murder." Remy reached across Fareeba to put a hand on Louis's shoulder. "You vindicated yourself, Zach."

The waitress brought bloody Marys, and they toasted Zach's fine work.

Zach had no idea whether it was day or night. Whenever he dozed off and woke, he had no idea how long he slept. He was very hungry and his stomach growled often. He figured he must be in a detention center, because he knew that all the jails in Louisiana were overflowing. Crime was high in New Orleans, and he assumed that most detainees were sent off to prison whenever accommodations were available.

In Jetson, he had read an article about Louisiana being the world's prison capital—more inmates per capita than any other state or country in the world. It had evolved into big business, often run by local sheriffs, and an inmate was worth twenty-five dollars a day in state money. They were a commodity to be bought or sold. He was now part of that system, one much harsher than the one he had just left.

Having no memory of what went on in Louis's hotel room, coupled with the bump on the back of his head, Zach surmised that Louis had overpowered him when he entered the room. Perhaps Louis knew he was being followed, and stood behind the door as it was opened. Louis must have knocked him out and dyed his hair blond. He was certain that Louis now had black hair, and had assumed his identity. Louis had fucked him again. It happened just as Louis said it would on the balcony of Muriel's—next time a murder occurred, Zach would not be a minor and would be awaiting his execution. He cursed himself for not paying more attention to Louis.

Sitting on the side of the bed, cold, hungry, and angry, Zach realized he'd only been out of Jetson two weeks. He made one promise to himself—he wouldn't be going down quietly this time—and he wouldn't be going down without a fight.

*

Fareeba insisted on staying with Zach and ensuring that he was okay. His sore throat was getting worse by the time they finished eating breakfast, and she thought his forehead felt awfully warm. Perhaps it was all due to the events leading to Louis's capture, but she felt she should stay with him. If need be, she'd call an ear, nose, and throat doctor.

Remy had no problem with Fareeba playing Florence Nightingale for the day, as he and Claude had things to do. He'd check with her later. The men left Fareeba and Louis sitting in the booth.

Fareeba's hand revisited the last place she had touched Louis. He was still rock hard. She stroked his erection. He placed his hand on her bare leg and felt her reaction.

"I'm concerned about the pressure all that testosterone is causin' on your system, Zach. I think you're about to blow like the Ninth Ward levees."

"Well, Fareeba, we wouldn't want the floodgates opening prematurely."

"We should have been better prepared. Isn't that the motto of the Army Corps of Engineers?"

"I'd like to see the surge occur when we're in the safety of my suite."

He slid his hand up the inside of her leg, under her dress, to her vagina. His fingers brushed against her wet panties. Fareeba emitted a soft groan and gripped his penis tighter. "Do you think you can make it to the suite before the breach?" she asked.

"Let's make a dash on three."

As soon as they closed the suite door, Fareeba was on her knees, pulling at his belt buckle and letting his slacks fall to the floor. She pulled his boxers down and looked at his erection.

She said, "What the—" and looked up at him. She hesitated for a moment then placed her mouth over his erection, moving her tongue under it, slowly taking it in, then pulling back and concentrating on the head. He exploded in her mouth as he groaned in pleasure. She touched herself between her legs and felt faint. She came immediately.

*

Louis sat on the balcony while Fareeba mixed two Cuba Libras. Lighting a cigarette, he let his mind replay that erotic scene. He had never been physically involved with a woman of such charms. The closest he'd ever gotten to sex with a beautiful girl was on the set of a movie in Hollywood. It ended with heavy petting followed by a hand job. He had been a virgin after graduating from prep school, and Harvard offered him very little—what wasn't already taken wasn't what he considered worth pursuing. His brief sexual encounters were spent with women he paid for, and he had usually left those furtive sessions feeling unsatisfied.

Fareeba brought out the drinks and placed one on the coffee table. She sat in a chair facing him. "You're smoking, Zach?"

"Once in a while. I feel I owe it to myself, after capturing Louis."

"Were you scared?"

"Naw," Louis said.

"What do you want now?" she asked.

"More of you," he said. "I want to fuck you."

"We can do that."

Later in the day, lying next to Fareeba, stroking her beautifully proportioned body, Louis knew he was where he should be for the first time in his life. All that Hollywood glitz held nothing compared to this city and the situation he found himself in. He vowed that he would do nothing to fuck this thing up.

Chapter 20

On Wednesday morning, Zach sat on the same wooden chair, wearing handcuffs and leg irons. Lionel sat at the other end of the table.

"Guard, state your name, the date and time," Lionel ordered.

The guard said, "Randall, Kenneth C., Wednesday, January sixteenth, two-thousand-thirteen, nine o'clock a.m."

Lionel said, "I am Sergeant Lionel Dugas, NOPD. I'm interrogating Louis Bujold."

"Louis," Lionel proceeded, "tell me where you were on Wednesday, January ninth, two-thousand-thirteen at four o'clock in the afternoon."

"Sergeant, I am not Louis Bujold. I'm Zachary Bujold," Zach stated firmly.

Lionel stared at Zach for a full ten seconds. He said, "You're telling me that you're not Louis Bujold?"

"Correct," Zach said. "Louis overpowered me when I entered his room at the Empress Hotel, knocking me out. When I became fully coherent, I was in this jail."

"So, the identification in the wallet you had in your possession is not correct?"

"Sergeant, I don't know which wallet was in my possession. When I became conscious, I was wearing this inmate uniform."

"Do you remember injecting heroin into your arm?"

"If heroin was injected into my arm, Louis must have done that."

"And you maintain that you're not Louis?"

"I'm not Louis. I'm Zachary Bujold. Let me take a polygraph. I'll prove it to you."

"I've read the psychiatric file of Zachary Bujold, Louis. Psychotic, schizophrenic, and delusional personality types can pass a polygraph when they are, in fact, lying."

"If I'm Louis, how would I know that Zachary hired Andre, or that Andre videotaped a conversation we had on the balcony of Muriel's?"

"You admit you had a conversation with Zachary. You may have had other conversations with Zachary. How would we know what Zachary shared with you?"

Zach thought for a few moments and said, "I assume Louis has taken over my identity. If he has, ask him when Miss Julie moved to New Orleans. I know she moved here just as Katrina hit."

"Louis, you could have gotten that information from Miss Julie before you strangled her."

"Lionel, stop callin' me fuckin' 'Louis.' I'm Zachary. I didn't kill Miss Julie. Louis did."

"Louis, stop callin' me fuckin' 'Lionel.' I'm 'Sergeant' to you, motherfucker. Randall, stop the recording."

Lionel leaned forward, his face as close as he could get to Zach's from across the table. He said. "Look, asswipe, I'm gonna get a confession out of you one way or another. I'll waterboard your sorry ass. You murdered a good woman, a friend of mine, and you're not gonna act crazy and think anyone will believe you."

"Well, Lionel, I'm sorry you think that way. I'm Zachary Bujold, whether you're too stupid to realize it or not. I'm done listening to your jive ass shit."

Lionel lunged across the table at Zach. He grabbed him by the throat and squeezed. Randall sprang forward and pried Lionel's fingers from Zach's neck. Zach fell back into the chair and coughed, attempting to clear his throat. He gasped for air, and then spat phlegm on the floor. Lionel stared at the man he knew was Louis Bujold and shook his head slowly. He stood and left the room.

*

Louis sat on the balcony of his Sonesta suite, smoking an American Spirit and sipping the Mimosa Fareeba had made him. It was 9:00 a.m. on Wednesday morning, and he watched as clouds formed in the eastern sky. It was cool out, but the jeans and Brooks Brothers sweater kept him warm. His feet were bare, but they weren't complaining.

It was impossible to spend time as he had and not be thinking about Fareeba. She was far and away the finest bit of tail he had ever had the pleasure to fuck. If Harvard women were nearly as appealing and accommodating, nobody would be graduating. He wondered how many lovers she was taking on behind Remy's back. He was simply happy to be one of them.

She had insisted that their pact, whatever that was, must remain in place, but that circumstances were just different these past few days. Remy was busy doing what Remy did, and it was her cycle to have sexual activity—*like some sort of locust*. He had consoled her, telling her it was only a tiny hiccup in the big picture. He could have backed it up with literary quotes, but thought that would be overkill.

Walking into the TV room, he sat on the couch. He felt comfortable being around Fareeba, knowing she had spent little time with Zach. He'd been following Zach for weeks, and had never seen them together. He had never been close to a woman like her before—one that was so welcoming. Most of his prior sexually-related conversations with women were with prostitutes. He watched as she walked out of the bedroom wearing a sundress. She sat on an armchair and swung it so she could face him.

As he took a long pull on the Mimosa, Fareeba said, "Zach, would you fuck me in the ass?"

He choked, and half the Mimosa went down his airway and half spurted out his nose. He groaned and ran to the bathroom, grabbed a towel and shoved it over his face. He coughed, blew his nose, and dried his eyes. He stared at his face in the mirror. *Did she actually say that?* After catching his breath, he walked back into the TV room and sat on the couch.

"Jesus, Fareeba, be more careful when you say something like that."

"Does that interest you, Zach?"

"Of course it does. I've never had the pleasure of that activity before. It's every man's secret fantasy."

"Have you had many women?"

"Not really, Fareeba. I've always been a little shy when it came down to it."

"But you're so handsome. Don't you think so?"

"I don't know how women perceive me. There are always good-looking men around."

"In New Orleans? Local people? You could have fooled me."

Careful, Louis, you're blowing it! "I don't know, Fareeba. I don't want to think about anything except your latest offer."

Fareeba got down on her hands and knees and faced the seat cushion of the armchair. Her dress was up around her waist, and her legs were parted. She said, "Oh, my, Zach, I seem to have lost an earring. Would you consider helping a girl in my position?"

Louis stepped out of his jeans and dropped his drawers, got on his hands and knees and crawled behind Fareeba. He said, "It's unlikely, but I might find it in here."

Fareeba buried her face in the leather seat cushion and moaned. After a minute, she said, "Aw, look harder, sugar."

*

Zach ate something unidentifiable—both texture and taste offered no clue as to whether it had parents or grew from the ground. He had thought that the food in Jetson was bad, but would now fight huge inmates for a chance at Jetson food. He had to get something in his stomach, but wasn't certain he could keep this food down. Finally, he put the tray on the floor and opened a bottle of water. He took a long swig.

He was rethinking his approach to the situation. If there was a next time with Lionel, he'd apologize and calmly try to use logic to sway the sergeant. The problem was that by having had encounters with Louis, he couldn't deny that as Louis, he could know anything. They thought he was Louis, and he had no way of proving he wasn't.

He'd been in detention for three days now. He knew he had the right to make a phone call, and he knew he had the right to a public defender. If he called Remy, he might get that same clueless attorney Remy sent him before. What he really wanted was a discussion with Remy. He could describe things from his childhood that involved Remy that Louis could never know. His real fear was that Louis, crazy bastard that he was, could flawlessly pull off being Zach. If that happened, Remy wouldn't consider speaking to Louis, who was now him. He was getting a headache just thinking about it.

He tried to sleep, but tossed and turned for hours. Finally, he heard a rap on the cell bars and looked up to see a different guard. He knew the drill, and walked to the bars and turned. Once the hardware was fastened, he shuffled quickly alongside the guard to the same room he had been in before. He was guided to the same wooden chair and sat, his eyes fixed on the door at the other end of the room.

Zach watched as Dr. Fadon entered the room and smiled at him. He sat down and placed a leather binder on the table. He opened it and slipped a pencil from its holder.

"Good afternoon, Louis. I'm Doctor Fadon. I'm a clinical and forensic psychiatrist working for the prison system of New Orleans. I'd like to keep this conversation informal, and I'll just make notes when I see fit. Do you feel comfortable with that arrangement?"

"Yes, I do, Doctor."

"You are Louis Bujold?"

"No, I am not, Doctor. I'm Zachary Bujold."

"The police think that Zachary Bujold found you unconscious from a drug overdose at the Empress Hotel, and that Zachary called the police."

"The police are wrong. When I entered Louis's room, he hit me on the head and knocked me out. He then switched wallets with me and dyed my hair blond. He dyed his blond hair black, and called the police. He must have injected me with heroin."

"That's a very complex set of actions that would have had to take place, by a man that you apparently surprised, during which time you were unconscious. How can you be so certain that this set of actions actually occurred?"

"Because I'm Zachary Bujold and I'm in here. How else could it have happened?"

"Perhaps the heroin and the ensuing drug overdose left you confused about your own identity. Have you considered that you just might be Louis Bujold, and that you're deluding yourself into believing you're Zachary because of guilt over things that you've done?"

"I don't believe that, Doctor. I know who I am."

"But you must admit that being Zachary at this point in time would be a lot safer for you now than being Louis at this point in time."

"You know what I must admit, Doctor Fadon?"

"What?" the doctor asked.

"That you were wrong seven years ago, when you diagnosed me as borderline psychotic. You told me there was no twin brother. Do you admit to making that mistake seven years ago?"

"I see you're becoming aggressive, Louis. That's a defense mechanism used when a person cannot deal with a situation appropriately."

"Wouldn't you become aggressive if you were falsely convicted of a crime based on the egomaniacal diagnosis of a doctor who was hired by a penal system because they could get him on the cheap? Where the fuck do they get guys like you? Shrinks are us?"

185

"Louis, based on your aggressive behavior, I'm going to terminate this session." Dr. Fadon stood and walked out the door.

Zach turned and looked at the guard. He said, "I think that went rather well. What do you think?"

*

Fareeba walked out of Zach's suite and took the elevator to the lobby. She walked out onto Bourbon Street and entered Fat Catz Bar. It was a quieter bar than most on Bourbon, and at 5:00 p.m. there were fewer freaks around. She walked to the bar and sat on a barstool. She ordered a double Johnny Walker Red over crushed ice.

Withdrawing a cigarette from a pack in her handbag, she slipped it between her lips and a lighter suddenly appeared in front of her face. She turned to look at the face of a smiling man. She said, "Get that fucking thing out of my face." Turning back to the bar, she groped in her handbag for a lighter, hoping she had one. She'd hate to have to call that guy back. Finding a book of matches, she lit the cigarette and inhaled deeply.

Her drink arrived and she took a long slug. The guilt was getting to her. She knew that she was weak when it came to sex—no matter what she swore she'd refrain from doing, she kept breaking promises to herself. What was the good of realizing you're a sexual addict if you don't want to give up the sex?

The fact was, she loved Remy but found the sex boring. Remy was boring. He wasn't imaginative when it came to dressing and when it came to sex. *How many men would object to fucking a woman that looked like her up the ass?*

If she was being honest with herself, she would admit that what she loved about Remy was the security. She'd been with Remy one year, and he still treated her like a princess. Before Remy, she had a long succession of lovers, none of whom wanted to let her go, but all of whom didn't know how to treat a lady—as if she could consider herself a lady.

This latest situation had her completely stymied. She couldn't just sweep this one under the rug. This one made her feel guilty like never before. She knew Zach was really Louis. She knew it when she pulled Louis's pants and boxers down to give him a blowjob after eating breakfast at the R Club. Zach was circumcised and Louis was not. Besides, Louis was totally inexperienced in terms of satisfying a woman. She thought he might be a virgin. He certainly knew nothing about foreplay. *What a waste of good looks.*

She had never encountered an uncircumcised penis before, and was mesmerized by its look and feel and by the change in dynamics when her tongue dealt with the foreskin. She wasn't proud of her toying with Louis after she knew for certain whom he was. She had wanted to gain some insight into the man, but she also wanted to experience his God-given penis in her anus and vagina. It felt like it had a French tickler attached.

What perplexed her was that Louis didn't seem much like a murderer. He was actually sort of sweet and naïve. She had, in fact, waited until he was drinking the Mimosa before asking him to fuck her in the ass. She knew he was Louis by then, and she wanted to see his reaction. It had the same effect that it had on Zach, and Louis didn't even react as confrontationally as Zach had. She realized she could be dealing with some psychotic personality here—Louis could split into some sort of maniac, but she just didn't get that vibe from him.

She figured that there must be some doctor's record of when Zach was circumcised. Remy would probably know about that. Her problem was that she would not only be admitting to Remy that she had sex with Zach, but would have to throw Louis into the mix. Furthermore, she gave Louis a blowjob the day she met him, knowing that he wasn't Zach. She knew Remy could never handle that. The police would have to be made aware of this difference in physical architecture. She could picture herself on the witness stand, in front of a courtroom full of spectators and the press, inspecting the penises of Zach and Louis, pointing, and declaring the winner by lack of foreskin to be Zachary Bujold. She'd be on Nancy Grace, for fuck sake.

She wondered whether Andre could be trusted with personal information of this sort. He had handed her his business card in Zach's suite, and he hadn't met Remy prior to the day they viewed the videotape together. She began rummaging in her handbag.

Chapter 21

Zach figured it to be Thursday morning. He was paying more attention to details such as the type of food he was being served, if that was determinable, and the few sounds around him. Criminals were coming and going, but he had not heard anyone mention today's day or date.

He knew his rights were being violated—being held indefinitely without being formally charged with anything—but the same thing happened in juvy. Prisoner's rights were violated all the time, and though inmates would grumble about it, and a few guards might act sympathetic, nothing was ever done to stop the transgressions. No one "out there" gave a rat's ass.

After the debacle with Dr. Fadon, he knew he had to make his next move count. He had to better control his temper. Mental health issues were part of this case, and he had heard the term "involuntary commitment" used on detainees at Jetson. Once a person was involuntarily committed, he dropped off the radar. He was certain Fadon considered "Louis" to be borderline mass-murderer by now.

He heard footsteps and inhaled deeply, held his breath, and exhaled. He tried to calm himself—reminding himself of platitudes he'd heard before—discretion was the better part of valor, don't go out with a fight, but rather, walk out with a whimper. He took note at how quickly he had changed his tune from fight to fright.

Lionel walked in front of the bars of his cell. The sergeant stood facing Zach with a wide stance, his arms akimbo with fists resting against hips. He had a very determined look on his face.

"Whoever you are," he said, "if you breathe a word of this to anyone, I will end you. Do you clearly understand me?"

Zach nodded his head and said, "Yes, Sergeant."

"Stand up."

Zach stood up from the bed and froze.

"Face me," Lionel said.

Zach walked a foot away from the bed and turned to face Lionel.

"Unzip your jumpsuit."

Zach pulled the zipper down to his crotch.

"Step out of the jumpsuit."

Zach followed his orders.

"Now drop trough."

Zach grabbed his boxer briefs and shoved them to his ankles.

"Get dressed. Not a word, remember?"

*

Remy pressed the doorbell of Zach's suite. He had talked to Philippe, and knew Zach was home. Philippe said Zach had just finished lunch at the R Club.

The suite door opened and Louis, wearing a cotton bathrobe, smiled at Remy. He stepped back to let Remy in. "Hi, Remy," he said.

"Hey, kiddo. I was just in the neighborhood and thought I'd stop in."

Remy walked into the suite and sat in an armchair in the living room.

"What would you like to drink, Remy?" Louis asked.

"It's early, but I didn't sleep well last night. I'll have a scotch neat."

Louis said, "Well, Uncle, I'll just have a scotch neat with you."

He walked to the pantry and pulled out a bottle of Johnny Walker Black. He poured three fingers of scotch into two crystal drinking glasses and walked to Remy, handing him one. Walking to the couch, he sat down.

"Why can't you sleep, Remy?" Louis asked, sipping the scotch.

Remy took a pull of scotch and enjoyed the burn of it going down his throat.

"You know, Zach, there's a lot to running an enterprise like mine—knowing who to trust, who to fear, and who is full of shit."

"I can only imagine," Louis said. He lit a cigarette and offered it to Remy.

"No, thanks, I'm tryin' to quit."

Remy reached into the inside pocket of his cowboy jacket and took out a folded piece of paper. He laid it on the coffee table and smoothed it out. He pulled a pen out of his pocket, stood, and walked to Louis, handing him the paper and pen.

"Read that carefully, Zach. It's a power of attorney form. There's not much to it. It simply says that in the advent of my death, you're able to act on my behalf."

Louis raised his eyes from the document and looked at Remy. "You're not planning on leaving us, are you, Remy?"

Remy laughed. "Not if I have anything to say about it. I just feel it's important to tie up loose ends."

Remy watched as the document was signed and dated. Louis stood and walked to Remy, handing him the pen and paper. Remy gazed at the signature. He nodded and folded the document, putting the pen and paper back into the pocket of his jacket. He reached under the left side of the jacket and withdrew a Beretta. He pointed the weapon at Louis.

"Louis, you almost pulled it off."

Louis sank back in the couch. He remained quiet and then said, "What gave me away, Remy? The accent?"

Remy shook his head. "The accent was good—you're a little flat, though. It's Zach's signature that you fucked-up on."

Louis raised his eyebrows. "I'm surprised. I practiced using the signature on Zach's driver's license."

"Have you ever signed for a driver's license?"

"Nope. I never needed a car at Harvard."

"You get a narrow strip to sign. Zach couldn't fit the capital 'Z' as he normally signs his name, with the lower loop. He began his signature with the letter 'Z' and no loop."

Louis nodded his head. He took a long slug of scotch.

"Just one more thing, Louis. Stand up and open the robe."

Louis looked at Remy curiously, but decided to acquiesce, considering a pistol was pointed at his gut. He stood and let the bathrobe slip to the floor.

"Now drop your drawers," Remy ordered.

Louis did so.

Remy nodded and pulled an iPhone from his pocket. "Come on in, Lionel, and meet the real Louis Bujold."

*

Zach walked into sunlight for the first time in four days. The sun was low and directly in his eyes. He put his right hand over his eyes, shielding them from the sun, and squinted as he walked to the limo. Remy exited with arms outstretched. "Come to Uncle Remy, Blondie," he yelled.

Zach walked into Remy's arms and hugged him tightly. "Remy. You don't know how much I missed you."

"That brother of yours is a trip. He almost had us fooled. Come on, get in."

Zach slid in the back seat and made room for Remy. He yelled, "Claude, good to see you."

"I'm glad you're out of that shithole, Zach," Claude said.

"Cigarette?" Remy asked.

"Sure," Zach replied. *Anything to alter the taste in my mouth.*

"Southern Comfort?"

"Gladly."

Zach inhaled smoke and sank deep into the seat. He felt more relieved after getting out of detention for four days than he had felt getting out of Jetson after seven years. Solitary confinement had deeply taxed him, not to mention the prospect of a looming lethal injection.

Claude began driving.

Remy handed Zach his wallet and cell phone. "I took these from Louis before they hauled him away."

"How'd you spring me, Remy?"

"It was Andre's brainchild. He had a guy hack into your medical records, and found one that stated you were

193

circumcised. The hacker searched Louis Snow's medical records in California, and couldn't find any mention of a circumcision. It was just a hunch, but it paid off. The main kicker was his attempt at forging your signature."

"Where is he now?" Zach asked.

"Right where you just came from."

"Do you think there's enough to convict him for Julie's murder?"

"Yeah, but I'm afraid he's crazier than a shithouse rat."

"I do, too," Zach said.

"Know what he said when he knew the jig was up?"

"What?"

"Impersonation of an individual is a misdemeanor. No jail time. That's what he expects to be charged with."

"What do they have on Louis regarding Julie's murder?"

"A sneaker print."

"That doesn't sound like much evidence," Zach said.

"You know, now that Lionel knows he's got the real Louis, I have a feeling Louis might just be confessing shortly."

"Remy, I'm sick of thinking about Louis. I did it in Jetson, and I'm still doing it."

"Wanna try our luck at Hold'em tonight?" Remy asked.

"I'd love to. I just want to be around people tonight. Right now, I need a good hair salon."

*

Fareeba knocked on the office door with "Andre Picard – Private Investigator" embossed on the glass.

Andre opened the door and smiled at Fareeba. He said, "Come in."

She walked into a small waiting room that contained several chairs and a secretary's desk, and she followed Andre into an office. As she entered, Andre closed the door and walked behind his desk, saying, "Have a seat."

She was wearing a simple house dress with heels on her feet. She sat and crossed her legs. Her long hair spilled over her shoulders and down her back.

"It all worked beautifully, Fareeba. We now have an indisputable method for distinguishing the Bujold brothers."

She laughed. "Instead of 'Hold 'em up' it'll be 'Drop 'em.'"

"It took courage for you to come to me with that bit of news. You know, Zach had no other way out. Lionel was dead set on a confession, and the shrink said Louis, or the man he thought was Louis, was an angry man capable of murder."

"How discretely was this handled, Andre?"

"Remy was told what the sergeant believes—I stumbled on the information using a hacker."

"And Remy won't be told anything different?"

"Not by me, Fareeba. No one else knows."

"I told you I'd make it worth your while."

Andre shook his head. "Zach's paid me too much already. You don't owe me anything."

Fareeba stood, walked around the desk, and knelt before Andre. She looked up at him and said, "I always pay my own debts."

She unbuckled his belt and unzipped his pants, tugging until they were lying around his ankles. She looked up at him while she pulled down his boxers and then lowered her eyes. Andre was fully aroused.

"My God, Andre, I don't know where to begin thanking you."

Chapter 22

Zach awoke to the familiar smells of jasmine and lilacs. He rolled onto his back and stared at the ceiling, happy to be back in his life again. He stretched his arms and legs, dozed for a short while and finally swung his legs out of bed.

He showered and shaved, then dressed in new jeans, sneakers, and a sweatshirt with the face of James Carville, the Ragin' Cajun, hand-painted on it. He walked through the suite, eradicating any evidence of Louis having stayed there— garments thrown on chairs or hung haphazardly in the closet and bowls used as ashtrays. Zach stuffed the clothing in a laundry bag and laid it near the entrance door. They would be dry-cleaned and hanging in his closet by tomorrow. He would be throwing the underwear and socks away.

He had a hunger for eggs St. Charles, and had seen a street vendor who advertised them. He'd have some breakfast and walk it off on the way to see Robbie. Walking out to the balcony, he felt a cool breeze blowing. He stood there for several minutes, enjoying the fresh air and the smell of the city. He grabbed his leather coat as he left the suite.

He walked leisurely to Loyola Avenue and found the street vendor by the smell of eggs, fillets, and Cajun spices a block away. He stood, leaning against a brick building, and ate the delicious concoction of eggs, trout fillets, hollandaise sauce, and spices. All he needed now was a beer.

The Eight Block Kitchen and Bar was a block away, and Zach walked there. He ordered a bottle of Abita Amber and sat on a barstool, savoring the malty lager. He thought of Julie and hated the fact that she was robbed of a life that they both treasured. To think that Louis murdered her just to implicate him in her death was infuriating. Louis didn't even know or appreciate the life he was snuffing out. He prayed that Louis had blond hair when he strangled Julie—the thought of her believing that Zach had his hands around her throat maddened him.

He walked along St. Charles Avenue, taking in the mix of new and old—a nineteenth century mansion with a late model Mercedes Benz in the driveway, a newly built streetcar resembling the transportation of a bygone era. The street was lined with oak trees, their branches struggling to touch the wood of an oak on the other side of the street.

As he approached the Bujold mansion, he saw long ladders with scaffolding and two figures standing on the long boards. Walking closer, he recognized Robbie and Leland. They were attaching a sign to the front of the house.

Zach opened the wrought-iron gate and stood looking at the sign. It was about twenty-feet long and two-feet high, centered over the front doors of the dwelling. The wood had been beveled along its edges, and "Miss Julie's Home for Cats" had been artfully carved into the wood in script. Zach felt tears welling in his eyes, and he brushed them away.

"Zach!" Robbie hollered from the scaffolding as he held one side of the sign. "Like it?"

"I love it!" Zach yelled, waving at Robbie's father, Leland. He walked closer.

"Hey, Leland, how are you?"

"Good, Zach."

"How'd you do the handwriting?"

"It's called a router," Leland said with a grin.

"That's beautiful work," Zach replied.

"Leland wants to stain the wood dark and paint the words white. What do you think, Zach?"

"Just keep doin' what you're doin'. It really looks great. Let's have a drink and toast Miss Julie's new home."

*

Hamilton sat on the floor in front of Zach in the sitting room. The cat was staring at him, and Zach wondered if he was asking him where Julie was.

"In a better place, if you can believe that," he said. He bent forward to grab Hamilton, but the cat would have nothing to do with it. It turned and moved further away.

He'd have to talk to Lionel about getting her pictures and plants over from her house. He wondered if the school might want to donate some class pictures of Julie's seven years teaching in the system. They could fill a wall with the pictures and accolades that he knew must be locked behind glass in the school's lobby.

Robbie walked into the room with two bottles of Bud and handed one to Zach. Leland walked in holding a cup of coffee. They sat and stretched their legs. Robbie and his father looked very similar despite the eighteen-year difference in age and Leland's gray hair. They were both handsome men.

"I want to apologize for not showing up earlier. I was locked up for four days until they figured out I was Zach and Zach was Louis. They have him behind bars now."

"Thank the Lord," Leland said.

"Did Louis murder Miss Julie?" Robbie asked.

"I'm sure he did, Robbie. He's one sick puppy."

"You okay, now?" Leland asked.

"I am. How have you been, Leland?" Zach asked.

"Like a boat without a rudder," Leland replied. "I'm away from my two mistresses—my wife and carpentry. Thank God I have a good son who stuck by me." He sipped coffee.

"Well, you've got one mistress back, Leland. Did Robbie mention the addition I'd like to have you build?"

Leland looked at his son. "No, he hasn't mentioned that."

Robbie said, "Dad, I didn't want to say anything until Zach was here. Maybe you two can come up with an idea."

"What are you looking to build?" Leland asked.

"I'd like some arrangement of decking around a structure that houses plants and cats, with access from the house and the garden, and plenty of glass. It'll need electrical lighting at night, maybe special lighting for the plant life. We'll need an architect and a building permit, and you to do the carpentry."

"Would you want it to blend in? Make it look like it was built at the turn of the century?" Leland was trying to contain his enthusiasm.

"Sure, Leland, whatever you think."

Leland leaned back in the armchair, lost in thoughts of the possibilities.

Robbie winked at Zach.

"Leland, I'd like you to be the curator of this house. It pays one-hundred grand a year as a starting salary. I'm giving your worthless son the same salary for the first year. Next year this time, I'll adjust his salary up or down as you recommend."

"That's not fair, Zach," Robbie interjected.

"Why not?" his father asked.

"'Cause once I start bringing in the two-legged tail, you're gonna get jealous and mean-minded, Father."

Zach smiled and said, "Leland, if you don't mind my asking, how much does your wife make in Houston?"

"She makes forty grand a year, Zach. That's why she's there and not here."

"We're gonna need a woman's touch in the redecoration of this house. The furniture is old, and needs replacing. It's all Victorian, which I myself detest, but Margaret could make up her own mind about that. You guys have to live with the furniture. So, her job would be decorator slash tour guide. You can offer her the position for sixty grand a year. Shit, you could offer her more, but you don't want her makin' more than you, right?"

"Absolutely not," Leland replied, smiling to himself. He lit a cigarette and shook his head. He said, "I don't know what to say, Zach. You've saved our lives."

"No, I haven't, Leland. You have. I've known you all my life to be a good Christian man and a hard worker. I wouldn't be offering this to any other family in New Orleans, I promise you."

Leland stood and walked toward Zach, careful not to step on Hamilton. He motioned with his hands. "Up," he said.

Zach stood up and they hugged. "You're a good man, Leland."

"Thanks, Zach. You've saved my family."

Zach grabbed his beer and took a long drink. "I've brought my checkbook. I'll write you both checks for fifty grand now, another fifty in six months. There should be a way to avoid paying Uncle Sam anything, 'cause this will be a non-profit, charitable organization. I'll get an accountant to handle the books. I'm going to Wells Fargo on Monday, and I'll set up a corporate account for you to draw money for expenses. I'll get you both debit cards. The account will have three-hundred grand in it to start with."

Leland said, "Let's go out back and get a feel for the sanctuary."

"Sanctuary," Zach echoed. "Why didn't you come up with that, Robbie?" he asked as he pushed his friend back into the armchair. "I told you he was worthless, Leland."

*

Robbie and Zach walked along Frenchmen Street. It was 11:30 p.m. and the music joints were hopping. Robbie suggested they have a few drinks in The Spotted Cat. It was crowded, but they found two stools at the bar. The place was seedier than some, but the jazz was said to be good and the drinks were cheap. Zach figured Robbie was attracted more by some of the obviously under-aged females on the dance floor.

Zach had never known Robbie to date white women, as so many of his brothers did. He preferred African-American and other women of color. Zach knew he would love the look of Asami. Robbie was attracted to Asian women, and before Zach could ask him what he wanted to drink, Robbie was on the floor dancing with a young Vietnamese woman.

"What'll it be?" a bartender asked Zach.

"Better make it three Long Island iced teas."

The drinks arrived as Robbie and the girl stopped dancing and walked over. "Zach, this is Hong."

Zach smiled at the pretty young woman and said, "That's funny. Women say Robbie's very hong."

She laughed and raised her eyebrows at Robbie.

"Do you like iced tea, Hong?" Zach asked.

"Of course," she replied.

"Well," Zach said, handing her one, "have a drink with us."

They danced and drank until 2:00 a.m. when the bar closed. The bartender didn't accept credit cards, and Zach paid in cash.

Hong had hung in there, and it looked like she would be spending the night with Robbie. Zach pulled him aside.

"Are you taking her home to the mansion?"

"Yeah. Leland won't mind."

"Good. I was gonna offer you my place, and I'd stay at Harrah's."

"Thanks, but I might as well get the old man used to it. I am twenty-two."

"You'll always be his little chocolate éclair, Mr. Cool."

"Someday you're gonna hafta tell me how you got so much of the money you're throwin' around, boy."

"Don't worry about the money, Robbie. It's clean, and courtesy of Uncle Remy."

"I guess you know how much it means to me, what you did today?"

"I think it's gonna do a lot for your father—maybe he'll get his sense of humor back. And you're not tied to it. You can do whatever you want."

"Thanks, brother. I'm takin' Hong to Julie's home in a cab. Want a ride?"

"No. I'll see you soon," Zach said, and began walking to the Sonesta.

Chapter 23

On Saturday morning, after breakfast at the R Club, Zach walked to the Rampart Street Police Department. It was a cold and cloudy day, and he was thankful to have the inner lining of his leather coat in place. It was 10:30 a.m., and he had no idea if Lionel would be there or would speak with him.

There was no officer on watch and Zach walked down the hallway to the Homicide bullpen. Only a few officers were at their desks. He looked into Lionel's office and saw that he was on the phone. He took a seat where the sergeant could see him. When he ended the call, Lionel waved him in.

"Zach," Lionel said, "sit down."

"Thanks for seeing me, Sergeant."

"I hope there're no hard feelings about the way I treated you in detention. You know I was sure I was dealing with Louis."

"Let's just say, Sergeant, that this whole identical twin business has complicated all our lives. My parents and Julie were murdered by my fucked-up brother, and I just got tired of defending myself for things that he did."

"I've misjudged you, Zach. I'm sorry for that."

"You were just doing your job. The shrinks are a different story."

Lionel raised his eyebrows and nodded. "While the DA will charge Louis with Julie's murder, there's no evidence linking him to the shooting death of your parents. I'm not happy about it, but it could be a moot issue. If he pleads innocent to the murder of Julie, I think he'll die by lethal injection. If he pleads guilty by reason of insanity, it'll be up to the judge and jury. That could be a cluster-fuck."

"That videotape may prove that Julie's murder was premeditated, even though her name wasn't mentioned," Zach offered.

"We'll see what the DA thinks."

"Another thing—I walked to Muriel's that night from Julie's house. Louis was following me. That's probably how he knew where she lived."

"That'll be up to the jury. This is gonna be one long, drawn out murder case."

"Yeah," Zach said, "he's an adult, which means cameras in the courtroom. This will be like the Menendez brothers' murder trial."

"And Louis is a Harvard Law graduate. I'm assuming he'll get the best of lawyers. Someone will take it pro bono."

"All you have is a shoe print?"

"Yep," Lionel said. "Your fingerprints were found, but not his."

"What about DNA?"

"Just hers and yours. Anything else, Zach? I got work."

"Did you know his DNA could be very close to mine? I've got his fingerprints on a drinking glass."

"I'll make sure the DA knows. We've got the DNA samples, and plenty of time to get experts in as needed."

"Is it possible to have Julie's pictures and plants sent over to the mansion?"

"I hear tell you're donating it in Miss Julie's memory."

"Her cats need a home."

"It's a nice gesture. I can have an officer do that. Will somebody be at the mansion?"

"Robbie Terrebonne and his father, Leland, will be there."

"All right, Zach. Get outta here," Lionel said, grabbing the phone from its cradle and punching in numbers.

*

Zach took a cab to Julie's new home, as he liked to think of it. He asked the driver to stop on the way, and bought a cold case of Abita Amber. He paid the cabbie and walked to the steps of the house. Not wanting to disturb anyone inside, he sat down on a step, opened a bottle of beer using his penknife, and sipped the brew. It was almost noon and the sun was getting stronger. He slipped his leather coat off and laid it on the steps.

Hong walked out of the front door and sat down next to him.

"Hong. Good morning."

"Good morning, Zach. May I have a beer?"

"Of course," he said, opening a beer and handing it to her.

"Have fun with Robbie?"

"I like him."

"He's a great guy, Hong. How long have you been in New Orleans?"

"I'm second generation," she replied, sipping beer.

"And you wear the ao dai? Isn't that very traditional?"

"My family is still very traditional. Most of our neighborhood in Avondale is, at least in our attire. When it comes down to it, it's just white pants and a top, right?"

"And you look very pretty in it."

"Thank you. You know what pisses my father off most?"

"That you're so pretty?"

She laughed. "No. That he captains a fishing boat made of fiberglass."

"He'd prefer wood?"

"Yes, but it's not economically feasible. Everything has gotten so expensive since the oil spill. You know, we still make our own nets."

"Does your father speak English?"

"Of course. Why?"

"I'm going to need boating lessons."

"I'll let him know," she said.

"Are you going to college?"

She nodded. "Tulane."

"What are you? Eighteen?"

"Actually, seventeen. I skipped two grades."

"Good for you. Is Robbie up yet?"

"He and Leland went out early. They're interviewing architects."

"On Saturday?"

"They made appointments," she responded.

"Can you stay here 'til they get back? Someone may be bringing stuff over, and I need someone here."

"Sure. I'll put a note on the front door that I'm in the garden. I'm studying there. I love that garden."

"I used to study there, too. Let me put this beer in the fridge, and check on Hamilton. I'm trying to wear that cat down."

"I'm afraid of him," Hong said. "He looks like a Malayan tiger cub. I keep looking around for his mama." Her laugh was pixyish.

Zach found Hamilton in the garden, lying in grass under a tree. Walking slowly toward him, Zach got down on his hands and knees and approached the cat. Hamilton raised his head, showing little concern. He allowed Zach to place a hand on his side and stroke him. Zach took his time, knowing Hamilton was mindful of his every move. He sat cross-legged next to the cat, waiting for him to make the next move. He hadn't heard any purring yet.

*

He walked along St. Charles Avenue to Remy's house. Fareeba came to the door. Opening it, she looked at him and said, "Zach?"

"Yes, Fareeba, I'm Zach."

"Care to prove it?" she replied, giving him a sexy look.

"Not out here on the porch, sweetheart," he said.

"Let's have a drink," she said, opening the screen door for him to enter. "Have you eaten?"

"Not since breakfast."

Walking to the kitchen, she said, "How about some Margaritas?"

"Sure. Do you have a mix?"

"In the pantry. You know where the liquor is. The blender is over there," she said, pointing to her right.

She began setting up lunch while he made them a small pitcher of Margaritas. They convened in the dining room. She brought in a Chilean sea bass, garnered with a Creole seafood sauce. "It's hot," she said.

"Where's Remy?" he asked, spooning a portion of sea bass onto his plate.

"He gets very secretive sometimes, Zach," she said, leaning back in her chair and drinking some Margarita. "I don't ask any questions."

"Is someone giving him trouble? Blackmailing him?"

"I think so. It must go way back, to the days when your father was alive."

"Has he mentioned the name Edna to you?"

"No. Why?" she asked.

"I'd help him if he asks," he said, ignoring her question and putting a forkful of sea bass into his mouth.

"Stay away from it, Zach. You haven't had time to breathe yet, with all of Louis's shit. Don't get involved with Remy's shit."

"Did you meet Louis when I was in detention?"

"Yes, I did. Remy and I had breakfast with him and Claude at the R Club." Fareeba played with her portion of seafood.

"What did you think of him?"

"I thought he was you. He sounded the same, and he acted like you."

"So, I guess we have a physical difference," Zach said, watching her eyes.

"Really, Zach? You could have fooled me," she said innocently.

"You know what, Fareeba? I think it would be very hard to fool you, ever."

"You're so sweet, Zach. You're so unlike the Bujold men."

"You've only had experience with Remy, right?"

"Yes, but everyone knows about the Bujold men—angry, vindictive, and cruel."

"Is Remy cruel to you?"

"In ways he knows hurts me most—usually by ignoring me."

"You gonna leave him?"

"I may. I may go home and start over," she said, looking at him.

"You know, as much as I might want to, I couldn't take you in, even if he kicked you out."

"Why not, Zach?"

"It would be a slap in the face to Remy. He's stood by me through everything. I couldn't do that to him."

"Well, a girl can dream, can't she?" Fareeba said, reaching over and kissing Zach on the cheek.

*

He began walking toward the French Quarter. Coat slung over shoulder, he walked along Loyola Avenue. On a whim, he entered the main entrance of the New Orleans Public Library and followed signs for the genealogy department.

He sat in front of a computer and thought of Julie, possibly sitting in the same chair, searching databases for facts regarding Bujold family members. He clicked on the genealogy button, and began reviewing methods of attaining information by family name. He found a link to "Digging up Roots in the Mud Files" and clicked on it.

"Mud files" were described as old Louisiana civil court records going back thirty-five years or more, when they were, in fact, stored on shelves and getting muddied. This information was currently available on the website NUTRIAS, with records dating back to the early nineteenth century.

As he drilled down into the archives, he began to realize how complex the civil court recording system was. Property suits and death certificates were available, but he soon found that some specific information was not easily attained, or perhaps unavailable. Information retrieved often required more information to bore deeper. He leaned back in the chair and tried not to become frustrated.

After several hours of digging, he came up with enough information to access the microfiche archives. He found a newspaper article describing the trial of Henri and Remy Bujold, and their ensuing conviction for gunrunning. This all happened when Henri and Remy were around twenty-one years old. They received a sentence of one year at Angola.

Zach thought back through his childhood, remembering events that his father and Remy would laugh about at the dinner table, much to Annette's chagrin. Zach was certain he had never heard them talk about a stint at Angola.

His interest was sparked, and he began searching for newspaper articles that described his grandfather's murder. He ended up spending more than six hours in the library.

Chapter 24

Zach woke from a dream in the middle of the night, his face sweaty and his hands balled into fists. It took him several minutes before he realized that his teeth were clenched tight, and he relaxed his jaw. His heart was racing, and he swung his legs out of bed and breathed in deeply and exhaled slowly, trying to control his heart rate. Walking to the bathroom, he urinated and grabbed a robe. He walked to the kitchenette, put on coffee, and walked to the balcony.

The dream brought him back to Jetson when he was fourteen. After six months of probing, the shrinks had made little progress in convincing him of the fact that he had indeed experienced a break from reality and had murdered his parents. Hypnosis had not accomplished a breakthrough. The team decided that some mind-altering drug such as LSD could be their answer, and Zach was set up in an observation room.

When he was twelve, Robbie and he had smoked grass and hashish, and both enjoyed the high. The hash was stronger than the weed and brought them into laughing fits that left them completely drained. At thirteen, Zach had experienced mescaline with a group of his friends, and he had discovered that he loved being outdoors while hallucinating. Everything he looked at seemed to be sharper and seen through a filter—the color of the sky, the rustling of leaves, the strobing of lights, and the intensity of the touch. He lay on the grass in Franklin Square, next to a pretty schoolmate of his, and gently kissed her lips, waiting several moments before kissing them again. She had smoked grass, and soon tired of what she considered to be teasing. She went off to find a real man, and Zach had been content to lie on his back and watch the spectacular cloud formations.

The acid trip in Jetson was anything but spiritual or pleasing, and, as the drug took hold, Zach had felt claustrophobic about being inside and confined. He wasn't tied down—he was allowed to sit on a metal chair, but couldn't leave the observation room. A portable john had been set up if he had to relieve himself, and a guard sat at the other end of the table and watched him continually.

The plan was that a psychologist would come into the room from time to time, ask him how he was feeling, ask a few questions, and leave him to write down his thoughts. As he began to hallucinate, he enjoyed watching the red and yellow paint squish out from the linoleum floor around the heels of an entering or exiting doctor. He attempted to strike up a conversation with the guard, but the man must have been ordered to remain silent.

He began drawing pictures, beginning with broad strokes of the pencil on the yellow legal pad, and then felt himself getting drawn into the detail. His teeth were tightly clenched, and he began tracing the images he saw on the pad—mouths with teeth in the shape of the letter 'V.' Mouths with razor sharp

214

teeth and tightly stretched lips, some with tongues hanging out, began populating the picture. He'd rip a sheet off the pad and crumble it, pitching it into the port-o-john, and he'd try again. The mouths reappeared and he traced them again.

Eventually, the psychologists morphed into high priests, and Zach was Michelangelo. A priest would enter the room and survey his progress, and, like any renowned artist, he grew angry at their lack of patience. He'd been working on the painting for five months and all he was getting was vacant stares instead of appreciation. The mouths he was tracing were angels, and he was exasperated that they couldn't see it. He finally asked them for a pencil sharpener and they brought him one.

Zach was only six hours in, halfway through the trip, when paranoia set in. He wasn't Michelangelo, and the priests were beginning to realize that. He was an imposter that would soon face the guillotine. He bolted for the door as a doctor was leaving, and the guard grabbed him. He stabbed the guard in the hand with a sharpened pencil. As the doctor turned to grab him, he shoved the pencil in the doctor's stomach and raced down the hallway. The corridor doors were secured, and he fell to the floor and began screaming, staring in horror at the blood on his hands.

Sitting on the balcony, remembering the events, he found the caffeine to be working against him. He switched to a stiff screwdriver, and walked inside as a light mist began making him shiver. He finished the drink quickly and crawled under the comforter, taking the fetal position that almost always brought him to sleep.

*

He met Asami for dinner at Bambu. He was dressed in brown slacks and loafers, with a maroon sweater and his suede jacket. Asami wore a designer outfit that accentuated her small breasts and shapely legs. They kissed in front of the restaurant and walked in. The hostess led them to a table.

"Now I know who you look like," Zach said.

"Michelle Yeoh?" she asked, nodding, hoping she was right.

"Lucy Liu, only younger."

"Well," she said, "thanks, but neither actress is Japanese."

A waitress stopped at their table. He asked Asami to order drinks.

She ordered two Van Gogh martinis and Zach began laughing.

"What?" she asked.

He shook his head and said, "Just a bad dream."

"What's new?" she asked.

"Obama gets inaugurated today. What do you think of him?"

"I think the country would have been better off with Romney," she replied.

"Why?"

"You probably won't like what I have to say, but the poor in America need a good kick in the ass. In Japan, people who work in factories don't expect to get rich, but they work nonetheless. They work to eat and clothe themselves and their families, and live in pods if they must. For a small country, Japan has the third largest economy in the world. Poor people in Japan consider themselves part of the middle class. They work, and live worse lives than unemployed Americans on welfare."

Their drinks arrived and Asami held her glass up to Zach's, saying, "To the poor."

"Jesus, Asami. That almost sounds like 'Let them eat cake.'"

"And what do you want for America?" she asked.

"I suppose I'm more of a laissez-faire sort of person in terms of our interaction with other nations. Maybe that's a simplistic approach in a world economy, but I think America should get its own house in order before it meddles in other nation's affairs—especially countries that hate us. And when did we start rebuilding a country's plumbing after we won the war? Where are the spoils of war? You know where? They're in the pockets of companies like Halliburton, instead of the pockets of the working class."

"Your two-party system, along with unlimited campaign funding and lobbyists will strangle your middle class," she said, and sipped vodka. "You're ripe for a government overthrow."

"By the American middle class?"

She shook her head. "Start learning Chinese. Maybe they'll let you be an interpreter."

"Wasn't it the Japanese that tried something like that before?"

She licked the tip of her index finger and drew an imaginary '1' in the air. "Are you going to college?"

"I received my GED in prison, Asami, and I've read a lot of books. I realize that doesn't say much in terms of my higher education." He watched for her reaction.

"I saw a brief rundown on your story on Nancy Grace. Identical twins?"

Zach nodded. "My twin is in custody now. It wasn't on 'Fox Eight News'?"

Asami shook her head. "Aren't you pissed?"

"I'm just tired of it all." He finished the martini. "Let's have another. Would you order food for both of us, please?"

She looked for the waitress and waved at her. She said, "I'd be pissed."

"Sooner or later, you realize that being pissed interferes with the rest of your life. I don't want to end up a bitter person."

She ordered two more martinis, the rack of lamb, and the Thai filet of fish.

"I was beginning to think I wasn't going to see you again," she said.

Zach laughed and said, "I was released exactly three weeks ago, and have attended the funeral of a woman I loved and spent four days in a prison I hated. I've been shot-up with heroin, and every day I seem to learn more about the crime family that spawned me."

She put a hand to his cheek and leaned over to kiss him.

He said, "Please tell me you've got some deep, dark secrets within your family."

She smiled and shook her head, saying, "What can I say. It's good to be honorable and rich."

They shared their entrées, and Zach found that he loved the taste of lamb. To his knowledge, Annette had never served it. The filet of fish was marinated and deep fried, and together they ate it all.

"Did your father visit you?"

She nodded and said, "He's still here. He's the 'honorable and rich' I mentioned. I'm his only child, and he loves to spoil me. I was born when he was forty. He's now seventy-two, and will not retire."

"You said his company makes lenses?"

"Optical equipment of every sort. He's just not ready to retire."

"And he never remarried after your mother died?"

She shook her head. "He still has sex, though."

"God bless you Japanese. How in the world can your population be declining?"

"People can't afford children, and there'd be no place to put them." She laughed.

"Are you going to let me spend the night with you?"

"My father will be sleeping."

"He stays with you?"

"I insist that he does. I won't have him forever, you know."

"We'll go to my place, if it's okay with you and your father."

"I think we should leave him here at the hotel. Don't you?"

*

Asami was very impressed by the accommodations at the Sonesta. Zach brought her in to Irvin Mayfield's jazz club and she seemed to like jazz. They sat and ordered Rum Runners, listened to the band, and talked with their heads touching. When they had enough, he took her to his suite.

"Ooh, Zach, I didn't know suites like this existed in New Orleans." She walked out onto the balcony and looked down. He walked behind her and moved into her body. She moved her body back against his.

"We can take a Jacuzzi here, or go swimming if you want."

"A Jacuzzi here sounds better to me. Do you have any rum?"

"I've got Bacardi Dragon Berry, and One-Fifty-One."

"One-Fifty-One?"

"That's the proof. It'll kick your ass."

"I need rum and a good ass-kicking."

219

"Tell you what. You fill the tub and I'll mix the drinks."

As he mixed the One-Fifty-One with the Dragon Berry rum, he thought of how pragmatic Asami was. He had expected her to be more liberal-minded, but wasn't displeased about her political views. Maybe America was getting soft.

He brought the drinks into the master bathroom and watched her bending over the tub, naked, fiddling with the water temperature. *That butt does not look thirty-two years old.* She slipped in and groaned. "It's hot, baby."

He placed a drink near her and put his on the counter. He undressed, grabbed his drink, and slipped in. "You're right," he uttered.

She tasted the drink and raised her eyebrows. "I like this."

He took a swig. "Wanna get schnockered?" he asked.

"I'm unfamiliar with the term."

"It's Jewish for balls to the wall drunk."

"You don't want to see me drunk, Zach."

"I don't mind, but, if you do, please consider the poor people down below. Don't puke over the balcony."

"You think I'm a rich bitch, don't you?"

"Asami, I think you're a remarkable young woman sitting naked across from me."

"I see by your erection that you're anticipating having your way with me," she stated coyly.

"I'll have it any way you want, and then some. I'm ready for you tonight."

"Have you ever play-raped someone?"

"No. How does that work?"

"You throw me down on the bed and act as though you're raping me."

"Do you fight me?" he asked.

"I struggle to get away, but don't really hurt you. I won't scratch your eyes out."

"And how aggressive would you want me to be?"

"I want you to try and rape me."

"What if you want me to stop?" he asked.

"I say 'Gonorrhea.'"

"That's a perfect word to make me stop."

"What do you think?"

Zach downed the rum drink and said, "Let the games begin."

Chapter 25

Lionel assumed his position across the table from Louis in the conference room of the detention center. He leaned back in the wooden chair, studying Louis.

"Are you comfortable in your cell, Louis?"

"The digs are great, Sergeant." Louis made a motion with his right hand as though he were smoking a cigarette, pausing to blow out smoke. "When can I make my first phone call?"

"Phone lines are down for now."

"Duly noted, Sergeant. This will all be duly noted."

"You're a very arrogant man. Where did you learn that? In prep school or at Harvard Law?"

"My experience at Harvard taught me that if you infringe on my rights, you'll only be hurting your case. Infringe away."

"You deny strangling Miss Julie Sykes?"

"I never had the pleasure of meeting her, Sergeant."

"Where were you on Wednesday, January ninth, at four o'clock in the afternoon?"

"That's something we'd have to discuss with my attorney present, Sergeant. I wish he were here so that I could answer your questions."

"Are you familiar with the story Zachary told the psychologists regarding the murder of your parents?

"Only whatever was printed in the newspapers."

"Do you admit being there with Zachary on New Year's Eve, seven years ago?"

"Of course I was there. That's how I know he killed our parents."

"And he said you did it."

"Didn't the psychologists label him a pathological liar and a psychopath, among other sordid things?"

"That was because no one thought you actually existed."

"I don't believe that a man can be diagnosed as a psychotic personality type by five different clinical psychologists and be a sane man. Do you?"

"Why didn't you make your existence known at that time? Why didn't you take the stand against your brother?"

"It didn't look to me like the prosecution team needed any help."

"Why are you back here in New Orleans now, Louis?"

"Sergeant, I talked to you about the murder of our parents because that case is closed. I'm imprisoned here for a reason I'm not even aware of. I will not speak with you about anything that's happened since I arrived in New Orleans without my attorney present."

"You'll be meeting with a public defender later today."

"Don't bother with that. I won't be using a PD. I know exactly who I'll be retaining to handle my defense."

"Well, I'm late for lunch. I hope you enjoy yours. I hear it's only been lyin' in the sun for three days." Lionel stood up.

"Let me know when the phones are back up, Sergeant, so we can talk about things more current." Louis took another suck on his imaginary cigarette.

"Play crazy all you want, Louis. It'll just extend your time here." Lionel left the room and Louis was escorted back to his cell.

*

When he returned to his office on Rampart Street, Lionel locked himself in his office and lit a Perique cigarette. He decided to bypass calling the sheriff and dialed D.A. Michael Riddle.

"D.A. Riddle."

"Michael, this is Lionel."

"What's up?"

"Louis Bujold is not talking. He wants to call an attorney."

"He's not acting scared?"

"He's an arrogant fuck."

"If you can't pressure him to confess, let him call an attorney. We can't screw this up. You'll have to play by the book."

"He's already starting to act crazy. Have you set up a meet with him and Doctor Fadon yet?"

"Yes, and that should happen today or tomorrow."

"So, he can make a phone call?" Lionel asked.

"Let him get his lawyer. The indictment is in, and he'll be arraigned tomorrow or the next day."

"He's lookin' to skate on this, Michael. He wants to end up in Alexandria for a coupla years."

"His brother will testify against him, correct?"

"Oh, yeah. Zachary will testify to Louis's murdering Miss Julie and his parents."

225

"Don't count on too much from all of that. He wasn't a witness, and he's got mental issues of his own."

"No, Michael, he doesn't. Not to my way of thinking. It was all Louis, all the while."

"Make sure Louis can contact an attorney today." The D.A. hung up.

∗

Remy called Zach and invited him to join them at Harrah's that evening. He had tickets to The White Stripes at 8:00 p.m. They could meet up for dinner prior to the show.

Zach sat at the bar at Pier Four-Twenty-Four and ordered an absinthe on ice. He was wearing his newly laundered slacks, shirt, and sports jacket. He had considered asking Asami to join them, but thought their relationship too tenuous to jumble in with the Bujold family dynamic. Besides, Asami might bring her father, and Zach could picture her proper Japanese father getting back slapped by Remy after asking, "Is it true they're slanted?"

Zach had to admit he was tiring of the cowboy outfits Remy wore. He watched as Remy sported one walking in with Fareeba on his arm. She was dressed elegantly in what looked like a Versace understated silk number, reaching her knees with a slit up the side. He could only imagine what she was thinking.

"Hey, kiddo," Remy said, placing a hand on Zach's shoulder and patting it. Fareeba smiled weakly at him.

"Remy, Fareeba, how are y'all?" Zach asked.

"Our table should be ready. Let's eat."

Fareeba and Zach selected Creole delicacies, while Remy chose Cajun. Zach watched Fareeba as she contributed little to the conversation. Her eyes told him that things were not right.

She had hardly touched her food when she asked to be excused. Remy nodded and she left. He looked at Zach and shook his head.

"Havin' problems, Remy?"

"She's embarrassed me. I think I'm gonna hafta let her go. It's time."

"What did she do?"

"It's not what she did, Zach, it's who. I've been told she did Andre."

"Aw, shit. I'm sorry, Remy. How did you find out?"

"Lionel told me Andre's secretary saw Fareeba givin' Andre head. She was walkin' back from lunch and passed his office window. She saw it all through the blinds. Andre's secretary is Lionel's cousin."

"Do you love Fareeba, Remy?"

"I did at one time, but if I can't trust her, I'd rather be doin' hookers."

"Does she know you know?"

"No, but I'm bein' mean to her. She knows something's up."

"That's too bad, Remy."

"What's the good of havin' a sexy woman around if all you picture is her with other men. I can't even get hard with her anymore."

"Listen, Remy, I don't want to continue with this evening. I've got a woman at the casino I may be able to see, and, if not, I'll gamble. You should spend time with Fareeba and be honest with her. Tell her your feelings. She's smart, and she'll understand. She's worth tryin' to keep, don't you think?"

"I don't blame you, Zach. I wouldn't want to be in the middle of this, either. Take off, and I'll handle it."

Zach walked out of the restaurant and to the casino. He found a quiet bar and ordered vodka. He called Asami, but her phone went to voicemail, and he disconnected. *She's probably with her father, and not taking calls from the male prostitute.*

He enjoyed being in the casino. It was an exciting feeling for him—the odds of winning at luck or love. It was an added benefit to not be concerned about losing. He thought it gave him an edge against the odds. He didn't have to play desperately, and he could bluff whenever he wanted.

He sat at a hundred-dollar-minimum blackjack table. It was just him and the dealer. He played for a while and lost a grand. He began walking through the casino and spotted Fareeba at a slot machine. She looked out of place in her fine clothing, flanked by two women wearing ratty jeans.

"Fareeba," he said from behind her. She turned and looked into his eyes. Her eyeliner was smeared and her cheekbone was red. She stood and turned, moving into his embrace. He grabbed her handbag and walked her to the ladies' room.

"Freshen up. I'll be right here."

Obviously, their talk had not gone well. He suspected Remy had punched her in the face.

She exited the bathroom and he led her outside. The fresh air felt good. A breeze was blowing in from the river, and he slid his sports jacket over her shoulders. He sat her on a bench, and she began weeping.

"I can't go home tonight, Zach. He'll kill me."

"No, he won't, Fareeba."

She raised her head and stared into his eyes. She didn't say a word.

"Let me get you a room here. I won't leave you, but I can't take you to the Sonesta. Remy's likely to stop by."

She stood and put her head against his chest, her arms circling around his waist. He kissed her on the neck and walked her back into the casino.

*

He removed two little bottles of scotch from the hospitality bar and poured them into drinking glasses filled with ice. He brought them to the coffee table and sat with Fareeba on the couch.

"Has he hit you before?"

She shook her head. It appeared as though she would have a shiner tomorrow.

"He's brought back his hand a few times, but never hit me. He slapped me once. He called me a cunt and a whore tonight."

"You said he'd kill you. Were you serious about that?"

She looked at him and raised her eyebrows as if to say something, then just shook her head and declined to talk about it. "He told me to move out of the house."

"I think its best you stay here for now. Is this room okay with you?"

"Of course, Zach," she said, looking down at her bare feet.

"Do you want anything?"

"I just want you to hold me. Can you do that for a while?"

Zach stood and took her hand, leading her to the bedroom. They disrobed and slid under the sheet and heavy comforter. It was cold in the room, and their bodies brought warmth and comfort to each other.

Chapter 26

Zach woke to a sweet smell and realized his face was buried in between Fareeba's breasts. He moved his head away to find her looking at him with one green eye and one closed eye. Her eyelid was swollen shut and the entire socket was blackened. She puckered her lips and kissed the air.

"Mornin', sugar," she said with an exaggerated Creole twang. "Don't I look special?"

Zach didn't have to look down to know he had a raging erection. He must have kicked the comforter off his body sometime during the night, and his erotic thoughts were evident to Fareeba. She smiled at him as she reached for it, moving her fingers softy over the head. He put a hand to her breast and rolled the nipple between his thumb and index finger. She rolled onto her back and spread her legs. He positioned his body between her legs, and she bent her legs to accept him. Entering her, he slipped his hands under the cheeks of her ass and pulled her up to meet his thrusts. She arched her back and moaned, and he kept going, making sure she came first.

He rolled over onto his back and waited for his breathing to slow down. She ran a hand down his chest to his belly. He turned his body to hers and said, "You are the sexiest woman I've ever had the pleasure of knowing, black eye and all."

"The pleasure is all mine, sugar," she said as she rolled out of bed. She walked to the bathroom and he sat up and ran his fingers through his hair. He swung his legs out of bed, stood, and walked to the armchair that he had tossed his clothes on the night before. Slipping on his boxers, he grabbed the brochure describing Harrah's amenities and reviewed their breakfast offerings. Fareeba walked out of the bathroom in a bathrobe. She walked to him and kissed him.

"Let's order breakfast," Zach suggested.

"I'll have the eggs Benedict, white toast, and orange juice, or a Mimosa—your choice."

Zach ordered breakfast and two Mimosas.

He sat on one end of the couch and watched as she curled her legs under her at the other end. She ran her fingers through her hair.

"Do you feel like talking about it?" he asked.

"What?"

"The blowjob."

Fareeba shook her head and said, "It began innocently enough. We were all sitting at the table at the R Club. You were complaining about a sore throat, and I said I'd stay with you. I thought you were running a fever."

"You mean Louis, right?"

"Yeah, but I didn't know that, then. Well, Remy and Claude left and we began touching each other under the table. You got really excited, and we thought you might not make it to the suite. We ran for it, and, inside, I pulled your pants down and gave you a blowjob."

"Louis," he said, correcting her again.

"Right. I honestly thought it was you until I saw your penis. I mean Louis's penis. It was uncircumcised."

"So, what did you do?"

"What could I do? I acted like nothing was wrong and I blew him. But now I knew that he really existed, and that it was you who was in jail. I couldn't let him know that I knew. I was afraid he'd panic and leave New Orleans."

"You and Remy never really thought Louis existed, did you?"

"Honestly, we had our doubts, Zach."

"So that was it?" Zach asked.

"Well," she said, and paused, "I never had experienced an uncircumcised penis before. It was like a party favor. I'm not particularly proud of it, but I encouraged Louis to fuck me. It turns out that Louis is very inexperienced."

Zach shook his head and looked away. Fareeba cursed herself for being so honest. He turned back to look at her and began laughing.

"You're taking this well," she said, somewhat annoyed.

"It's pretty funny, from my perspective," he said.

"Why?"

"Because that wasn't the blowjob I was referring to."

"Oh, you meant Andre?"

"How many blowjobs did you give during my four day incarceration?"

"Just Louis and Andre," she said defensively.

Zach shook his head and grinned. "Is Andre circumcised?"

"Yes, but the surgeon must have had to use a meat cleaver on that dick."

"Big?" he asked.

Fareeba extended her hands in the air and separated them as a fisherman would as he described a very big catch.

"Jesus," he remarked. "Did you have any reason for blowing Andre? I mean, other than opportunity?"

"Don't you judge me, Zach. I couldn't very well tell Remy I had blown both his nephews, could I? 'Yeah, Remy, Zach's is clear-headed and Louis's has a French tickler attached to it.' So, I approached Andre. I told him you were in jail instead of Louis, and how I knew. That made Andre check on your medical records. I had to pay him for his services, and he got enough money from you. I'm the reason you're a free man, buster."

"The way I look at it, honey, Louis's dick is the reason I'm a free man."

"You're splitting hairs," she replied and went to open the door for room service.

After the waiter left, they held their Mimosas in the air.

"To foreskins," Zach toasted.

"I'll tell you one thing, Zach. I've never seen Remy look at anyone like he looked at me last night."

"How do you mean?"

"To say it was a cold stare wouldn't do it justice. It was more of a 'If it takes eating my firstborn to wring your neck, I'll do it,' kinda look."

"That's the Bujold slow burn," Zach replied. "Dark eyes."

*

At noon, Zach left Fareeba and took a cab to Julie's home. Robbie and Leland were sitting on the front porch, drinking

Abita Amber. Zach walked up and sat with them. Robbie went inside and came out with a beer for Zach.

"What are the proprietors of Julie's home up to today?" Zach asked.

"We had an architect over this morning and another will come by late this afternoon," Leland said.

"Any progress?"

Leland nodded. "It's too soon to show you, but it will be a good-sized room with a deck wrapping around it. I've got a lumberyard ordering all the deck railings, and the structure will look like it was built one hundred years ago. There'll be enough space to place tables and chairs around. The decking will be stained and weather-coated, and all the wood should be painted white."

"That sounds great," Zach said. "You'll be accommodating the cat lovers and the cats."

"That's the idea. People willing to spend time with cats will want contact with them. They could adopt them right here."

Zach handed two plastic cards to Leland. "That's your debit cards. They'll post against a corporate account I set up at Wells Fargo. And how about the missus, Leland?"

"She took you up on your offer, Zach." Leland couldn't hold back a grin.

"It's your offer, Leland. You're running this show."

"Your uncle came by," Robbie said. "He asked for you to go see him. Don't you have your cell phone with you?"

"No. I'll go see him, after I finish this beer."

"Remy didn't look himself," Robbie said.

"He's havin' trouble on the home front."

"Fareeba?" Robbie asked.

"You met her?"

"I've seen her with him. Outrageous lookin' woman."

"I'm sure it's just a lover's quarrel," Zach said dismissively.

Leland said, "Come around back, Zach. I want to show you the overall layout, and show you where we'll have to move some of the garden's bushes."

Zach inhaled deeply, not particularly wanting to see Remy right now.

*

He opened the door to Remy's mansion and stepped into the vestibule. The house was quiet. He shouted, "Remy!"

He heard his uncle yell, "Out back."

He walked in and through to the kitchen. Remy was sitting outside in the garden. Zach walked down the steps and joined him, sitting on a concrete bench.

"Remember Uncle Etienne?"

"Sure. My uncle with the mole on his face."

Remy grunted. "The mole everyone wanted to bite off. Remember when I told you about your father and me going legit nine years ago?"

"Yeah," Zach replied.

"How it cost us one-hundred million bucks?"

"I remember."

"That money bought silence. By taking the money, a family was taking an oath of silence in regard to what Henri and I had participated in. We, in turn, promised to never rat on them to the Feds. It was all because of RICO."

"Okay," Zach said.

"Uncle Etienne wouldn't take money. He wanted a judge killed. The judge wouldn't budge on a sentence regarding Etienne's business partner. So, I killed the judge to buy Etienne's silence."

Zach remained quiet, waiting for Remy to continue.

"I know your father and I never spoke of our business in front of you, but I always suspected you knew of things going on around you. I know there's an undercurrent of gossip regarding our family circulating in this city. Now you're an adult, and part of this family. There's no sense in sugar-coating things we did to attain what we have."

Zach said, "What does Uncle Etienne want now?"

"Fifty million not to mention my name to the Feds."

"What are you gonna do?"

"Kill him," Remy said.

"Why not pay him?"

Remy looked at Zach. "Do you think your father and I made our money by giving it away to anyone who had something on us? Do you think the family made their money that way?"

"But now you're out of it, Remy. You can afford to pay him off. Why risk everything for some principal devised by a fucked-up family of murderers?"

Remy stood up and stared down at Zach. He started walking around the sidewalk circling the birdbath. He said, "Don't criticize the family until you know more about the times. This city has been corrupt since the beginning of its founding."

"That doesn't exactly absolve the crime of murder, Remy."

Remy shook his head vehemently. "Look, Zach, it's not fair that Etienne does this. Don't you get it?" He began throwing his arms in the air, saying, "We're all family, and he's doing this to me? After I paid for his silence? It's not right, Zach. He's betraying me."

Zach felt a wave of nausea overcome him. He felt dizzy. He gripped the edge of the concrete bench and squeezed, watching his knuckles turn white.

"Stop, Remy. Please stop."

"Stop what?" Remy screamed.

"Calm down. Sit, and discuss this thing rationally."

"I don't need you to tell me what the fuck to do, Zach. What do you know about this kinda shit?"

"I know that if you go off half-cocked, you're liable to do something you can't take back."

"Oh," Remy said, groaning a laugh, "I won't want to take it back."

"You're risking everything for a man who's not worth it. Please, Remy, sit down."

Remy looked at Zach and sat. He stared ahead, taking on the slow burn, his eyes going dark.

Chapter 27

Louis sat on the commode in the holding cell of the detention center. He figured it was Thursday morning. He had spent Wednesday afternoon and evening with his head in the toilet. Early Thursday morning, any liquids left over were coming out his other orifice.

He was certain he had stomach poisoning. He had never experienced it before, but the ever-widening bands of excruciating pain that ended up surrounding his stomach in spasms could be nothing less. He had thought of Lionel's comment on road kill more than once over the past twenty-four hours, even going so far as to thinking Lionel intentionally poisoned his food.

His attorney, Jeffrey Lightner, was due in town this afternoon, and Dr. Fadon would be giving him a psych evaluation sometime this morning. Lightner had told him that he wouldn't be allowed to sit in on the evaluation, and for Louis to be completely honest as long as it didn't compromise his defense.

His rectum was on fire from the acidic fluids that he had excreted. His system was devoid of any external matter, and yet he wasn't hungry—he just felt empty. He was in fear of taking anything in. His last attempt at drinking water had put him back on the toilet seat.

Lying on his back, staring at the ceiling, he wondered what it was going to take to extricate him from this mess. He began questioning why he ever decided to return to New Orleans. Louis wasn't always certain he was being completely honest with himself.

A guard told him to approach the bars, and Louis walked there and turned his back to the guard. He was handcuffed and shackled. *What's the hurry?* he thought as the guard dragged him down the corridor to the conference room. He sat in the wooden chair, looking out the window at rain pouring down, and waited.

Dr. Fadon walked into the room and placed his leather binder on the table. He smiled at Louis and sat down.

"Good morning, Louis, I'm Doctor Fadon."

"Good morning, Doctor Fadon."

"I'm a clinical and forensic psychiatrist working for the prison system of New Orleans. I'd like to keep this conversation informal, and I'll just make notes when I see fit. Do you feel comfortable with that arrangement?"

"Yes, Doctor."

"Louis, I'd like you to answer my questions as honestly as possible. Will you do that?"

"I will, Doctor."

"Did you murder Julie Sykes?"

"No, sir, I didn't."

"Did you murder your parents seven years ago?"

"No, sir, I didn't."

"Do you know who might have killed your parents?"

"Yes. It was my twin brother, Zachary Bujold."

"Did you see him kill them?"

"No, but I had left him with them. When I left, they were alive."

"And where was Zachary before you left?"

"He was drinking scotch in the garden, talking to himself."

"Did he have gloves on his hands?"

"No," Louis said.

"Do you remember being mad when you were in the garden with Zachary?"

"Yes. I was mad that our parents had separated us. Identical twins shouldn't be separated."

"Do you remember pacing around, throwing your hands in the air, saying how it just wasn't fair?"

"I just remember being mad."

"Have you ever felt like you've had an out-of-body experience, Louis?"

"No."

"Have you ever felt as though you had a break from reality?"

"If I had a break from reality, how would I realize it?" *You moron.*

"I sense you're getting angry now, Louis."

You bet, you stupid motherfucker. "I'm not angry, Doctor."

"Are you feeling intimidated?"

"Certainly not, Doctor. Not by you."

"Now you're being dismissive. That's a symptom of hostility. Why are you being hostile now?"

"If you just spent the last day puking and shitting road kill, Doctor, you might be a little hostile now."

"But you're channeling your hostility toward me, Louis. I didn't serve you bad food."

"Can we move on from the road kill, Doctor?"

"We were discussing the anger you felt at your parents for separating you from your twin brother, Zachary."

"I was feeling anger at the situation, not necessarily at my parents."

"But your parents made the decision to separate you from Zachary. They also decided to keep Zachary and give you up. Wasn't that the real source of your anger?"

"No. Get this through your head, Doctor. I felt anger because I think identical twins should not be separated."

"So, you would have been okay with everything if your parents had given you both up? To be adopted together?"

"Absolutely."

"But they didn't, and yet you deny being angry at them."

"What the fuck is the difference, Doctor? I didn't kill my parents."

"So that means Zachary killed your parents, correct?"

"Yes."

"Even though he wasn't the one who was mad at them?"

"Maybe I made him think about it, and he got mad at them. I don't know. I simply know that they were alive when I left."

"They were alive when you remember leaving, Louis."

"What is that supposed to mean?"

"People can have time-outs from reality, Louis."

"Doctor, I took abnormal psych classes just like you. I know about psychotic episodes and schizophrenia. Based on where you're working, I might know more than you. I did not have a fucking psychotic break from reality."

"There goes that anger again."

*

Dr. Fadon sat in Lionel's office after his interview with Louis. The blinds were closed and they both smoked cigarettes.

"So, how'd it go?" Lionel asked.

Fadon shook his head. "He shows classic signs of denial in terms of his dealing with his expulsion from the family. He has a lightening quick temper. His emotions turn on a dime."

"Did you question him about Julie's murder?"

"As soon as he said he didn't kill her, I dropped that line of questioning. I didn't want to alienate him."

"But he got mad at you anyway?" Lionel asked.

"As soon as I mentioned breaking from reality, he turned on me."

"Didn't that happen with Zachary seven years ago?"

"It did, but not immediately, rather, later on."

"Isn't that because you guys kept telling him he had no twin brother?"

"That would have added to Zachary's hostility. After watching the videotape of the two brothers interacting, I've come to the conclusion that we made a mistake with Zachary. I now believe Zachary was telling us the truth about what happened."

"Now that you have Louis."

"Don't criticize what you know nothing about, Sergeant."

"Well, all I can say is you and your buddies better get your stories straight. Louis's attorney is one of the best criminal defense attorneys in the country, and he'll be discussing your fuck-up seven years ago with the jury."

"Sergeant, we're not dealing in an exact science. When you get five psychologists to agree on something, it's usually a correct diagnosis. Don't forget your own duplicity in this."

"Duplicity?" Lionel repeated. "What form of deception are you talking about, Doctor?"

"Someone from your bureau was asked if Zachary Bujold had a twin brother."

"And it was determined that Louis Bujold must have died as an infant. No medical or adoption records existed for the child."

"Well, he didn't die. He was given up for adoption, or just given away. Finding that out wasn't our job."

"So the Homicide Bureau is to blame?"

Fadon raised his eyebrows, saying, "We were told that Zachary Bujold did not have a twin brother. What sort of a diagnosis were you expecting from us?"

*

Zach knocked on the door of Fareeba's suite. She opened the door wearing a bathrobe. He walked in with a large plastic bag. "I hope they fit, Fareeba."

"I just can't wear what I have here again. It grosses me out to wear clothing twice without washing them."

"You'll have your dirty clothes back this evening, all dry-cleaned. Monique was at the boutique, and knows your measurements. She picked out clothes you should like. I think you'll be okay. Try them on."

He walked to the hospitality fridge and looked inside. "We're out of scotch."

"I've got someone coming to replenish the bar. Have vodka."

Zach pulled two small vodka bottles out and poured vodka into a glass. He walked to the couch and sat down. "Remy is a crazed man, Fareeba."

"Tell me about it," she said, turning to him and attempting to wink her swollen eyelid.

"It makes me wonder about my father. He could have been as crazy as Remy."

"From what I hear, they were inseparable."

"That's what made my mother give up Louis."

"I wouldn't be so sure of that, Zach," Fareeba said, sitting next to him and taking a sip of his drink.

He lit one of her cigarettes and handed it to her. "Do you mind if I have one?" he asked.

"Not at all."

He lit a cigarette and inhaled, then said, "What do you know that I don't?"

She took a drag and said, "Remy was pretty drunk one night about six months ago, and probably told me too much. He was talking about how he and Henri had both graduated from high school, pretty much with the same grades, neither of them wanting to go to college, and Henri acting aloof, above it all. Remy said Henri had an air of aristocracy about him which was just plain bullshit."

"What does that have to do with my mother giving up Louis?"

"Be patient. None of you Bujold's ever learned patience. Anyway, Henri was dressing up, acting classy when he met Annette. Now, Annette was a thoroughbred from the aristocracy of New Orleans. She really had class. She fell in love with Henri, and despite her family's horror about her choice, they got married."

She took a slug of his drink, and he walked to the fridge to find more vodka. He returned and sat down, running his hand up her bare leg.

"Stop it!" she said, "I want to finish my story before I ravage you. So, now they're married, and, of course, she gets to know her step-brother Remy all too well. She witnesses his uncouth behavior, his swagger, and his leers at her. According to Remy, she was getting wet just being around him. He was drunk when he told me all this."

"So what happened?"

"What happened was happening every day. Annette was coming over to his house while Henri was out and about, having his affairs, and they were fucking like rabbits. Remy said he finally had to lay down the law."

"Okay," Zach said, lighting a cigarette without realizing he had one burning in the ashtray.

"Nine months after he laid down the law, you were born."

Zach sat staring at her. He felt blood in his face and heard a pounding in his ears. He said, "Remy is my father?"

"He was drunk, Zach. I had never seen him really drunk before, and couldn't tell if he was making it up or not."

"Did he say anything else?"

"Yes. He said one more thing. He told her, 'Annette, if you have twins, take the second born and drop him out the hospital window.'"

Chapter 28

Jeffrey Lightner sat across the table from Louis in the conference room at the detention center. He was a robust man with cherub cheeks and big, brown eyes. His eyebrows were slanted down to the bridge of his nose, giving him a hawkish appearance. He looked out of place and uncomfortable in the tight Brooks Brothers suit he was wearing. He held a handkerchief in his right hand, wiping at sweat when it began dripping.

"They'll arraign you shortly, at the courthouse. The guards will take you to an area adjacent to the courtroom. When your case number is called, they'll escort you in. You'll join me at the defense table. The judge will read the complaint. He'll ask you if you understand the charges. You will say, 'Yes, your Honor.' No more. He'll ask you how you plead. You will say, 'Not guilty, your Honor.' That will be all you say. Got it?"

Louis nodded and said, "Got it."

"The judge may set bail, or may consider you a flight risk. That depends on what the prosecutor says about the events of seven years ago."

"The murder case of my parents is a moot issue, Jeffrey. My brother was convicted of that crime. How can they now consider that I fled the scene?"

"Seven years ago, Louis, no one thought you existed. Now they're faced with the fact that you do exist. That's not simply a nuance in this case. It will pervade this case, as well as the decisions made prior to and during your trial."

"Are you going to ask for a change of venue?"

"Of course I will, but I don't think we'll get it."

"Because?"

"The tabloids are going insane over this case. First of all, it brings to light a possible injustice perpetrated against a local, popular boy named Zachary Bujold seven years ago. He was born of a family which has given millions in charity to New Orleans post-Katrina. Secondly, the woman you're accused of murdering was a saint in New Orleans. 'Miss Julie' came down as Katrina hit, and stayed to help. She got the local children through middle school and high school, with grants and scholarships to colleges across the country. This has become a very big case, and the locals want to try you, Louis."

"I didn't kill this 'Miss Julie' character. I didn't even know her. The only thing I'm guilty of is impersonating another individual, who, by the way, was not a police officer. It's a misdemeanor offense."

"Has anyone discussed the video and audio clip they have on you?"

"No."

"I saw it early this morning at the office of Sergeant Lionel Dugas. The DA was there. You were videotaped on a balcony of a restaurant named Muriel's, talking with your brother. You basically threatened him by saying if anyone else turns up dead, he's an adult now, and he'll be executed. It's an undeniable threat, seen as such by a team of clinical psychologists, and the murder you mention happening would have to implicate Zachary. You were following Zachary, who was dating Julie Sykes. In fact, you followed Zachary from Julie's house to Muriel's."

"I didn't know who lived in that house."

"That would be for the jury to decide."

"What was my motive in murdering Julie Sykes?"

"To put Zachary behind bars as Louis, and to masquerade around as Zachary. We can't deny that, because you've already done that. You did it for money and opportunity."

"I switched our identities because I was being followed."

"You did it, Louis. The jury will not care why. You promised a 'shit-storm' and you delivered on that promise."

Louis put his elbows on the table and face in his hands. He remained silent while his attorney left the room.

*

Remy sat in the Lincoln across the street from the Bujold family safe house in Lafayette County. It was near dusk and the weather was cold. Rain was pouring down. He watched as Etienne walked down the side stairway and onto the sidewalk. Remy flashed the Lincoln's headlights and hit the horn twice in rapid succession. Etienne walked across the street and slid into the passenger's seat.

"This fuckin' rain won't let up," Etienne complained, pushing the hood of the rain slicker back off his head to rest on his shoulders. He rubbed his open hands together.

"Well, Etienne," Remy said, "it'll be hot where you're goin'. Put your seatbelt on."

"I'm just gonna slip away to Miami, Remy."

Remy steered the Lincoln down to the end of the street and made a right. He was headed to the wetlands.

"So the Feds are looking for you now, Etienne?"

"Yeah. You got the money?"

"I've got two million in a briefcase in the trunk, and I'll wire transfer the rest when you give me the account number. I see you got the mole removed."

"And the tattoos. Some dental work as well. With your money, my boys and I will live well."

"See, that's the rub, isn't it, Etienne?"

"What?"

"It's my money."

"But you know this whole thing started in your neck of the woods, on your watch. None of this shit would be goin' down now if you were bein' careful. Now I'm gonna be charged with killing a judge."

"Well, Etienne, this 'thing' has been corrected in my neck of the woods. You're the only 'thing' I have to deal with now."

"In a minute, you're gonna drive us both into water, Remy," Etienne remarked, pointing ahead.

"No, Etienne, just you." Remy pointed the pistol in his left hand at Etienne's chest. He pulled the trigger twice. The noise was deafening in the air-tight rental. He parked the car and rolled down the front windows. Stepping out, he closed the door and threw the car in drive. The Lincoln hit the water and slowly began to submerge.

Remy walked back onto the dirt road. He turned and said, "Slip away to hell, Etienne."

Claude pulled up in a Mustang. Remy opened the passenger's door and slid in. He said, "Let's get some crawfish before we hit the highway."

*

Zach asked Fareeba to join him in the casino, gamble a bit, and eat at Bambu. She kissed him and declined, saying she was embarrassed to be seen with a black eye, and hated wearing sunglasses indoors.

He played blackjack for an hour and won three hundred dollars. He walked away feeling annoyed to have spent the hour grinding out some money when he could be lying next to Fareeba. She seemed to have no limit in terms of physical contact—not just sex, but also hugging, touching, and holding. She had a hold on him, and he knew it.

He walked into Bambu and took a seat at the bar. Ordering sake, he opened the menu and looked for the specialties. He requested a shrimp appetizer, and looked out over the room full of diners. There was a large contingency of Japanese patrons, which made him think of Asami. Now that he had Fareeba to himself, he couldn't imagine being with another woman.

He felt a hand on his shoulder, and heard Remy say, "Hey, kiddo."

Zach turned to look at Remy and smiled. "Hey, Uncle. Sit with me."

Remy sat on the barstool to Zach's left and faced him. He was wearing a dark blue Armani suit with a white shirt and red tie. He had wing-tipped shoes on his feet.

"Well, you're dressed differently, aren't you? How'd the interview go?"

Remy laughed. He ordered a drink from the bartender.

"I had to change my image, Zach. No more cowboy clothes. No more Fareeba. How is she, by the way?"

Zach put his drink on the bar and stared at Remy. "Are you having me followed, Remy?"

Remy shook his head and laughed again. "It's okay. She's irresistible. Don't I know it?"

"But really, Remy. You have someone following me?"

"What do you think Claude's real job is?"

"I'm guessing now that it's surveillance."

"He does what I ask, and gets paid very well for doing it. He's been with me forever, and we think alike."

Zach's food was placed in front of him. He had lost his appetite. He pushed the plate between them. "Eat, if you're hungry."

"So, what's goin' on, Zach?"

Zach sipped sake and said, "Are you my father, Remy?"

Remy shook his head and said, "That Fareeba. The whore has one secret and spills it the day I kick her out."

"Well, are you?"

"Yes, Zach, I'm your father."

Zach nodded and asked the bartender for a double Stoli's on ice. "Did Henri know?"

"I never knew for sure. It was never mentioned. Annette thought he didn't know, but the math didn't work in his favor. He was gone most of the time you would have been conceived, and when he was around he was cheating on Annette. Does it bother you, Zach?"

"You being my father? No, actually, it doesn't. You meant as much to me as Henri, maybe more. I told you things I would never tell Henri."

"That's 'cause he acted so damned proper."

"And Mother shared both your beds." Zach took a long drink of vodka.

"I never approached her, Zach. She always came to me. Annette was a goddess, you know that. I wasn't going to disappoint her."

"And you never knew she had twins?"

"I had told her twins were a possibility for her, since the gene existed throughout the Bujold clan. I wasn't there for the birthing—that was Henri's job. Then I was in jail. Annette and Henri never told me they had twins."

Zach took a gulp of vodka. He felt unclean. He threw a fifty on the bar and walked out.

*

He and Fareeba followed the busboy down to the lobby of Harrah's and out to valet parking. A cab was waiting, and the busboy placed Fareeba's clothing in the trunk. Zach tipped him and they slid into the cab. "The Royal Sonesta, please," Zach said to the driver.

Zach had valet help with the clothing, and they took the private elevator to the concierge floor. Philippe said, "Welcome back, Zach, your suite is ready for you." He smiled at Fareeba as she walked by.

Inside, after her clothing was hung in the guest bedroom closet, Zach opened the pantry and asked what she wanted.

"Let's have scotch and watch a movie," she replied.

Zach poured scotch over crushed ice and carried the glasses to the couch. He sat next to Fareeba and kissed her hard. "Welcome home," he said.

"And you think this is safe, Zach? Remy's not going to freak out?"

"If he's going to, what difference does it make where we are? He's got Claude keeping tabs on us."

"I guess you're right. He admitted to being your father, eh?"

Zach nodded and drank scotch. He powered on the flat-screen and began scrolling through the menu of movies. "It doesn't matter to me, Fareeba. I'm the product of a crime family—the whole fucked-up Bujold legacy."

"He does love you, Zach."

"Yes. And he has always stuck by me. He's even letting me have what I want most."

"What's that?" she asked.

He turned and looked into her big, green eyes, and said, "You."

Chapter 29

Louis met with his attorney on Saturday morning, the day after his arraignment. They sat at the conference room table. This was Louis's eleventh day in detention. He had been eating sparingly, and he figured he'd lost ten pounds.

Jeffrey Lightner was seated to his right. He unbuttoned his suit jacket and let his paunch ease down over his belt. He loosened his tie and pulled his collar away from his neck, allowing his jowls room to spread out. Louis watched as Lightner reviewed his notes, and worried about the concerned look on his attorney's face.

"Where will they send me next?" Louis asked.

"Orleans Parish Prison, on Gravier Street."

"And all efforts to get me out on bail have been denied?"

"Yes, Louis, I'm sorry. The judge is adamant about it."

"Not even with a GPS ankle bracelet?"

"I'm sorry, but, no."

"What will you do next?"

"I have the make and model of the sneaker they maintain you were wearing at Julie Sykes house. The sneaker has earth on it which is present in the garden surrounding her house. Only one print was found on the front porch. We will have the make and model run through a database of sales which will be limited to Louisiana. My assistant is involved in that now, and will be involved in the analysis afterwards. I've retained the services of a private investigator whom I've used before. This effort will be made in the hope of finding another match on the size and shoe print, preferably here in New Orleans, trying to find a person with a motive for murdering her."

"And all they have is the shoe print, right? No other evidence that I was ever in the house?"

"That's correct," Jeffrey nodded.

"I've walked almost every street in the French Quarter. I've stopped to talk with people on their porches. For all I know, it could be my shoe print. It seems like pretty flimsy evidence of a murder, Jeffrey."

"It ties you to the murder scene, Louis. Have you given any thought to pleading temporary insanity?"

"With the way that public opinion is skewed, it might be my only chance."

"It's your only chance to avoid life in prison or the death penalty. You're going to go through a battery of psychiatric tests over the following months. None of these jailhouse shrinks are at the top of their game, and you're a very smart individual. I think you know how to convince them that you had no specific intent behind the murder, that you acted impulsively, blah, blah, blah. And, don't forget, we'll be bringing in the big guns. They'll all be board certified, all Ph.Ds, and all with specialties in psychotic behavior. You'll be coached well."

"I hope the food is better at the prison."

"Nobody has died of malnutrition there, Louis. You're gonna have to suck it up for a while. If you don't, you'll be spending years on death row, followed by a lethal injection."

"I didn't do this thing, Jeffrey."

"At this point, Louis, that fact is completely irrelevant."

Louis put his elbows on the table and face in his hands. He remained silent while his attorney left the room.

*

Zach was getting used to the walk from the Sonesta to Julie's home, and would vary the route depending on what the street vendors were offering. They knew enough to keep the locals interested, and were always situated close to a bar.

After lunch, Zach stopped in for a beer at Eleven-Thirty-Five Decatur. It was a trendy bar, but they offered pint draughts. He watched as Anderson Cooper discussed Louis's capture with some legal expert on CNN. Zach had found new methods of avoiding the press. The Sonesta offered a number of ways in and out, and Zach was using them all. He turned his attention away from the TV and enjoyed the cold brew.

Walking along St. Charles Avenue to the mansion, he felt himself finally relaxing. Louis was behind bars, Robbie and Leland were making the mansion right, and he had Fareeba alone to himself. He found a real softness in Fareeba, and planned not to think more than one day at a time with her, much like an alcoholic would treat sobriety. She was, indeed, addictive.

The front door was open and he stepped inside, yelling, "Hello?"

Hamilton walked out from the sitting room and stared up at him. He bent down slowly and ran his hand over the cat's back. He was surprised to see Hamilton raise his back, and Zach

257

slipped his hands under the cat's belly and picked him up. Hamilton had come around.

"Out back, Zach," Leland hollered.

He walked through the house, cradling Hamilton in his arms, and looked out through the bay window. Construction, or destruction, had begun. He walked to the back door and looked around. The back porch was gone and footings had been poured. He stepped down onto a temporary back step and then stood on the ground. Walking toward Leland, he saw Robbie extricating himself from under to house. Hamilton struggled to be free, and Zach set him down on the grass.

"Break time!" Robbie announced and walked to a Styrofoam cooler. He pulled out three Abita Ambers and passed them around.

Zach looked at the father and son team and said, "Jesus, you guys are a mess."

Leland laughed and pried off the cap from the bottle. "When did these go from twist off to pry off?"

"About five years ago, Dad," Robbie stated, smiling at Zach.

"Wait 'til you smell me, Zach," Leland said, taking a swig of beer. "I found out where the old septic tank is, the hard way." He laughed. "Talk 'bout bein' knee deep in shit!" He laughed again.

"Wanna see the plans, Zach?" Robbie asked.

"No. Just tell me about it."

Leland stood and walked to the back of the house. "There'll be a door on either side of the bay window to a deck that surrounds the sanctuary." He began walking off the outer edges of the structure.

"The building itself will be stand-alone, but right up against the house. We don't want an old structure supporting a new one. It'll be wood-framed with Kolbe custom glass panes, electrically operated from inside the mansion. The roof will have similar glass panes which open downward, to let in sunlight and rain. A rollup canvas awning will cover the deck when it's raining. The cats will have doorways to the garden and full access to the house. There'll be plenty of electrical outlets for portable lighting if the plants need artificial sunlight."

"Looks like you thought of everything, Leland," Zach replied. "When's Margaret coming down?"

"Today. I've gotta get my shit together and pick her up at the airport." He finished his beer and climbed up into the house. "I'm gonna take a shower."

"Shower well, Leland," Zach said, after getting a whiff of the man, "and burn the clothes." He watched as Leland walked into the house.

"He's getting his sense of humor back, Robbie."

"Oh, yeah. Dad's on a roll. He got drunk with Hong last night. I think she wants him."

"Margaret will make short work of Hong."

"I found something I didn't want my father to see," Robbie said, looking concerned.

"What is it?"

"Follow me," he said, walking through the garden. He stopped at the birdbath. There was a metal box set on a concrete bench.

"What's in it?" Zach asked.

"Pistols."

"Where'd you find it?"

Robbie pointed to the back of the house. "It was buried so just the top was at ground level. I found it when we dismantled the old porch."

Zach walked to the box and flipped the top back. It held four pistols. He studied the weapons. He picked up a Smith & Wesson .38-caliber pistol by the barrel and laid it on the bench.

"My parents were shot with a thirty-eight-caliber gun. There's one twenty-two-caliber Ruger, one forty-five Colt, and a Beretta nine-millimeter. The Smith and Wesson's the only thirty-eight."

"At your trial, the prosecution said you could have hid the weapon anywhere," Robbie stated.

Zach looked into Robbie's eyes. "You think I hid the gun, Robbie?"

"It was just you and Louis, Zach. How would he know about the box?"

"You think I shot my parents?"

"Zach, that doesn't matter to me. You'll always be my friend."

"If I hid the gun, Robbie, I'm crazy. You don't need friends like that."

"Hell, we don't even know that's the gun that killed your parents. We all know the Bujold family business. This could just be your father's arsenal."

"Well, I'm gonna put this in a plastic bag and find out who shot it last. I'm taking the Beretta and the Ruger, too."

"You sure you wanna do that, Zach? Why not just let sleeping dogs lie?"

"I've already done the time, Robbie. Maybe I'll prove who did the crime."

*

He sat outside Lionel's office and waited to be waved in. Feeling nervous and out of sorts, he couldn't help but wonder if he was opening up a can of worms. Perhaps Robbie was right about leaving the whole thing alone. He'd thought of approaching Remy with the weapon, but wasn't particularly in the mood to see Remy now.

Lionel raised an index finger and beckoned Zach. He walked into the office and sat facing the sergeant.

"What's up?" Lionel asked.

"Robbie Terrebonne and his father, Leland, are working behind my house, building a sanctuary. Robbie discovered a box which was hidden under the old porch, containing some pistols. I brought one with me. It's a thirty-eight-caliber revolver."

Zach reached into the pocket of his leather coat and withdrew the weapon, sealed in a plastic bag. He placed it on Lionel's desk.

Lionel looked at the revolver, saying, "That's an old Smith and Wesson."

"How can you tell it's old?" Zach asked.

"I know guns. That pistol is a Model Twenty-three Outdoorsman with a six-and-a-half-inch barrel. It was manufactured during the first-half of the twentieth century. It's worth at least three grand. It's very rare and deadly accurate."

"You'll have ballistics take a look at it?"

"Yep. Looks like Miss Julie might have been right. I'm gonna hafta locate the evidence warehouse and find the bullets after all."

"This could just be part of my father's stash."

"We'll see," Lionel said. "Anything else?"

"How's Louis holding up?"

"I think he's about to break. I can see it in his eyes."

"Any chance he'll get out on bail?"

"No chance, Zach. He's headed for Orleans Parish Prison on Monday."

"Good," Zach said and stood. He walked out of Lionel's office.

Chapter 30

Late Sunday afternoon, Zach was sitting in the Desire Oyster Bar when he saw Claude walk by on Bourbon Street. He waved at the big man but Claude didn't notice him and continued walking. Zach turned toward the lobby and watched as Claude made his way to the private elevator. He began to shout out his name, but held back. Zach stood and walked out of the bar as the elevator doors shut. He walked to the elevator and waited for it to descend. Stepping in, he wondered why he was getting an unannounced visit from Claude.

When the doors opened, he stepped out and looked down the corridor to his suite. There was no concierge at the desk, and Zach walked to the door of his suite and slipped in the keycard.

Claude had Fareeba on her back on the tiled floor of the TV room. He was kneeling over her, his back to Zach. Zach grabbed a vase from the living room coffee table and ran at him, smashing the vase against the back of Claude's head. The vase shattered, and Claude grunted as he fell forward over

Fareeba's torso. He moved forward on his hands and knees, struggling to stand up.

Zach moved in front of the big man. He was several inches shorter than Claude, and about sixty pounds lighter. He knew he couldn't let Claude face him one on one. As Claude raised his head, Zach threw a punch at his Adam's apple. Claude stood up straight, clutched his throat with gloved hands, and gasped for air. He looked at Zach with desperation in his eyes, and then fell to his knees. Zach kicked him on the side of his head and Claude fell to the right, crashing into the glass coffee table and shattering it.

Zach knelt down beside Fareeba and felt her chest for a heartbeat. He touched her throat and felt a pulse. He began giving her mouth to mouth resuscitation, wishing he had another person pushing down on her chest. As he blew into her mouth, he could feel her lungs expand, and knew she had no blockage. He kept it up until he felt her head move. He looked into her eyes and saw recognition. She had abandoned the lifeless stare, and was looking into his eyes.

Zach put a hand to her cheek and said, "Can you breathe?"

Fareeba swallowed several times, and whispered, "Yes." She coughed, closed her eyes and covered her mouth.

He stood and put his hands in her armpits and brought her head and torso up. "Still breathing okay?" he asked.

"I'm okay, Zach."

He helped her stand and slowly walked her to the couch. She sat and put her head back, taking in long breaths. Looking at Claude spread over the shattered coffee table, she said, "Is he alive?"

Zach walked over and stood beside Claude's body. Blood had travelled along the tile, from Claude's head toward the balcony. A shard of glass was embedded in his neck, and blood was oozing from the wound. Zach reached down and felt his wrist for a pulse. He opened one of Claude's eyelids, saying, "Fucker's dead."

He walked to the kitchenette and withdrew a bottle of vodka from the freezer. He filled two glasses with ice and poured the vodka, walked to Fareeba and handed her one, then sat near her in an armchair. He took a swig and Fareeba sipped.

He grabbed a pack of cigarettes from the end table, slid one out, and lit it. He took another drink of vodka. He held up his hand and watched as his fingers trembled.

"I'm gonna go after I calm down, and you have to call the police. Tell them I killed Claude in self-defense, and I'll talk to them later, okay?"

Fareeba nodded. "Where are you going?"

"To get some answers from Daddy Dearest," he said, staring at Fareeba. "I love you, Fareeba."

"I love you back."

*

The full moon was shedding light over the mansion when Zach arrived. He realized that the last time he looked at a full moon was on New Year's Eve, one month ago. He paid the cabbie and pushed the wrought-iron gate open. He turned the power off on his cell phone. Checking his watch for the time, he walked to the porch. Placing his hand in the pocket of his coat, he gripped the Beretta with his right hand and withdrew it. He opened the screen and front doors, walked in, and left the inner door ajar. He stood in the vestibule, listening.

The house was dimly lit. He didn't know if Remy was expecting him to be dead alongside Fareeba, but he was certain Remy expected her to be dead. He walked slowly in sneakered feet, hoping not to step on a loose hardwood panel. He walked down the hallway to the kitchen, hearing sounds coming from somewhere further down the hall.

He could hear the TV in Remy's study, and walked on carpeted flooring to the doorway. Remy was sitting back in an easy chair, and his eyes were closed. Zach walked in front of Remy and stood looking down at him. He placed the Beretta to the side of Remy's left ear and pulled the trigger.

The gun blast echoed though the room. Remy's body bounced up in the upholstered recliner as his eyelids opened and he screamed. He lurched forward and tried to stand, but the footrest caused him to fall back in the chair. He screamed, "What the fuck!" and put a hand to his ear.

"That's what I wanna know, Remy. What the fuck have you done?" He stood there with the weapon aimed at Remy's chest.

Remy removed his hand from his ear and stared at blood on his palm. "You shot out my eardrum!" he screamed.

"I'll talk louder. What the fuck have you done?" Zach hollered.

"What are you talking about?"

Zach walked to the bar and poured four fingers of scotch into two glasses. He walked to Remy and put a glass on the end table. He turned and walked to a chair at the conference table. Sitting down, he had six feet between them and a clear shot at Remy.

"Let's start at the beginning. Papa Pierre."

"What about him?" Remy asked.

"He never took you or Henri into the family business. Why not?"

"Because he was a prick. Mama Teresa must have told you that." Remy grabbed the glass of scotch and took a gulp.

"My grandmother never said a bad word about anyone. Don't even mention her name. You and Henri were arrested for running guns when you were twenty-one. I was two at the time. That wasn't family business. You both served a year in Angola. When you got out, Pierre was shot dead. You two did that, didn't you?"

"We did not kill our father, Zach," Remy stated emphatically.

Zach pointed the Beretta at Remy's right shinbone and hollered, "Put down that gun!" He pulled the trigger. Remy screamed and lurched forward, the glass of scotch flying from his hand. He grabbed his shin with both hands. He groaned and looked at Zach in disbelief. "What the fuck are you doing?" he hissed between clenched teeth.

"I've got thirteen more bullets, Remy. Reconsider your last statement." Zach took a pull on the scotch, and aimed the Beretta at Remy's stomach.

"Enough! Stop shooting me. We killed our father, okay?"

"Why?" Zach asked.

Remy grimaced in pain, grabbing his shin tighter, saying, "He was denying us our birth right."

"You both wanted his money, and murdering him was the only way you'd get it."

"He deserved what he got."

"And Henri and Annette? Did they deserve what they got?"

"I swear to you, Zach. I didn't do that."

Zach aimed the Beretta at Remy's right shoulder. Remy yelled, "Wait!"

Zach lowered the Beretta and took another drink of scotch. "Remy, be careful what you say next, because I'm not gonna run out of bullets before you run out of blood. I'm only looking for the truth."

Remy grabbed a pack of Cohibas from the end table and withdrew one. He lit it and said, "Would you pour me another scotch?"

Zach shook his head.

Remy glared at Zach and finally nodded. "When you were thirteen, Annette had another argument with Henri about his screwing around. He told her to fuck off, and she said she had, with me, and that you were my son. Henri didn't take the news well. He hired a hit man to kill me, but Claude intercepted the guy. So, now I knew Henri wanted me dead. I never mentioned this to Annette." He took a deep drag on the cigar. "Please, Zach. Another drink? My leg is on fire."

Zach stood up and walked to the bar, poured scotch, and handed the glass to Remy. He walked back and sat at the conference table.

Remy took a long drink of scotch. "I planned to kill him on New Year's Eve. You were supposed to be on a date. I was wearing a costume and mask. I walked in the front door and found them on the couch in the living room. I shot them and walked out the back door. That's when I found you in the garden. I put you in the hallway and left."

"What kind of costume were you wearing?"

"What the fuck does that matter?"

Zach pointed the Beretta at Remy's head and said, "Just answer the question."

"The Grim Reaper. I thought it was appropriate."

"How did you drug me?"

"I put a morphine tablet under your tongue."

"Why did you kill my mother?"

"She fucked me, but she loved Henri. She could never be trusted. She would have called the police in a heartbeat."

"And you let me take the fall."

"You were fourteen. I figured you'd be out by eighteen."

"You sent me a shitbag attorney."

"You had to be convicted or the investigation would have continued. I'd be looking at a death sentence."

"Why did you murder Julie?"

"That bitch and her meddling got Etienne charged with the murder of a judge. I had to kill her to satisfy the family. Besides, she would have worked her way up to me."

"Did you strangle her or did Claude?"

"Claude," Remy stated.

"And you threw a going away party for her, you sick fuck."

"It wasn't a personal thing, Zach," Remy said, grimacing. "It was about survival."

"You had Claude attend her funeral. Why the fuck would you do that?"

"Appearances."

"And you threw your son, Louis, under the bus, too."

"Louis is no son to me," Remy said maliciously.

"How did you get Louis's shoeprints on the porch?"

"Claude did that. He knew where Louis was staying."

"And Fareeba?"

"That was personal."

Zach nodded, yelled, "Drop the gun!" and shot Remy in his left shinbone. While Remy screamed, and the glass of scotch flew out of his hand, Zach said, "Andre, did you get all that?"

Andre stepped into the room and said, "We have the audio."

"That didn't sound coerced, did it?"

"Not at all," he agreed.

Zach reached into his coat pocket and withdrew a plastic bag containing a pistol. He handed it to Andre. Andre removed the .22-caliber Ruger by the barrel and walked to Remy. He placed the grip of the gun in Remy's right hand and squeezed Remy's hand around the grip. He wiped the barrel clean and slipped the gun back into the plastic bag.

"Better call Lionel," Zach said.

Andre walked off and Zach looked at Remy. "Hell of a father you turned out to be."

*

His suite at the Sonesta was sealed tight, and Philippe had found Fareeba a smaller, vacant one.

She was sitting on the balcony when Zach arrived. She entered the room and he held her tight.

They sat on the couch.

"Remy killed them all."

"Good God. Is he in custody?"

"Yeah. Will you spend some time with me, Fareeba?"

"Of course, sugar."

"I need you now. I've lost my whole family."

"It'll pass, honey. I don't see how anything else could go wrong."

"Do you want to move back into the mansion?"

"You know, Zach, I love it there—the solitude of the place, the garden, the master bedroom just the way I want it. This would be a time when I can have that without Remy. You do know that I loved him, don't you?"

"I'm not sure how anyone could love a Bujold man."

"He had his moments, Zach. But I wouldn't want to live there without you."

"Do you really think you want a relationship with me?"

"Zach, I've only known you a month, but, you have to admit, it's been one hell of a month. You learn a lot about a person when there's a crisis. I'm in love with you."

"I'm afraid to be in love with you. I do love you, and I'd really like to give it a try."

"All we've got is time, Zach. We have to try this. I'd never forgive myself if I didn't try."

"The allure of sex can wear off, Fareeba."

"Are you afraid that I'll cheat on you, or that I'll get fat?" She closed her mouth and blew air into her cheeks, raising her eyebrows.

He laughed. "We shouldn't begin this by making promises we can't keep. I include myself in that. Let's just start with good intentions."

"I can do that. You'll see that my intentions are good," she said, moving closer to him and kissing his mouth.

What do we have to lose? he asked himself.

*

Zach received a call on his cell phone just short of midnight. Fareeba had drifted off and he walked out of the bedroom before he spoke.

"Sergeant, don't you ever sleep?"

"Not when I've finally got Julie's murderer to discuss things with."

"Thanks for letting me take the evening off, Lionel. I'll be available anytime beginning tomorrow. The experience I had with Remy and the things that I learned are gonna take some time to absorb."

"You'll have to come in for a deposition sooner or later. I'll see when the DA is available. For now, just hang tight and don't leave the city."

"Does forensics have the thirty-eight?"

"Yeah. Remy's fingerprints are on the weapon, and I've got people assigned to find the evidence warehouse that the bullets are stored in. His confession will be enough to hang him, but the ballistics will be a nice added touch. He's probably killed other people with it. There's no way he's walking away from this, Zach. I don't know how you stopped yourself from shooting him between the eyes."

"I nearly did when he called Julie a bitch. I shot him in the shinbones knowing he'd require surgery and a long convalescence. He killed a judge some years back, and I'm assuming he recently killed his cousin Etienne up in Lafayette County. I just want him to suffer, Lionel."

"There are some gang bangers up in Angola who will be happy to oblige. I'll tell them he's a pedophile, and proud of it."

"No way he bails out, right?"

"No way, Zach. I'd shoot him myself if he ever gets out."

"Thanks for your help, Sergeant."

"I owe you one, Zach."

Chapter 31

Tuesday morning, two days after Remy was carted away by the police, Zach received a call from a restricted number. "Zach," he answered.

"This is Louis."

"I was wondering when you'd call," Zach said.

"I thought we might meet for a drink, and talk."

Zach paused to think about it. "I'm at the Sonesta. You know the suite," he said, sardonically.

The crime lab had finished their forensic roundup in his suite, and Philippe had seen to it that the place was immaculate. Zach dressed in jeans over alligator boots, slipping on the James Carville T-shirt. Opening the French doors to the balcony, he watched the rain coming down hard.

He had locked down the suite yesterday, as soon as it became available to him. Reporters were still trying to get interviews with him, and he felt comfortable in the cocoon-like setting, with no extraneous lights or sounds to distract him. He had wanted time alone to think, and had asked Fareeba if she wouldn't mind moving back into the mansion.

He had kept the rooms dimly lit and ordered room service. Pieces of the puzzle were now making sense. He remembered Henri's unsettling behavior days prior to his death, and knew now it wasn't due to the aftermath of Katrina or Rita, as Henri had stated, but rather, he was in fear of retaliation by Remy.

He remembered an occasion when he had walked into the kitchen to find Annette and Remy in a furtive discussion that ended when they realized he had entered the room. He visualized relatives looking over their shoulders at him, and wondered now how much they knew at the time. He couldn't remember a time in the last month prior to his arrest when Henri and Remy were together.

This whole business had a mental hold over him for such a long time, and he was finally getting free of it. He didn't want to walk away from all of it feeling nothing but hatred, yet most of his revelations brought him to that one emotion—hatred, and bitterness for being played the fool.

He walked out onto the balcony, holding a glass of vodka on ice in his hand. The sounds and smells of the city rose up to him as the rain poured down, missing most of his body but soaking his boots. It felt good to be just where he was, both physically and mentally. He was to be an escapee from all the Bujold family insanity.

He heard a noise behind him and turned to watch Louis entering the suite.

"I felt it appropriate to sneak up on you, Zach," Louis said, placing a keycard on the end table in the TV room. "That's been my MO from day one."

Zach approached him, feeling uneasy. He didn't know what to do or say next. He lamely extended his right hand and Louis shook it firmly.

"Like a drink?" Zach asked.

"Whatever you're having," Louis said, as he walked to the balcony, stood in the rain, and looked down at Bourbon Street. He stood there for a full minute, then walked back inside, ran his hands through his black hair, and wiped rainwater from his face.

Zach handed him a glass of vodka and sat in an armchair. Louis sat on the couch. Zach swung his chair to face Louis.

"We could find humor in some of this shit, you know," Louis said.

Zach smiled and said, "Sure, it's like and old 'Road Runner' cartoon, except that *I'm* Wile E. Coyote and the Acme safe is always falling on *my* head."

"I have to admit, you certainly got the brunt of it."

"I could have done without the heroin."

Louis nodded and said, "From my point of view, Zach, you had to have murdered our parents. Why should I care if you overdosed? I just didn't want you talking to the cops at that point in time. I wanted you unconscious and behind bars."

Zach nodded. "I've come to the conclusion that Julie didn't die because of me. Remy had her killed for things she put in place before I ever came on the scene. You don't know how certain I was that you murdered her."

"I know you must hate me for setting you up to look like me and drugging you, but I was acting on instinct. I knew I was being followed, first by a black guy that turned out to be Claude, and then by you. I knew you killed our parents, and I knew you could convince people that I did it, so I acted accordingly—I became you." Louis took a drink of vodka.

Zach said, "And I knew you killed our parents and Julie, and would have killed you myself if I could have gotten away with it."

They both remained silent, taking sips of vodka.

"You know what I feel most guilty about?" Louis asked.

"What?"

"That you had to spend seven years with Doctor Fadon. What a fuckin' idiot."

"And he was the head idiot. His team was worse."

"I can see why you hated me," Louis said.

"There's something you don't know about Remy," Zach said.

"What?"

"He's our father," Zach said. He stood and walked to the balcony. The rain had stopped, and the street smells were musty.

"There goes our gene pool, right down the toilet," Louis said.

He joined Zach on the balcony, lighting a cigarette, and placing a hand on Zach's shoulder.

Zach fought the urge to recoil from Louis's touch.

"Is it possible to reconstruct some sort of family after all this, Zach, or should I just go away?"

Zach turned to look at Louis. He said, "Stay, Louis. Let's see what we can build from this."

*

Louis opened the wrought-iron gate. He looked at the four large columns that adorned the front of Remy's mansion, supporting the roof and the second-floor balcony. He walked up the steps to the front porch, and rang the doorbell. Zach opened a door, and Louis opened the screen door. He followed Zach into the vestibule and through to the kitchen.

"Fareeba, I believe you met my brother, Louis."

Fareeba turned from the sink and gazed at Louis. She smiled and said, "What's cookin', sugar?"

"Hi, Fareeba."

Zach said, "Fareeba, would you bring Louis and me some coffee and Kahlua?"

"Sure, honey."

Zach led Louis to the study. He turned on a light over the small conference table, walked to the desk, and returned with a crystal ashtray. He walked to the shelf of books and returned with two hardbound ledgers. Finally, he retrieved a humidor from the desk and placed it on the table.

"Let's sit side by side," he said, bringing a chair to Louis's right side and sitting. He opened the humidor and rolled out two cigars. "Cubans," he said. "Put up with me, Louis. This is something our father and I went through only once."

Hamilton walked into the study and jumped up onto the table. He stretched his body and curled up near to where Louis sat.

"I hate cats, Zach. Can I shove this thing off the table?"

"No," Zach ordered. "Leave him alone. I've adopted Hamilton, and he's here to stay."

Zach adjusted himself in the chair and said, "Remy split everything down the middle with me. Now, that's what I'm doing with you."

Fareeba walked in and Zach stopped talking. She placed a glass mug of coffee to Zach's right and then a glass to Louis's left. He smelled a lilac scent coming off her. His head was at the level of her belly. He inhaled through his nose and felt dizzy. She bent and kissed Zach on the ear and let a finger trail over Louis's shoulder as she left the room.

Zach handed Louis a cigar and stuck one between his teeth. He produced a lighter and lit the cigars. Leaning back in the chair, he blew out a smoke ring and took a minute to himself.

Reaching for the ledgers, he placed the ledger labeled "Remy Bujold" in front of Louis. He slid the ledger labeled "Zachary Bujold" in front of him and opened it. Louis followed suit.

"Each page represents a year of income and expenses. I've only been given last year. See the balance forward amount?"

Louis looked at the opening balance at the top of the page and counted the zeroes. "One million dollars," he said.

"Every dollar amount is rounded off by one hundred. It makes things easier."

"One-hundred million dollars?" Louis's voice increased an octave.

"Look at my balance forward."

"One-hundred million dollars," Louis repeated.

"The investments now are very conservative—gold, silver, and oil. You basically get around ten percent on your invested money every year, and you have to pay taxes on it. They never went crazy with tax-sheltered money, but they donated big to local charities. Look at it this way for now—if you only spend two million a year, you'll never run out of money in your lifetime."

"Fuck!" Louis exclaimed. "We're the next generation Koch brothers."

"Coca Cola's got nothing on us, Louis."

Louis turned to look at Zach and said, "We're gonna have to get you educated, brother."

Zach relaxed on the living room couch while Fareeba and Louis cleaned the kitchen after dinner. Hamilton sat next to him, looking up at him and purring while Zach brushed his whiskers back with his thumb.

"Don't worry, boy. You'll always know who I am. I'll be the one who's not kicking you." He put his hand on the top of Hamilton's head and brought his hand down his neck and back. Hamilton purred louder.

He watched as Fareeba looked up into Louis's eyes and laughed at something he said. Louis had certainly acted charming during dinner, talking about his time at Harvard Law, downplaying his scholastic standing at graduation to his brother with the GED from the University of Jetson. Fareeba seemed delighted to be part of this new, young tag-team of brothers. The hard times she'd faced recently with Remy seemed to be well behind her.

Zach watched as they moved around each other's body, grabbing another plate to be washed or a plate to be dried and put away. He witnessed the unintended touch that would naturally occur whenever two people negotiated a small space, and observed the undeniable reaction to the touch they both experienced but wouldn't acknowledge.

He wondered how he would fare with Louis. They had been raised so differently. That crack Louis made about getting Zach educated hadn't gone unnoticed. Zach had felt that to be a condescending and presumptuous statement. He also felt uneasy about having Louis around him and Fareeba. He felt as though he was being upstaged by his own shadow.

While he felt comfortable with his own sexual prowess, he couldn't deny that Louis had an inch on him. The fact that Louis was sexually inexperienced didn't give Zach much comfort. Louis would be putty in the hands of Fareeba. She could mold him into whatever she wanted.

He looked at Fareeba and tried to remember their latest pact. They certainly had blown their first pact to smithereens, hadn't they? What was it now? Lovers with good intentions?

Zach watched as Louis exhibited his intentions. He knew that Louis wouldn't be doing the dishes one week after he had Fareeba all to himself. Zach had to admit that Louis was going to be a problem for him and Fareeba, not to mention Hamilton.

He never felt the slow burn washing over him as he stared at them, and was completely unaware that his eyes had gone dark. Hamilton jumped off the couch. Mardi Gras was right around the corner. He could go as the Grim Reaper. That might just be appropriate. He'd have to buy a shoulder holster for the Beretta. He patted the sofa and Hamilton jumped back up. *It's just you and me, Hamilton.*

THE END

ABOUT THE AUTHOR

Peter Jensen lives in Naples, Florida with his three soft-coated Wheaten terriers.